THE ROOM WAS SMALL AND SMELLED CLEAN...

He saw that his possibles and cased rifle were on the floor near the bed. She asked him if the room suited him and he said it did. So she shut the door and asked him if he wanted to sit down and test the bedsprings.

Longarm figured he was stuck with the bed for the night, even if it was full of rattlesnakes, but to be polite he sat down and bounced a couple of times, saying, "It's a grand old bed, Palomina."

She blew out the candle and said, "Oh, my candle has gone out."

He didn't answer. He wasn't sure what in thunder he was supposed to say.

The next thing he knew, little Palomina was in his lap... "Oh, *Señor*," she gasped, "what are you doing...?"

Also in the LONGARM series from Jove

LONGARM
LONGARM ON THE BORDER
LONGARM AND THE AVENGING ANGELS
LONGARM AND THE WENDIGO
LONGARM IN THE INDIAN NATION
LONGARM AND THE LOGGERS
LONGARM AND THE HIGHGRADERS
LONGARM AND THE NESTERS
LONGARM AND THE HATCHET MEN
LONGARM AND THE MOLLY MAGUIRES
LONGARM AND THE TEXAS RANGERS
LONGARM IN LINCOLN COUNTY
LONGARM IN THE SAND HILLS
LONGARM IN LEADVILLE
LONGARM ON THE DEVIL'S TRAIL
LONGARM AND THE MOUNTIES
LONGARM AND THE BANDIT QUEEN
LONGARM ON THE YELLOWSTONE
LONGARM IN THE FOUR CORNERS
LONGARM AT ROBBER'S ROOST
LONGARM AND THE SHEEPHERDERS
LONGARM AND THE GHOST DANCERS
LONGARM AND THE TOWN TAMER
LONGARM AND THE RAILROADERS
LONGARM ON THE OLD MISSION TRAIL
LONGARM AND THE DRAGON HUNTERS
LONGARM AND THE RURALES
LONGARM ON THE HUMBOLDT
LONGARM ON THE BIG MUDDY
LONGARM SOUTH OF THE GILA
LONGARM IN NORTHFIELD
LONGARM AND THE GOLDEN LADY
LONGARM AND THE BOOT HILLERS
LONGARM AND THE BLUE NORTHER
LONGARM ON THE SANTA FE
LONGARM AND THE STALKING CORPSE
LONGARM AND THE COMANCHEROS
LONGARM AND THE DEVIL'S RAILROAD
LONGARM IN SILVER CITY
LONGARM ON THE BARBARY COAST
LONGARM AND THE MOONSHINERS
LONGARM IN PRISON
LONGARM IN BOULDER CANYON
LONGARM IN DEADWOOD
LONGARM AND THE LONE STAR LEGEND
LONGARM AND THE GREAT TRAIN ROBBERY
LONGARM IN THE BADLANDS

TABOR EVANS

AND THE
LAREDO LOOP

A JOVE BOOK

LONGARM AND THE LAREDO LOOP

A Jove Book / published by arrangement with
the author

PRINTING HISTORY
Jove edition / June 1981
Second printing / November 1981
Third printing / September 1982

All rights reserved.
Copyright © 1981 by Jove Publications, Inc.
This book may not be reproduced in whole or in part,
by mimeograph or any other means, without permission.
For information address: Jove Publications, Inc.,
200 Madison Avenue, New York, N.Y. 10016.

ISBN: 0-515-06583-8

Jove books are published by Jove Publications, Inc., 200 Madison
Avenue, New York, N.Y. 10016. The words "A JOVE BOOK" and the
"J" with sunburst are trademarks belonging to Jove Publications, Inc.

PRINTED IN THE UNITED STATES OF AMERICA

Chapter 1

It was never easy to get to work on time, but this one old morning was a pisser. Longarm rose early with good intentions. He'd struck out the night before with that snooty little redhead from the Black Cat Saloon. So, waking up at dawn with a clear head and a hard-on, he decided to get to the office early and tell his boss he'd reformed.

He washed down his goosebumps with a wet string rag dipped in cold water. He woke up some more when he brushed his teeth with Maryland rye. He'd shaved the evening before, not knowing then how the redhead felt about gents who didn't own at least a silver mine. So Longarm ran a thumbnail along the angle of his jaw and decided the hell with it. He didn't expect to meet anybody at the office prettier than the prissy young dude who played the typewriter in the front room, and Longarm had never been that desperate yet.

He put on a fresh hickory shirt, even though it was only the middle of the week. The shirt he'd worn the night before was still reasonable as far as clean went, but he knew his boss, U.S. Marshal Billy Vail, liked to play at detective work, so he'd likely comment on the violet stink. Longarm had told that infernal barber he only wanted bay rum to spruce him up for that match with the redhead, but the romantic Eye-talian barber had convinced him that gals liked stronger stink-pretty on a man. So here it was, the middle of the week, and he had to change his shirt.

As he buttoned up, he growled, "A lot you know about redheads, you damned old gondolier. She'd have let me smell like cowshit if I could have told her I owned the Diamond K. We were getting along just swell until I told her what Uncle Sam pays a deputy marshal these days!"

He caught himself scowling in the mirror and suddenly he laughed. He nodded to his reflection and said, "Morning. That was close, old son. You know no gal is interested in a man's salary unless she has dishonorable intentions."

He sat down and hauled on his tight tweed trousers and stovepipe boots as he pondered the infinite treachery of womankind. It was getting so a man couldn't feel safe with any of 'em, these days. You'd think a saloon gal who painted her face would be less anxious to rope and hogtie a friendly old boy. But they were all the same. A man figured the game was won and over about the time he got a gal between the sheets. But that was where the game just started getting interesting to a gal. They didn't figure *they'd* won till they could show their girlfriends a diamond ring.

He stood and strapped on his cross-draw rig, checking the five rounds of .44-40 in the chambers as he did every morning. Nobody had ever stolen his bullets while he slept alone, but a man in Longarm's line of work couldn't afford sloppy habits.

He put on the sissy string tie they made him wear around the Federal Building in Denver. He'd never gotten used to the new rules of President Hayes's reform administration. He buttoned his brown tweed vest over the ends of the tie and took a long gold-washed chain from the dresser top. There was an Ingersoll pocket watch at one end of the chain and a brass derringer at the other. The watch kept fair time and the derringer fired two .44-caliber rounds on occasion.

He put the watch in the left pocket of his vest and the gun in the other, leaving the chain draped across his chest sort of elegant-like. He put on his dark brown frock coat and smoothed the collar where it was a mite frayed. He'd been wearing his federal shield pinned to the lapel more than usual, lately. Billy Vail had been using him over at the federal courthouse as a prison-chaser since the suit had last been cleaned and pressed. He'd had his badge pinned in his wallet the night before, of course, but the redhead had likely noticed the threadbare lapel while going over his accounts with those knowing green eyes. They'd been getting along like fury till she'd gotten around to his job and how much it paid. He'd been caught off-guard, thinking he was among friends. If he had it to do over again, he'd tell her he hadn't had time to change, coming from his mine up in Leadville. For treachery deserved the same in return, and he was willing to bet she'd settle for being the play-pretty of a rich old married gent, even if an honest working bachelor wasn't her notion of a bright future.

Longarm put on his flat-crowned Stetson and left the rooming house on the unfashionable side of Cherry Creek. It was a bright sunny morn, and as he crunched along the cinder roadway, a meadowlark perched on a fence cocked its beady eye at him and whistled saucily. Longarm said, "Aw, shut up. It ain't that pretty out, and I face a long hard day at the office."

He was almost to the Cherry Creek bridge when he heard the sound of gunshots—a *lot* of gunshots—coming his way from somewhere near the Burlington Railroad yards to the northwest.

Longarm knew better. He was a federal lawman and the Denver Municipal Police had ears. He took out his watch and consulted it. The office wouldn't open for almost an hour, but he'd intended to eat some chili con carne for breakfast on Larimer Street. What was happening yonder was none of his business.

Another shot rang out. It sounded like a ten-gauge scattergun. The first shots had been .44s or .45s from a handgun. He heard the whipcrack report of a Winchester, making it at least three folks shooting over there. This was getting sort of interesting. So, though he knew better, Longarm started legging toward the sounds of gunfire. Longarm legged good. He was over six feet and long of limb, with a mile-eating stride most men had to trot alongside to keep up. Working more on foot than the average cowhand, he favored low-heeled army stovepipe boots without spurs, so he moved cat-quiet, too.

But there was no need for pussyfooting this morning. He

spotted the police line a full block away as he rounded a corner. They had the Burlington yards covered, and their blue backs faced him as he approached. Longarm knew most of the local coppers, but not all, and there was a fool city ordinance about wearing public guns these days. So he took out his wallet and pinned his federal shield to his lapel before he moseyed up to them, .44 double-action in hand, to ask pleasantly and politely what the hell was going on.

A police sergeant he knew turned with a frown, saw who it was, and said, "Howdy, Longarm. You remember the Terrible Tracy Twins?"

Longarm nodded. "Yeah, they ain't really twins, but they sure acted terrible the last time they held up the Drovers Savings and Loan."

"Well, they just tried to do her again."

"Do tell? It's a mite early to make a withdrawal, gun or no. The banks ain't open yet, are they?"

"Nope. The Tracy boys grabbed the head teller at home, aiming to make him open early, I reckon. Teller spotted one of our patrolmen on Lincoln Avenue as they was frog-marching him down Capitol Hill. He was either a brave or foolish man, for he let out a holler and it's been sort of interesting ever since."

"You say *was*?"

"Yeah, the teller was killed on the spot. Our patrolman took a round in the leg, but hit one of the Tracy boys as he went down. They must have lost interest in our fair city about then, for, as you see, they headed for the tracks out. Another copper swapped some shots with them as they run across the schoolyard of Evans Elementary, and now he's on his way to the hospital too. Them Terrible Tracys are right good shots."

Longarm traced a mental route from the old brownstone school to the nearby railyards and observed, "Interesting is a mild word when you consider one damn long running gunfight, Sarge. How the hell did they ever get this far, still standing?"

"They run and fight pretty good. We figure they've both been hit a few times, and, as you see, we've got 'em boxed in the yards now. Our orders are to keep 'em there whilst the captain figures out the next move. They can't get out and we don't aim to lose any more men this morning."

Longarm moved to the tipped-over wagon the police were

using as a shield. He stared into the railroad yards beyond. There was nothing to be seen but the maze of tracks and stationary rolling stock. Way up the tracks a switch engine stood quietly, venting an occasional plume of steam. He asked the sergeant, "Who fired that shotgun I heard?" and the copper said, "Railyard bull. He ain't with us no more. See that caboose yonder? He fired from there as the Terrible Tracy Twins ran betwixt them other boxcars. One of 'em nailed him with a lovely offhand shot. They swapped a couple more shots with another railroad dick before the fellow decided he'd feel safer somewhere else. Now the ornery sons of bitches are anywhere among all them railroad cars, and it figures to be a waiting game."

Longarm glanced at the sky and commented, "Well, you have a full day and at least one of them's wounded. What happened to the yard bull they put on the ground? I fail to see him over by yonder caboose."

"Oh, a couple of yard workers carried him out. We yelled at them to take cover, but they must have been fond of him. The Tracy Twins never shot them. Don't ask me why."

"Don't have to," Longarm said. "They've moved up the line between the cars. You boys have the whole yard surrounded, huh?"

"Of course. The yards is big and sprawly, as you can see. But there's no way out we haven't got covered. We can't go in and they can't come out."

Longarm looked at his watch. "Damn," he said, "I meant to beat old Billy Vail to the office this morning, too."

The sergeant asked, "Why don't you, Longarm? You can see this figures to take all day and what just happened wasn't a federal crime."

Longarm replied, "What happened earlier *was*. The Terrible Tracy Twins are wanted on a couple of federal warrants too. They sure shoot good, but the brainless bastards *will* hold up post offices when they can't find a bank open. Killed a federal employee, last time they did it."

He put the watch away, but not the .44, and stepped around the end of the wagon bed. As he started walking toward the tracks, the police sergeant yelled, "Come back here, dammit!" But Longarm didn't have to obey any old local lawman. So he didn't look back.

5

"Goddammit, that's suicide, and suicide is agin the law, Longarm!" called the copper behind him. Longarm eased over to the caboose they'd been discussing. He saw by the blood on the ballast rock at his feet that they'd told him true about the yard bull. He had a good view up the line from here. The cars stretched in a broken line to some loading chutes a furlong north. He couldn't see what lay beyond, but there was nobody shooting at him between here and there. He hadn't expected there would be. The open stretch was covered by the coppers infesting the jagged line of fences, buildings, and such that were facing the cars on the track.

Longarm made his way into a slowly settling cloud of dust inhabited by some Denver cops, railroad men, and a herd of sheep penned in a loading corral beside a halted string of stock cars. The critters had been spooked by the gunplay and were still milling and cussing, but they'd started to settle some, so you could talk. Longarm nodded to a Denver P.D. captain he knew and asked what they were doing, if it wasn't herding sheep.

The captain said they'd chased the Tracy Twins this far and lost them in the infernal dust. He added, "It looks like they ducked under the wheels of this stock train, and now God knows where they are out yonder."

Longarm stared thoughtfully at the halted rolling stock in the vast yards and said, "They couldn't get in any of the sealed freight cars. But the railroad sends empty boxcars back down the line unlocked and regular. If I was one of the Tracys right now, I'd be hunkered in some empty car, hoping for a free ride out before anybody got to it."

"Hell, ain't no cars going in or out until we catch the bastards," the police captain replied.

A railroad man nearby said, "The hell you say! We got melting ice and uncared-for livestock to think about, even if we didn't run this here railroad on a timetable."

The captain looked at Longarm, who shrugged and said, "It ought to be safe to let sealed cars through your cordon. Might clear the field of action too, if we could narrow her down to the empty rolling stock the owlhoots figure to be hiding in."

The police captain turned to one of the civilians nearby and asked him, "Do you Burlington gents have a list of empty, unlocked boxcars?"

The railroad man said, "Not on me. But we'd have one at the dispatcher's." He turned to one of his helpers and added, "Owens, run over and get today's orders." Then, as the other man sprinted away, he turned back to Longarm and the copper to say, "I can tell you they ain't in that string of stock cars there. So what about it?"

Longarm glanced at the nearby string of cagelike stock cars, then turned to study the milling sheep penned beyond them all, at the base of a loading chute with its gate closed. He didn't answer. The police captain said, "I don't know."

"Dammit," the railroad man said, "we got a timetable to keep, you know. Them sheep should have been on their way to K.C. half an hour ago!"

The police captain asked Longarm, "What do you think?"

"I'll take a look," Longarm replied as he drew his gun again and stepped over to the short line of stock cars. The sides of the cars were made of horizontal slats with wide spaces between them, and he could see clean through to the far side. He hunkered down and had a look at the undercarriages. Nobody was riding the rods. He'd have been surprised if he'd seen anyone, considering.

He walked back to the fence and said, "Short train, all stock cars with no caboose or tender at either end. I reckon it's safe to get those sheep out of the sun, but how do you aim to move 'em anywhere worth mention?"

The railroad man said, "Oh, this here's a special order of spring lamb."

"Yeah? Some of those sheep look as old as the lamb I was fooling with at the Black Cat last night. But what the butcher won't tell 'em, they likely won't know. I see no reason not to load 'em on board. That switcher is standing by to haul 'em out of the yards, right?"

"Yeah, we're fixing to run this short string around to Fitzsimmons, northeast of town, and add 'em to an eastbound UP freight. That other train will be leaving *without* these here sheep if we don't get cracking, too!"

Longarm stared over into the tightly packed woolly-backs. "I'll move up and make sure nobody we're interested in is hiding in the coal tender and such," he told the captain.

He climbed over the loading chute, not touching his boots to the sheepshit-covered bottom planks as he forked his legs over the rough rails on either side. He moved up the short line, checking each empty stock car as he passed. Someone must have signaled the engineer in the tender, for it started backing as he walked to meet it. He hunkered down to peer under the moving wheels as the tender's coupler snapped on to that of the forward car. The colored fireman was staring down curiously. Longarm walked over and mounted to the cabin, putting his gun away. He told the two crewmen who he was and what was going on. They said they doubted like hell he'd find any outlaws hiding back in the coal, but he looked anyway and, seeing they were right, dropped off to rejoin the others back at the chute.

They'd already started loading. A yard rider on a bored-looking pinto cutting horse was hazing the woolly-backs by riding back and forth along the far rails as a couple of Mex kids poked them up the chute into the first car. It took little time to fill the car and drop the gate. But Longarm knew his office would be opening about now, and if Billy Vail believed this story, he'd believe anything. Had Longarm known he'd be spending the morning this close to sheep, he'd have left his old shirt on. You couldn't get near the critters without walking away smelling like a sheepherder. They were heated and sweated up from being packed so close. They bitched and butted each other to crowd away from the pony that was hazing them; this activity added floating, fuzzy lumps of lint to the dust they were stirring up. Longarm figured there was no sense brushing himself off until the last of them were aboard and out of his way. Moving this line of cars might simplify the search, but he knew they had a lot of work ahead and the damned day was starting to be a hot one.

They got the last sheep loaded and the switch engine slowly started to move them off to market, poor critters. The man they'd sent for the papers returned with the list of empty, unlocked cars. As they were going over them, another uniformed copper ran up the now-empty line the stock cars had been standing on. He called out, "We got one, Captain. Old Tinker Tracy bled hisself to death just down the line. One of the boys noticed blood running out of a door. So Colson and his men moved in. They found the rascal as dead as a turd in a milk bucket."

"What about his brother Tiny?" the captain asked.

"Not a sign of the other twin, Captain. He must have left

his brother to die. He sure ain't in any car near enough to matter. Old Colson's sort of encouraged, and he's been looking."

The captain snorted. "Well, run back and tell Colson to move careful. We only got one to deal with now, but Tiny Tracy is mean as hell."

He turned to Longarm and said, "We'll get us some boys and start at this end, slow and easy. There's just no way he's gonna slip through us, but old Tiny's desperate and he might try anything."

Longarm nodded as he fished out a cheroot and lit it. He flicked the match stem into the trampled sheepshit of the now-empty yard. Then his eyes narrowed as he stared down at the countless hoofmarks and he muttered, "Son of a bitch! I just wasn't awake yet!"

The captain asked him what he meant, but Longarm was moving too fast to answer. He called after the stockyard rider who was walking his pinto away. The man reined in, and as Longarm caught up, he told the stockyard man to get the hell off that mount, adding, in a politer tone, "I'm on federal business, and you'll be paid if I bust your brute up."

The other man made no move to dismount as he asked Longarm what the hell he was talking about. Some men were like that. So Longarm swore, grabbed him by the belt, and hauled him off bodily. He forked his own leg over the saddle as the former rider sat up, spitting dust and cussing. Longarm heeled the pinto into a flat run without looking back to say he was sorry.

The pinto had seen better days and was surprised as hell to be tearing through the streets of Denver at a full gallop, but as Longarm had suspected, he was an old cow pony, and the day was young, so what the hell.

The old plug's hooves struck sparks as they pounded on the pavement when they reached the politer side of Larimer Street and kept going. Longarm started lashing with the rein-ends as they tore past a streetcar heading east on Colfax. The folks riding inside stared out like they'd never seen a fast rider before.

A dray wagon was blocking the way near Broadway, so Longarm rode up over the sidewalk, nodding politely to a couple of surprised-looking gals walking along with parasols. A man in a derby jumped out of the way and shouted, "Damn drunk cowboy!" as Longarm flashed by. The pony caught a shoe on the streetcar tracks running along Broadway. For a scared split-second, Longarm braced for an ass-over-teakettle fall. But the horse recovered his balance and made it across. Longarm guided him off the paving of Colfax to lope up the grassy grounds of the State House, atop Capitol Hill. A boy mowing the lawn with a quartet of sheep called out, "Hey, cowboy, you ain't allowed to ride on the grass!" But Longarm kept going without looking back.

Capitol Hill was really the edge of a vast mesa, with its far side too far off to worry about. So, once they'd made the top, it was flat running. Longarm whipped the pony faster, snapping, "Come on, dammit, *move*, you useless mess of crowbait!"

The trouble with Denver was that the streets atop Capitol Hill were laid out in a grid running east and west and north and south. Longarm wanted to head northeast. So he did. He tore between two houses and busted through a clothes line, yelling back that he was sorry as a woman came out waving a broom at him.

There was a solid wall of housing along Seventeenth Avenue—running east and west, goddammit. He swore and loped toward Aurora, where he didn't want to go, till he spied another gap and tore through to Sixteenth, swerved around a house and across a vacant lot to Fifteenth, where he was once more forced to ride due east for three damned blocks before he came to a water-filled construction site and splashed through, cursing, at a northeast angle.

He left an awful lot of housewives cussing in his wake. The kids on their way to school thought it was neat to see a cowboy gallop by, and waved at him as he passed. That meant it was nearly nine o'clock and he was in trouble with his boss, too. It was sobering to think what might have happened if the Terrible Tracy Twins had crossed that schoolyard down yonder a mite later in the morning!

He saw a mess of little kids ahead and cut sideways through a yard to avoid them. A woman watering her garden out back gasped, "What on earth . . . ?" He saw that the rear of her yard was fenced, and jumped his lathered pony over the pickets without taking time to tip his hat to the lady.

The houses were spread thinner now, so he was able to make better time as he zigzagged between them. Chickens scattered and dogs chased him, snapping at the pony's heels, which was all to the good, as it encouraged him to keep moving.

The old stockyard horse was only good for eight or ten miles at this pace. So when Longarm spotted a gent sitting in a carriage by a house, he reined in, tapped the federal badge on his lapel, and said, "Howdy. I need that perky-looking chestnut pacer, friend."

The man shot a startled glance at the carriage horse between his own shafts and gasped, "This here's not a saddle horse, officer."

"Sure he is. Help me saddle him up, goddammit!" Longarm said as he dismounted and proceeded to unhitch the fresher animal. The man made no move to help, although he knew better than to resist an obvious lunatic as big as Longarm. It took a few minutes to unhitch the carriage horse and saddle it. So he told the man what was going on while he did it. A worried-looking woman in a sunbonnet and Dolly Varden dress stuck herself out the side door of the house to ask what was going on. Her husband said, "Get back inside. I'll tell you later."

Longarm told him where to ask about his chestnut, if he never saw it again, and told him to hang onto the pinto. Then he mounted the chestnut and saw that the man had been right. It wasn't a saddle horse and it had no intention of being one. So, by the time they got that settled, they'd made a mess out of the front lawn and flower beds with its bucking hooves. But when he finally got the chestnut settled down and headed the right way, he saw he'd still gained some time. The fresh mount was fast as well as ornery. Longarm admired its long-legged pace. He didn't try to lope it. He saw they were making smart time at the pacer's comfortable gait and, praise the Lord, the houses were thinning out and spread far enough apart so he could set a beeline for Fitzsimmons Siding.

The small town of Fitzsimmons was planning to be a Denver suburb one of these days, but Denver still had some growing to do, so they were soon riding over open prairie, navigating by the sun in the sky and the smoke of the locomotive dead ahead. Longarm didn't think the smoke was moving, but he lashed the pacer into a full run anyway, and as he raced into Fitzsimmons he saw he'd timed it close.

He tore through the yards to rein in the lathered chestnut

by the UP Baldwin just as the engineer was sounding his departing whistle. He yelled up, "Hold your steam, old son. This here train is under arrest. I'll tell you all about it directly. Right now I'm busy."

He dismounted and tethered the chestnut to a grab rail. As he started down along the tracks, another man wearing a badge came to meet him warily, and said, "Morning. Did you have some reason for riding through my salad greens just now?"

"I did," Longarm said. "I'm after Tiny Tracy, who just left Denver after committing crimes too numerous to relate. You'd best stand clear unless you take that badge serious, pard. He's in one of those stock cars down the train."

The Fitzsimmons lawman drew his antique Patterson Conversion .45 and said, "Whither thou goest, so shall I follow, Uncle Sam. But how come you boys let him get this far?"

"The train pulled out before I remembered a story I read when I was a little shaver. Let's keep it down to a roar. Stay back and cover me while I play Bo-Peep."

Longarm eased in on the first stock car. He hunkered down and peered through the slit closest to the straw and the sheep-shit-covered decking. He nodded and moved to the next car to repeat the process. Then he motioned to the man backing him to stay put as he crouched even lower to crawl for the door. He turned the handle and slid the door open as he called out, "All right, Ulysses. It worked on Cyclops and it worked on Denver, but it never worked on *me*! Come out of there with your hands held high and we'll wash that sheepshit off you before we lock you up with our less imaginative prisoners."

Tiny Tracy didn't see things Longarm's way. Sheep exploded out the door to leap, bleating and running, in every godamned direction. The outlaw followed, cussing and shooting.

Longarm had sort of expected it, since one of the few tiny things about the big bastard was his brain. He'd moved away from where he'd spoken, so, as Tiny Tracy put a couple of bullets through the side rails of the car and the space Longarm had vacated, Longarm fired back, taking more time to aim. Tiny Tracy came out anyway, not getting the message that he was dead until he'd landed facedown in the trackside dust.

Longarm rolled him over with his boot and told the awed town constable, "He must have read the same story. It was writ a long time back. Lucky for the rest of us, I noticed the drag marks in the Denver yards. He hunkered down amid a herd of sheep being loaded. Lay on his back and held two together, clinging to their wool as they were hazed aboard. It was sort of slick. Who in thunder would ever think to look for a rogue cowboy under a mess of sheep?"

The town law said, "You did."

Longarm shrugged. "Well, I read books from time to time. I always admired those Greek gents for the slick way they snuck out of that giant's cave. We'd best get some help and round up them scattered woolly-backs. If we herd 'em into those pens down the way and have the train back to the chute, we ought to see them safely on their way again."

"What about this owlhoot you just shot, Uncle Sam?"

"He ain't in shape to herd sheep with us, now. Later, I'd sure be obliged if you can scout me up some water to pour over him and a tarp to wrap him in. I got enough explaining to do, back at the office, without coming in smelling even worse than I already do."

What with one thing and another, it was well past noon by the time Longarm faced the thunder of his boss, U.S. Marshal Billy Vail, across the desk in Vail's office at the Denver Federal Building. Longarm had never been quite this late to work before, but the pudgy older lawman wasn't really sore. He'd heard about the morning's events before Longarm left the morgue, and had already given a statement to the newspapers about the brilliant law enforcement of his top deputy. He likely wouldn't get the complaints and demands for damages for a day or so.

He waited until Longarm had settled back and lit a smoke before he said, "Well, old son, you've had your fun. It's time I put you back to work for the taxpaying public again."

Longarm blew a smoke ring and said, "That sounds fair, Billy. I'd best change my pants and shave if you want me to ride herd over at the federal court the rest of the afternoon."

"Never mind. You're a mite gamy, but you can freshen up aboard the train. The Denver & Rio Grande has washrooms on their coaches now. Will wonders never cease?"

"So I heard. Am I supposed to be going somewhere on the D&RG, Billy, or do I just climb aboard and marvel at the wonders of the modern age?"

"Oh, I forgot. You were out amusing yourself when the wires came in. Some sons of bitches stole some government beef off the army at Fort Bliss. I want you to go to Laredo and check it out."

Longarm studied the end of his cheroot as he said, "Billy, the last time I looked, Fort Bliss was right outside El Paso."

"Hell, everybody knows that."

"Laredo *ain't*. Laredo is over five hundred miles southeast of both El Paso and Fort Bliss."

"Everybody knows that too. Mexico is just a spit and a holler south of all the places you just mentioned, old son. Army chased the banditos who lifted their cows as far south as the army is allowed to go, and they were last seen raising dust in the land of hot tamales. Surely you know about the Laredo Loop? I sent you down along the border to check it out a short while ago, remember?"

"Yep. It was sort of interesting. Billy, I told you then and I'm telling you now, the so-called Laredo Loop is a notion of some Wild West writer like Buntline. That other case had nothing to do with this Laredo Loop stuff. I met up with a self-elected sheriff who had to be taught some constitutional law."

"Yeah, they say his funeral was well attended. Forget that side issue you got mixed up in the last time. This time I want you to pay attention and do the job you're sent to do!"

"I'm willing, Billy. But I'm already mixed up. Let's go over that Laredo Loop business again."

Vail sat back and ran a hand over his bald dome as he replied, "It ain't complicated. You know the Díaz administration down Mexico way don't allow folks to steal Mex cows."

Longarm grimaced distastefully. "Porfirio Díaz don't allow much more than breathing, and he'd tax that, if he could figure how. *You* may call his dictatorship an administration, Billy. Me and a mess of decent Mex folks call it hell!"

Vail waved a pudgy hand as if brushing a fly away. "Whatever. The point is that while the *rurales* will blow you out of your pants for running a Mexican brand, they ain't too particular about what happens to a cow calved on this side of the border."

"You mean they hate our gringo guts, don't you?"

"Some Mex lawmen *can* get sort of sullen. Anyway, the way the Laredo Loop works is like this. An American cow gets

14

stolen. It's spirited down to some Mex ranch and given a new brand. A legal brand, in Mexico. The *rurales* ain't interested in the old brand, as long as it ain't on their list of stolen cows."

"Don't you mean they're in on it, Billy?"

"Whatever. What they're pulling is legal, in Mexico. The new Mex owner keeps the cow for a time. Then, when its new brand heals, he sells it, legal, to a licensed buyer passing through."

"Licensed by Mexico and working with the cow thieves," Longarm said.

"Of course, but try telling that to the folks running things down there. Anyway, the buyer moves the beef sideways in a big sort of loop through old Mexico, where nobody can question a trail herd's lawfully registered brands. It's called the Laredo Loop 'cause Laredo is the port of entry where the cows come back across the border to be sold with a lawful bill of sale. You know the price of beef is up, back East. So there's many a buyer for the meatpackers waiting to get a good buy on slightly cheaper Mex cows."

Longarm snorted derisively. "Yeah, and who's about to let his conscience stand in the way of a good buy? But what about the Texas Rangers? Last I heard, they were still fairly honest. How would you flimflam a ranger with a fancy new brand and some pretty papers writ in Spanish? What about the old brand they can still read on the critter, if they take the trouble to look? Don't they keep a record of stolen cows, Billy?"

"Sure they do. Stolen *Texas* cows. No cows stole in Texas are ever sent back through Laredo. *They* wind up getting sold in Arizona. That's the other end of the loop. Cows stolen west of the New Mexico line don't have brands registered in Texas. Lawmen out in New Mexico or Arizona don't keep tabs on Texas brands. This loop, trail, whatever, shuttles American cows stolen in one part of these United States to some other parts where it's safe to sell 'em, see?"

"I see some of it. Not all. How come they call it the Laredo Loop if Laredo's only one end of the secret passage? Where do they unload the Texas cows?"

"Nobody knows for sure. We've only found out recent about the plentiful Mex beef crossing at Laredo. The Western territories ain't as settled as old Texas. So they likely smuggle them through more than one border crossing out there. What you *call* the racket ain't our problem. Our problem is to find out who's doing it and make 'em stop."

Longarm took a drag of smoke before replying, "That sounds reasonable. But you're still sending me the wrong damn way, Billy. If those last cows were snitched near El Paso, they'd have Texas brands, wouldn't they?"

"No, and the army is sort of sheepish about that. Fort Bliss is a supply depot. So they furnish beef for smaller posts all over the southwest. You don't exactly get a top hand for thirteen dollars a month and beans. The government herd was run sort of, uh, informal."

"Jesus, you mean they didn't even have the usual U.S. brands?"

"Some may have. Most had just been purchased and had whatever old brand they came with. The fool purchasing officer didn't keep a record. So the stolen herd could be packing just about any brands, or none at all."

Longarm whistled silently and said, "Billy, you are wasting my time and the taxpayers' money by sending me all the infernal way to Laredo! In the first place, those cow thieves might have run them west, the other way. In the second, I wouldn't recognize one of those particular cows as stolen if I had it for supper! What in thunder am I supposed to do, stand on the corner in Laredo and ask every cow I see if she's new in town?"

Marshal Vail looked down at his desk blotter and said, "Well, you're a sort of ingenious cuss, and they're expecting me to do *something*."

"That's another question I've been meaning to ask. How come *us*? Don't they have a district court and a U.S. marshal down El Paso way, Billy?"

"They do," Vail said. "Washington asked us to handle it because the matter is sort of delicate. They, uh, ain't sure about the federal men along the border."

"You mean Washington suspicions them of being in on it with the other crooks?"

"Dammit, Longarm, I sure wish you'd learn to talk more polite about our fellow peace officers! Nobody's saying any border lawmen are working with the crooks. They'd just feel safer about it if they knew for sure. This office is far enough from the border to make us above suspicion. I don't want to swell your head, but you might as well know, certain folks in Washington have heard about your habit of getting results. So they told me to put you on the case, and that's what I'm trying to do, goddammit."

Longarm nodded. "All right. But going to Laredo for openers is still dumb. Why don't I just run down to El Paso and start looking for sign where the cows were stolen?"

"Uh, I sure wish you wouldn't. You remember Colonel Walthers?"

"Sure, that asshole army man I can't seem to get along with for some reason."

"I noticed. He's in charge of the investigation at Fort Bliss. He runs the military police there."

Longarm laughed and said, "Shoot, Colonel Walthers might be able to get his socks on without help, but whatever he might think he's doing for the army down there, he sure ain't *running* it! I'll stay out of his way, Billy. I'll stay off the army post and just sniff for sign along the border."

Vail shook his head and said, "No, goddammit, I don't want you anywhere *near* El Paso! We know where the cows crossed the Rio. I want you to head 'em off, not chase 'em."

"Hell, Billy, you ain't listening. Those cows could come back anywhere! I ain't tall enough to see the whole infernal border from any one spot. If I went down into Mexico and found the hideouts where they change the brands and all—"

But Billy Vail was rearing up behind his desk, red-faced, as he cut in, "Goddammit, Longarm, you are the one who isn't listening! I ain't sending you to Mexico. I want you to stay the hell *out* of Mexico! That's a direct order, damn your eyes! The last time you were south of the border, you caused all sorts of problems that ain't quite died down yet. You may be a lawman in these United States, but in Mexico they still have papers out on you for murder!"

Longarm shrugged and grumbled, "Hell, I never murdered anybody down there, Billy. Maybe shot up some asshole *rurales* who were acting truculent, but—"

"But me no buts," Vail interrupted. "This time you're to go where I send you, and go after the folks I send you after. You're to do your whole and entire investigation on this side of the border. Is that clear?"

Longarm puffed his cheroot and said he'd catch the 8:15

south. Billy Vail sat down again and said, "Right. You change at Alamosa for the train to Laredo. And Longarm?"

"Yeah, Billy?"

"Please don't get us into another war with Mexico."

Chapter 2

Longarm knew that Marshal Billy Vail had ridden through fire, salt, and Comanche in his day, and could still hold his own on the rare occasions when he was called from his desk to work the field. But old Billy really spent too damned much time behind that desk these days, and paperwork was as rough on a lawman's brains as it was on his rump.

Billy Vail's plump body could have used more excitement, and his brain needed to simmer down a mite. A working lawman knew better than to make a game of chess out of a situation that was likely checkers. But old Billy had crossed all the bridges ahead of his overworked and underpaid deputy, and here Longarm was, going way the hell out of his way aboard a dusty southbound train, approaching Laredo from the wrong direction. Longarm was willing to admit that a stranger arriving from Fort Worth aboard the Missouri Pacific might look less like a lawman from Denver than he would swinging down from El Paso. But if anybody in Laredo was expecting him, it would hardly matter, even if he arrived aboard a free balloon.

Billy was fond of sending his deputies into the field undercover, and Longarm could see the advantages of that too, if it was true that Justice had reason to suspect its local agents along the border. But while desk theory was one thing, getting it to work out in the field was another. A novice outlaw might not have heard of Longarm, but the tall deputy wasn't given to false modesty and he was aware that he had a rep among his fellow peace officers. He knew he'd been described, in hushed tones, to many an apprentice gunslick as a Western phenomenon to be avoided or, if that didn't work, fired upon from the rear. Billy Vail had suggested he buy a new hat or shave his mustache before leaving Denver. But Longarm liked his pancaked Stetson just fine, and while he could always grow another, he knew that a pale, freshly shaved upper lip against the saddle-leather tan of his weathered face would attract far more attention. So he'd just lit out, changing trains all over Robin Hood's barn, but looking pretty much the way he normally did. If he was spotted, he was spotted. If he didn't run into anyone who knew him personally, he'd likely not be. What the hell, it wasn't as if he had two heads. He was just a tall old boy with a West-by-God-Virginia way of talking and a thoughtful way of walking that made more knowledgeable lawmen and owlhoots think twice before they messed with him. He had his badge and ID tucked away, and lots of gents packed a double-action .44 in a cross-draw rig. He figured he'd just check into whatever cheap hotel there might be in Laredo and play the tune by ear as it might be requested.

Texas was tedious, as well as a mite bigger than it really needed to be. He'd left Fort Worth on the late-afternoon train, and as he sat alone in a coach seat, watching the sun go down, it promised to get duller looking outside. It was a modern combo with a newfangled dining car and some Pullman cars up forward. Longarm had considered booking a fold-down bunk, but had decided it might be an unjustified abuse of the taxpayers, since the whole shebang figured to arrive in Laredo about 3:00 A.M. He knew that after sitting bored and restless for days, he'd never get to sleep before midnight, and rising to get dressed again after two or three hours of sleep seemed more uncivilized than comforting. He had plenty of smokes and a couple of books to read. So he reckoned he'd tough it through, get off in the wee hours, and be checked in and bedded down before sunrise. He'd planned it that way. Three in the morning was an infernal time to arrive anywhere. Most of the other passengers would be going on through to Mexico, to get off in Monterrey at a more sensible hour. He'd probably be the only gent detraining in Laredo, and the usual railroad-depot loafers wouldn't be on the scene to speculate when he got his gear from the baggage car and had to ask directions.

The flat range outside was turning purple in the gloaming, and way off in the distance Longarm spotted the glimmer of orange light in a settler's window. They were likely sitting down to supper, and Longarm wondered who they were, and why he cared. He always got sort of wistful this time of the evening, when he passed a lighted lamp in the window of some settled-down-for-good family. He wondered why. Those folks over yonder likely wished they were aboard this train, going someplace more interesting.

Up ahead, the locomotive whistled at a grade crossing. Longarm smiled, thinking back to the boy he'd once been, and how often at night he'd lain restless in bed, listening to the distant call of a passing train and wishing he was aboard her, going someplace, anyplace. Another day of routine chores was a horrid thing to think on when you were trying to go to sleep after a day in the fields with a hoe.

"Grass is always greener..." he murmured half-aloud, as he got to his feet and headed for the dining car. He wasn't really hungry, but the office had vouchered him three meals a day, and what the hell, if those infernal nesters were having supper, he'd have one too, and likely a better one.

He moved through the Pullman cars ahead, noticing that most of the seats were empty and only half of the coal-oil lamps were lit. Some well-dressed Mexican folks were arguing quietly about something as he approached, but hushed themselves as he passed. Longarm didn't look down at them; he figured he didn't look like he savvied Spanish, so there was no call for him to comment on the awful thing the gent in the silver-conchoed *charro* suit had said to the pretty *señorita* in the seat across from him. Longarm figured the gal had to be his wife or daughter. No other gal would have sat still for his mean-mouthing. As Longarm opened the door at the end of the car, the man in the *charro* suit lit into her again. He was accusing the gal of having bedroom eyes around Yanquis. Longarm hadn't looked close enough at the señorita to have an informed

21

opinion on this. She'd had her profile to him as he passed, and although he'd admired her dusky cameo features, he doubted he'd remember her the next time he saw her. She was one of those pretty but unremarkable little things, like you saw made out of plaster in the plate-glass windows of the Denver Dry Goods Department Store. She'd likely bought her outfit someplace like that. She'd been dressed more American than the men and the other woman with her. He knew any Mexicans booked aboard a Pullman had money. They were *ranchero* folks, most likely. He wondered if they sold beef legally, or if they might be part of the racket he'd been sent to investigate.

He put the thought on a back burner as he passed through another sleeping car and entered the diner. Anyone aboard this train would be traveling on, and there was no way he was about to start up a conversation with a pretty *señorita* and her jealous husband or fiance or whatever. He found an empty table near a window on the sunset side and hung his hat on the hook above it before sitting down, riding backwards. He didn't care one way or the other which way he faced aboard a moving train, but he liked to have his eyes on the entrance as he sipped his soup. He opened his frock coat and adjusted the gunbelt on his hip before the black waiter got to him with the menu.

The Missouri Pacific sure was getting fancy. The icewater didn't seem to have a price tag, but everything else cost an arm and a leg aboard this infernal train. Even the coffee was a la carte and cost a penny a cup. He decided he'd have some anyway and save on the salad. Everybody seemed to be serving salad lately, as though they thought their customers were a herd of cows. Longarm scanned the menu and decided he'd have liver and onions with mashed potatoes. He'd rather have had a steak, but he'd eaten a steak on a trian one time, and what the hell, what could they do wrong to liver and onions?

The waiter took his order and moseyed off, walking like a schoolmarm. Longarm didn't know if the waiters they hired were sissies or just trying to look high-toned, but they sure acted funny.

The dining car was half empty, but Longarm figured it would be sort of impolite to light up one of his cheroots while he waited for at least some coffee, for God's sake. So he sipped his icewater and tucked his napkin in his collar to keep himself occupied. It was almost dark outside now, and when he tried to look out the window, he only saw the interior of the diner, reflected in the glass. He spotted a female wearing a big picture hat coming in, and examined her discreetly by staring at her reflection instead of right at her. She looked sort of interesting, either way. The hat and her dress were both widow-black, but she had black ostrich plumes on the hat and her waistline was cinched in to an impossible eighteen inches. Longarm knew enough anatomy to know that no woman born of mortal flesh had an eighteen-inch waist, lacking whalebone and a heap of vanity-induced discomfort. But he figured that with her corset off, she had maybe a twenty-two- or twenty-four-inch waist to set off her ample bosom and nicely rounded hip bones. If she was a widow, she was a young one who hadn't had many kids. Her face wasn't bad, either. As he studied it in the reflection, he noticed she was looking his way with eyes as big and dark as those of a doe in heat. He managed to keep his own eyes blank as he noticed that she was joining him at his table and had to look directly at her.

He started to rise, but she murmured, "Please stay seated, sir. May one presume this seat is not taken?"

"I'm glad to say it ain't, ma'am," Longarm said, as the gal in black sat down with a demure smile. Looking openly at her now, he saw that she was a study in black and white, for her skin was the color of Jersey cream and her hair was as black as a raven's wing.

"My name is Petunia Blair and I'm on my way to Laredo," she said by way of introduction.

"Uh, my handle is Custis Crawford and that's where I'd be headed too, ma'am," he replied. "You, ah, live in Laredo?"

She dimpled slightly and murmured, "No, I'm going there on business."

The waiter brought her a menu before she could say more. Longarm asked the waiter if they could have some coffee while they waited for the cook to rustle them some grub. The waiter shot him a snooty look and said he'd see what he could do. Then he ignored Longarm as he took the gal's order. She asked for salad and poached trout, which didn't surprise him; he'd figured she couldn't pack much away, wearing that corset.

There were other things he couldn't figure. Like why she'd sat down at his table when there were a couple of other empty ones nearer the door. He could see why she hadn't wanted to sit across the aisle with the sullen-looking gent in the big Texas hat. The fellow was well dressed, but a man who ate while wearing a hat was either Jewish or impolite, and he didn't look Jewish. The demure-looking Petunia didn't seem to be sending any smoke signals or playing high-buttons under the table. He'd thought she looked sort of interested when she'd first spotted him across the room, but now that they were seated face to face, she just acted like she wanted to eat and coffee up. He was glad he wasn't playing poker with her.

The waiter brought their coffee and told Longarm his liver was ready if he wanted to start ahead of the lady. Longarm told him to serve them both at the same time, and the waiter nodded as though he approved.

"I don't mind if you want to be served now, sir. After all, you were here first," Petunia said.

"That's all right, ma'am. My folks raised me polite in the first place, and I was only killing time in the second. We face a long, slow night aboard this rattler, and the longer it takes to eat, the less I have to read. I picked up this book by a French fellow named Verne, but to tell the truth, I can't get into it. It's about this jasper who's built himself an airship, and now he's out to conquer the world with it."

"It sounds exciting, Mr., ah, Crawford."

"That's likely the trouble with it. I was in a war one time. The notion that folks could fight a war up in the air just won't go down. I can't buy airships dropping bombs on cities from way up on high like this crazy man in the book. Seems to me that if some owlhoot flew over me in such a fool contraption, I'd be more amused than scared."

He noticed that the Mexican family had come in and taken a table. The pretty *señorita* sat with her back to him, so Longarm still didn't know whether she had bedroom eyes or not. He noticed she had a rose in her hair, though. It was dark hair; he reckoned you could call it black. But it wasn't nigh as black as Petunia's. He wondered if Petunia dyed her hair to get it so stove-black and shiny. He suspected she did. That *señorita*'s hair was the natural black hair of a gal who had dark coloring. Petunia's skin was too white for a natural brunette. He wondered how on earth she kept it that pale in Texas. Even wearing big hats, a gal had to pick up *some* sunshine if she ever went outside in the daylight. He remembered another foreign book he'd read, and he smiled at the spooky notion he'd just had. He'd just seen the gal's reflection in glass. That Carmilla gal in the story about vampires had had no mirrors in her house and, come to think of it, never ate salads or poached trout, either.

The waiter brought them their orders on a tray, and as he was serving them, the man across the aisle in the big hat scowled toward them and growled, "Hey, nigger, where's my damned supper?"

The waiter stiffened slightly and tried to ignore the lout until he'd finished pouring the coffee, but the man in the big hat repeated, "Nigger! I'm talking to you, nigger!"

Petunia grimaced and shot the uncouth bully a disgusted look, which he apparently missed. The waiter turned his head to the man across the aisle and murmured, "Your order's coming directly, sir. The cook needs time to prepare so much."

"Yeah? How come you served them folks ahead of me, then? I was here afore either one of 'em, goddammit."

Longarm knew better, but enough was enough. He smiled over at the man in the big hat and murmured, "Watch the lingo, pard. Ladies present."

The man in the big hat swiveled in his seat, exposing the ivory grips of the Peacemaker he packed in a shoulder holster under his frock coat as he glared at Longarm and rasped, "I wasn't talking to you, cowboy. I asked this nigger where my vittles was, so crawfish *out* unless you're serious about getting *in*!"

Longarm felt his cheeks flush as he realized everyone else in the car was now aware of the exchange. He knew the gal across the table was expecting him to show off, but he'd gone way the hell out of the way to arrive in Laredo quietly, and this wasn't the way to do it. The waiter seemed to take the situation more seriously. He murmured something and sidestepped out from between them to vanish into the cooking compartment. The man in the big hat stared thoughtfully across at Longarm and said, "I'm waiting for an answer, friend."

Longarm smiled benignly. "I'm not about to prod a man from push to shove over a blue-plate special, mister. It's a free country and I reckon you've got every right to complain about the service aboard the Missouri Pacific if it don't please you."

"Then why'd you take that nigger's side agin me? Are you

a goddamn Black Republican, boy?"

Longarm took a deep breath, let half of it out to control his voice, and said, "I figure our waiter's man enough to take care of himself. My only objection to the way you voiced your free opinion was in your choice of words."

"My, my, ain't you the delicate son of a bitch?"

Longarm didn't answer. But Petunia did. She said, "Drop it, Pecos. You don't know who you're talking to."

The man in the big hat looked surprised and asked her, "Hey, you know who *I* am, little darling?"

Her voice was cold and flat as she replied, "I do, and I know your reputation. My, ah, escort has a reputation too, and he's right about this being a silly set-to over nothing."

The man called Pecos turned farther in his seat, legs braced under him, as he eyed Longarm and opined, "You must be new in these parts to take a nigger's part agin me, friend. The little lady is right about my rep. I'm interested in hearing yours."

"I'm nobody special, and my liver and onions are getting cold. So let's all just forget it, shall we?" Longarm suggested mildly.

He knew better than to turn away completely until the other man simmered down, but he made an effort at cutting his food with the fork in his left hand as he wondered who in hell Petunia was, and how she knew so much about him. She'd said she was getting off at Laredo, so there went all the time and trouble he and Billy Vail had wasted in sneaking him in quietly. She'd said she was a businesswoman; she knew the local gunslicks on sight; she kept U.S. federal deputies in her file too. That explained why she seldom went outside in broad daylight. Too bad. He'd just started to like her, too.

Pecos didn't want to let it drop. He looked at Petunia and said, "I don't remember seeing you along the deadline in Laredo, neither, honey. But you and me can get to know each other come Saturday night or so. You said your boyfriend here is a man capable of doing wonders and eating cucumbers, but I disremember a handle to go with his awesome rep. You want to tell me who he is and why I should quail at the sound of his name?"

Petunia toyed with her salad and muttered, "He's hardly my boyfriend. We just met. But a working girl at the Silver Dollar in Denver pointed him out to me one day, and they say he's nobody to mess with."

Pecos laughed. "She says I'm not to mess with you, boy. How do you feel about that?"

"I don't like to contradict a lady, but let's just forget it."

Pecos sneered at Petunia and demanded, "Lady? You aim to call that gal a lady, boy?"

Longarm's own smile was as friendly as a coiled sidewinder as he replied, "Any female I'm having dinner with is a lady until I say different, and before you say another word, I'd best tell you I've had just about enough of this foolishness."

Now, of course, if Pecos had had any sense at all, he'd have known better. But he'd started his brag with a lot of folks watching, and since the next stop was his home territory, he just didn't know how else to end it. So he came up out of his seat red-faced and slapping leather, and Longarm just as naturally whipped his own .44 out and fired first.

The round took Pecos under the heart and slammed him back against the bulkhead behind his overturned chair. Longarm rose, gun trained at nobody in particular, but ready if anyone else wanted a piece of the action. The man in the big hat slid slowly down the bulkhead, leaving a wet red streak on the polished mahogany paneling. The Mexican family rose to vamoose as others either ducked for cover or remained frozen in place.

A long, quiet moment passed as the wheels clicked under them and the late Pecos settled into a quiet puddle out of sight between the tables. Longarm swore softly under his breath and lowered the muzzle of his smoking gun. None of the hired help seemed interested in coming out of the cooking compartment, but a worried-looking man wearing a conductor's hat entered from the next car, shouting, "What's going on? I heard a gunshot."

Then he saw the gun in Longarm's fist and went as silent as everyone else.

Longarm felt drained and disgusted with himself as he faced the conductor wearily and said, "I just had it out with a gent you'll find yonder, under the tables. He went for his gun first."

A little fellow in a checked suit piped up, "That's right. We all seen it. It was that Laredo badman, Pecos McGraw. He started up with some of your help, and then he started mean-mouthing this gent and his ladyfriend there."

The waiter who'd been serving them came out when he heard the voices of reason. He looked relieved when he saw that it was Longarm still on his feet, and not the other man. He told the conductor, "That Pecos McGraw was at me again, cap'n. I tried to stay clear of him, like you told me the last time. But when he couldn't git at me, he just naturally went at these white folks."

The conductor eased past Longarm and had a look at the body on the floor between the tables. After a moment, he straightened and announced, "It's McGraw, right as rain. I'd be a liar if I said I was sorry." Then he turned to Longarm and said, "You'd be the Crawford who planned on getting off at Laredo, right?"

Longarm took a spare cartridge from his coat pocket to reload before holstering his .44 as he said, "I'm still getting off there, if I'm not arrested first. I reckon you'll wire the law at the next stop?"

The conductor nodded. "I'll have to report it from the water stop at midnight. That's where I'd get off, if I was you. You sure don't want to get off in Laredo, now!"

Longarm smiled thinly and started to reach in his coat for his wallet and ID as he said, "I'm not worried about getting arrested, if that's what you mean."

But he decided to let his badge stay put for the time being when Petunia said, "They can't arrest Mr. Crawford for what just happened, sir. It was sheer self-defense, and I mean to swear to it before a judge, if need be."

The conductor waved away the suggestion. "Ma'am, a judge and jury's the least of anyone's worries right now. Pecos McGraw wasn't one of the Missouri Pacific's favorite passengers, but he did seem popular in certain circles along the border. When word gets out that Mr. Crawford here put old Pecos on the carpeting, they'll likely want to settle the matter sort of informal."

He looked back at Longarm and added, "Nobody at the midnight jerkwater will bother you about what just happened. But I'd avoid the climate of Laredo for the foreseeable future. If the water don't kill you, McGraw's friends surely will."

Longarm never got to find out what the liver and onions he'd ordered tasted like. Petunia said she'd lost her appetite too, but that she had a bottle of Old Crow in her compartment. So while the train crew cleaned up the mess in the diner, Longarm followed the black-clad woman to her private compartment at one end of the second Pullman car. The porters were just starting to make up some of the bunk beds.

Her own seats in the small room had been made up into a bunk already. She apologized by saying she hadn't been expecting company, and told him to have a seat while she did the honors with the Old Crow. Longarm liked Maryland rye better, but bourbon, especially *good* bourbon, would do in a pinch, and there was something about this gal in black that didn't set right. She'd said she knew him, but she kept introducing him to folks as Crawford, the alias he'd given her. He decided to find out how well she knew him before he told her the story of his life.

Her own story didn't seem too complicated. Her face was bitter and a little pink as she took off her big hat and placed it on top of the same steamer trunk she packed her booze and tin cups in. She poured and handed him his drink before she said, "Well, I suppose you want to know how a nice gal like me got into such a business, eh?"

He sipped the drink, neat, and replied, "Everybody's in some business or another. Fortunately, yours and mine don't set us on opposing sides."

She shot him a confused look as she joined him, seated on the bed, with her own cup. He noticed that she took a healthy swig, considering they had no water to chase it. She said, "Well, I know you're sort of an aristocrat, next to me. But I'll have you know I don't work the cribs anymore. As you can see, I've saved my money, and when we get to Laredo I mean to do things right. I've already picked a good location and sent some nice things on ahead."

"What kind of things, Petunia? Blondes or redheads?"

"Silly, I'm talking about my furnishings. You know the trouble with places like the Silver Dollar or Madame Moustache's, in Dodge? They're too cheap and gaudy looking. I mean to have a respectable parlor house, with no red velveteen or dirty pictures on the walls. I figure a man away from home needs a, well, a more *wholesome* atmosphere. I mean to hire a good cook too. I'll have the usual refreshments at the bar downstairs, but I think a good home-cooked meal now and again is just as important as the, you know, other stuff."

Longarm nodded absently as he tried to put this crazy situation together in his head. They had maybe six or eight hours before Laredo to talk about the "other stuff," and right now what he wanted to know was how she knew so much about him and, more important, if it was going to be possible to get her to keep some of it to herself.

He took another sip and said, "You say a gal at the Silver Dollar in Denver pointed me out to you, Petunia? That seems fair, but the reason I'm curious is that I've never visited the Silver Dollar as a . . . customer."

She laughed. "I know. They say Madam Jacobs takes care of you personally. You were coming out of her office one afternoon when I first saw you. I was with two other girls near the piano, and I guess you didn't notice me. I was wearing a red shift, and my hair was different then."

"I thought I remembered the pretty eyes," he lied, "but of course I never connected 'em up with a house of ill repute. I'm just trying to remember the last time I paid old Ruth Jacobs a visit."

"It was only a few months ago. The Silver Dollar was the last place I had to work as crib girl. I told you I've been saving up to go into business on my own as a madam. I guess you won't believe this, but I haven't had to sell my body for a good six or eight weeks, and it does feel good to be done with that part of the business."

"So I hear. You say you saw me and Ruth Jacobs coming out of her office? Wait a minute, I do remember owing her a favor a while back."

Petunia nodded and said, "The girl who told me who you were said you and Ruth had sided one another in a gunfight a short time before. She didn't know your name was Crawford, but she remembered Madam Ruth saying anything you wanted was on the house, and of course she knew the line of work you were in."

"I was afraid of that," he sighed, sipping some more Old Crow.

Petunia noted the worried tone and put a hand on his knee as she assured him, "Don't worry. I'd be drawn and quartered before I'd tell the law on you. You were awfully sweet, back there in the diner."

Longarm felt more puzzled than sweet right now. His relationship with the notorious madam of Denver's biggest whorehouse was not something his superiors would approve of, but it was hardly illegal. Prostitution was not a federal offense in the first place, and Ruth Jacobs paid off the Denver P.D. regularly in the second. "Well, your friends likely had me mixed up with somebody else," he said cautiously.

"I doubt that," Petunia laughed. "You're a more exciting-looking man than one usually meets in a place like the Silver Dollar. Madam Ruth called you Custis as she said goodbye to you, too."

"All right, I just admitted being there."

He noticed that her hand was moving up his thigh as she said, "Don't act the coy virgin with me, Custis. I know who and what you are, but I said I'd never tell."

"That's nice to hear. Who and what in thunder did those gals tell you I might be?"

"Oh, we both know you're a notorious coin counterfeiter, Custis. I've seen some of your work. The other girls said you were a dangerous gunhand too."

Longarm sat silently thunderstruck as the brunette suddenly took one of his rough hands in both of hers and marveled, "My, you'd never know to look at your hands that you were so artistic. But I just saw how slick you move them with a gun. How do you get all those itsy-bitsy letters so neat with such big fingers?"

Longarm suddenly laughed, a trifle wildly, as the penny dropped. It was too funny for words. But he saw, now, how Petunia and those other whores had made their grotesque mistake. The tough and cool Madam Jacobs hadn't spilled enough to matter, and they'd put two and two together to come up with six.

As a lawman with a nose to the street, he naturally knew the denizens of the Denver underworld better than any Sunday-school teacher might have approved of. Ruth Jacobs had given him more than one good tip on a suddenly wealthy saddle tramp whose uncle apparently died about the same time a federal payroll was being held up. Also, a while back, she'd saved his ass by pointing out a bushwhacker literally behind a bush on the Denver State House grounds, and so he'd owed her.

Like many such establishments, the Silver Dollar minted its own tokens in lieu of cold cash to be taken up to the cribs and possibly mislaid in the course of an evening's trade. The Silver Dollar sold its customers mock coins, and the customers paid the girls upstairs with them. Talking to Ruth Jacobs after the shootout, he'd been told that the madam was having trouble with someone making crude copies of her "pussy pennies," so, helpful cuss that he was, Longarm had arranged to have new dies made for her by an employee at the Denver Mint whose wife had a lot of headaches. He'd been impressed at their artistry. Madam Ruth had wanted to pay him in cash or kind, but he'd settled for a drink, and only a drink, that afternoon in her office. (Madam Ruth was sort of long in the tooth and couldn't have been good looking when she was even younger than Petunia.)

Old Ruth Jacobs and her close confederates, by talking discreetly about their friendly neighborhood lawman, had left this other gal with the impression he was some sort of counterfeiter, and, of course, since old Ruth had boasted about her part in a wild-and-woolly gunfight, they'd gotten the idea he was a shootist, too!

Petunia lowered his hand to her own lap as she sighed, "I hope you'll be safe with me in Laredo, Custis. I'm worried about what the conductor said about Pecos McGraw's friends."

He didn't think she had anything important on under the black taffeta skirt, although he could feel the lower edge of her whalebone corset with the back of his hand as he said, "I was figuring on holing up at the hotel until I contacted some gents from the other side of the border, honey."

He was keeping his hand polite, so she sort of moved it back and forth between her thighs as she said, "They'll come looking for you there. But nobody would think to look for you in my place. We're not open for business yet, and I hardly know anybody in Laredo."

"Oh? Who *do* you know, Petunia?"

"Just the usual. A lawyer I hired up north contacted an associate down there to set things up with the local law, of course. I told you I mean to run a decent place, so none of the people I know will be in with riffraff like that nasty Pecos."

"That figures. He was sort of ornery, now that I study on it. By the way, since you seem to have a scrapbook on all us ornery rascals, just what did old Pecos do for a living when he wasn't trying to throw down a gent who already had the drop on him?"

Petunia said, "Oh, he wasn't a *real* outlaw like *you*, dear. It's my understanding he was a cattle dealer with an ugly streak. Like the Thompson Brothers. You've heard of them, haven't you?"

"Yep, had words with 'em in Dodge one night."

"Heavens, and you're still alive? Oh, Trixie was right, you really must be as rugged as you look!"

He moved his hand experimentally as he found it deeper between her trembling thighs and muttered, "You, ah, like your men sort of tough and ornery, huh?"

"Oh, that feels good, but let me take off my clothes if we're going any further, Custis."

She rose and started undressing as he smiled up at her, wondering how long this winning streak was likely to last. To his surprise, the first thing that she took off was her hair. It was a wig. In the warm coal-oil light he saw that she was a towhead blonde with close-cropped hair. He started to ask her why, but decided that would be stupid. Some whores liked to wear masks too, if they had friends and relations anywhere. Should anyone back East hear about a woman who answered to a missing gal's description, the jet black hair in the tale should throw them off.

Petunia folded her dress and placed it neatly on a shelf before she turned with a puzzled look and asked him, "What about you, dear? Don't you even mean to take your gunbelt off?"

He felt a little awkward as she stood over him, for she was indeed wearing no drawers or anything else under her dress except the black corset and long silk stockings. He noticed she still had her high-button shoes on, too. He said, "Uh, I was waiting for you to finish and give me some elbow room."

She laughed and climbed on the bed beside him to say, "Silly, this train will reach Laredo before the night's half over, and it takes me hours to get in and out of this fool corset." She moved closer to take his hand again and put it between her thighs as she purred, "Hurry. I'll let you see my bellybutton all you want after we get to my place in town."

He laughed and proceeded to shuck himself like an ear of corn. He let the duds fall on the floor near his feet. He wasn't quite as casual about it as he might look, for he made sure the gunbelt was on top and he palmed his derringer and tucked it between the pillows and the headboard when he took her in his arms to kiss her. She wrapped her arms around him and kissed him back, hungrily. Her breasts, naked above the black corseting, flattened against his own suddenly heaving chest. As she leaned toward the mattress, Longarm followed, cocking a leg over to get in position as she sighed and spread her milk-white thighs. As he mounted her, he glanced down to see where he was going. It looked wild as hell. Her tiny waistline had been purchased at the price of considerable displacement of the rest of her. Her pink-crested breasts rode proudly on a roll of flesh squeezed up under them from where it belonged around her rib cage. Her belly flesh had been extruded out from the bottom rim of the black-lace-and-whalebone corseting to form another roll on her normally flat belly above her flaxen pubic thatch. As he tried to fumble his way in, she reached down between them to guide his shaft to glory. Her eyes suddenly widened as she felt him experimentally. "Oh, there's more to you than meets the eye. Be gentle, will you? I haven't done this for a while."

Then she got him aimed, thrust her hips up to envelop him to the roots, and hissed, "Oh, yessss!" as she wrapped her legs around his waist and proceeded to buck like an unbroken bronc.

He knew he couldn't fall out of *this* saddle, so he didn't try to grab leather. It felt strange and interesting to have parts of him rubbing against black lace that sort of scratched and other parts encased in sugar and spice. Her thighs above the stockings were soft as marshmallow, but her leather shoes, crossed over his rump, felt like somebody in boots was kicking him in the butt with every bounce. He didn't know what celibacy did to a gal in Petunia's line of work, but he'd been doing without for days on the infernal trains old Billy had made him ride, and he came so fast it was downright insulting.

He knew there was more to come as soon as he got some wind back, so he stayed in her and she hardly seemed to notice he'd stopped moving, between the way she was thrusting and the funny vibrations the train wheels offered when their pubic bones met. He decided he'd had all the rest he needed and got his feet against the footboard of the small bunk to move at another angle. It sure felt nice to let his toes do most of the work now. Her little round belly felt like a warm, smooth pillow against his own as he went up and down on his toes in a horizontal position. She laughed and asked, "Is my corset scratching you? You're moving sort of like... I don't know, like a lizard or something."

He remembered a circus sideshow he'd been to one time, and made his voice like the barker's as he teased, "Hurry, hurry, hurry, for one thin dime, one tenth of a dollar, you will see Lulu the Crocodile Dancer. The last living descendent of the Crocodile Dancers who danced for old Pharoah in the shadow of the Sphinx!"

She giggled again, then moaned and sobbed, "Oh, Jesus, it's happening. Don't stop! Don't ever stop!"

Then she had a long shuddering orgasm and sighed, "Oh, please stop. I'm too excited. I have to get Petunia back."

So he stopped, or sort of stopped, as the train swayed under them and the wheels clicking over the rail-ends kept tingling their close-pressed bodies. She unhooked the booted ankles above his ass and he was afraid for a moment that she really wanted to stop, leaving him halfway to second base with a hard-on, but then she slid her thighs up his flanks to hook a silk-clad knee in each of his armpits as she said, "Oh, I can take it all now. Do you like it?"

He thought it would seem crude to ask her if she was trying to take him balls and all, so he kissed her some more and said, "Yeah, you sure have limber legs, for a gal in armor. How can you bend your waist in that getup?"

She started moving, inside as well as outside, as she cooed, "I don't have to bend my waist, dear. As a matter of fact, it sort of gives me some leverage I hadn't suspected."

"I noticed. Are you saying you don't usually do this with your corset on? Never mind, I don't reckon I really want to know."

She stiffened, as if hurt, then moved teasingly and said, "Maybe I should have charged you. You men never beleive any woman can do it just for fun, the way you do. We're either supposed to be in love with you or expecting to be paid for the hire of the hall when you want to play a tune on your old organ."

Longarm didn't answer. When a man was coming, he either had to say something mushy, which seemed sort of silly right now, or just buckle down and do it, which he proceeded to do.

Petunia responded to his increased passion in kind, so he

35

did his best to please a lady, and by the time she'd simmered down to a steady lope again, he was out of breath and going soft. So he suggested that they rest and share a smoke.

She said she'd admire that and seemed pleased when he held her head on his shoulder and put his cheroot to her lips every other puff. She told him it made her feel romantic to be treated friendly afterwards, and so he knew she hadn't been offended by his only coming twice for now. Gals who knew him better would have been. He was a mite offended himself, for she really was a damned fine lay. He figured part of it might be that she spooked him. Longarm wasn't letting on that he was spooked, and he didn't know *why* he was spooked, but he was alive this night because he'd learned a spell back that when the hairs on the back of a man's neck started to tingle, it was time to be on guard, and if there was one time when a man's defenses were down, it was in the middle of a good lay.

Petunia let the rank smoke trickle out through her nostrils as she cuddled closer and handed the cheroot back to him, saying, "I was so afraid you'd go cold and snooty on me as soon as you'd had your pleasure."

"Why would I want to act so uncivilized?" he asked.

"Oh, you know. I told you I was semi-retired, and I swear I haven't given myself for fun or profit in over a month. But you men are all alike when it comes to us businesswomen."

"I thought you said you weren't hiring out as a whore anymore."

"Well, we both know more than I should have told you. 'Fess up. You'd like me better if you thought I was an innocent widow woman, wouldn't you?"

He blew a smoke ring thoughtfully and said, "An innocent widow woman is a contradiction in terms. To be a widow woman, a gal has to have been married up at least once, and I've met damned few men who never slept with their wives fairly regular."

She started to say something else, but he put the cheroot in her mouth to hush her as he continued, "I'll tell you something else. It puts a man's passion off its feed to hear about any other old boy sharing the wealth. I met this widow woman up in Denver one time who really put a damper on my enthusiasm by talking every infernal night about her damned dead husband. She was young and pretty too, but it did get to feeling like there was three of us in her four-poster. I asked her polite to stop comparing us in the middle of some otherwise tolerable fun. But she must have figured I'd be complimented to be told in the middle of the act that I did it better than the dear departed." He took the cigar back, blew another ring, and added, "She was wrong."

Petunia began to caress his belly as she asked, "Oh, was this widow woman as good in bed as present company?"

He laughed and said, "There you go. You didn't like hearing about me in another lady, much. We're all sort of dumb that way. There ain't a human being who ain't a mite jealous and a mite fickle-hearted. We'd all like to have exclusive privileges to the entire opposite sex, provided nobody tries to make private property out of *us*!"

She moved her hand farther down and said, "I do sort of wish I'd found you in an egg, ready to hatch out pure, with a hard-on you knew how to use. It was sweet of you to call me a lady, though."

Her hand wasn't acting very ladylike at the moment, but he hadn't finished his smoke and the strangeness of the situation seemed to be having an odd effect on him. He was damned if he could see why his flag wasn't running up the pole right now, considering that a pretty blonde in black lace was trying to hoist it with considerable skill. He took a drag of smoke and said, "I'm going to tell you a story, and then we'll say no more about who might be a lady and who might not be."

"Can't you tell me later? We have to think about getting dressed by two-thirty or so."

"I know. It's still early. And you've got to get over this bullshit about the line of work you used to be in. So, like I was saying, there was this waitress up in Leadville. Nice gal, thirty or more, but still sort of pretty."

"Oh? Did you have your wicked way with her?"

"No," he lied, "but that ain't the point. I'm trying to tell you about a notion that vexed her. You see, she came out West during the Pike's Peak Rush, looking for gold in Cripple Creek with her old man. Only they never found any gold and the old man died of cholera, leaving her sort of stranded. There was lots of money changing hands in the gold fields, and an egg cost a dollar up in Cripple Creek. She offered to take in laundry, but they had some Chinamen who did that better. So, what with one thing and another, the poor gal had to sell the only thing of value she had."

"You mean her pussy?"

"Well, nobody wanted to buy her calico dress or sunbonnet. Anyway, she worked a couple of weeks as a woman of the town and then she got this job as a waitress. When I met up with her she'd been a waitress, and a good one, for a dozen years or more."

"Is there a point to this rambling yarn, Custis?"

"Yep. You see, what bothered her was that for a dozen years or more the boys in Leadville had been calling that poor lady a whore, and not once had anybody ever called her a waitress!"

Petunia laughed bitterly. "I know how she feels. And speaking of feeling..."

Longarm felt it too. He hadn't expected it just now, but he wasn't all that surprised. Any man who couldn't get it up under such circumstances had to be dead or dying. Petunia kept stroking as she sat up to fork a long, silk-sheathed leg over him and settle down atop him. That got his undivided attention. The soft lamplight was kind to her pretty but hard young features as she grinned down at him and started to move up and down on his shaft.

She moved slowly and sensually, a mite slower than he wanted her to. So he put his hands around her waist to help her. Her impossibly cinched waist was so tiny he could touch the tips of his long fingers together over her spine as he dug his thumbs into the lace between the whalebone stays over her navel. The black lace afforded him a good grip, but he didn't want to hurt her, so he asked her if he was causing her pain. She shook her head and said, "Oh, no, I like it. You're strong as a bull and it's sort of exciting."

He found himself eye to eye with an erect pink nipple, so he started kissing it to be polite as he ran his hands down over her bare derriere. He found he could move her better that way, with a soft buttock cupped in each palm. Petunia came quietly this time, which made it better. He was getting there himself, but it grew sort of tedious, even when a gal was light, to lift her on and off like a pretty feed sack. So he rolled her over, meaning to mount her properly. She landed face down and breathing helplessly, so he reconsidered, got out of the bunk, and hoisted her into a dog-style position, with his hands gripping the stout corset. The lamplight on her upthrust, naked rump made it look as pretty as two harvest moons rising side by side. So, standing barefoot on the vibrating floor, he got inside her throbbing flesh to finish his own pleasuring as he enjoyed the view. He could see what she meant about the corset being hard to get in and out of. It was laced down her spine and tied in a bow knot over her tailbone. He resisted a wicked impulse as he started to pound her, for they really did have to get off this infernal train at 3:00 A.M., and while it would be interesting to watch her explode out of that black lace and whalebone, it would be one hell of a chore to stuff her all back in.

That reminded him about what she'd said about him staying with her at her place in Laredo. He wasn't sure it was such a grand notion, but he sure couldn't wander about a strange town in the small hours after shooting one of the local citizens. The friends of the late Pecos McGraw would be laying for him at the regular hotel if they aimed to lay for him anywhere, so he figured he'd best go home with Petunia for now and see how he felt about it in the cold gray light of dawn. This unexpected orgy was doing wonders for the kinks he'd picked up, riding all these damned old trains. A few hours' sleep and a good breakfast should put him in shape to go back to work for the taxpayers. He thought about doing all this in another bed with all this black lace stuff off Petunia, and it seemed he could see her long, white, naked back as he thrust in and out, gripping the stays over her rounded hipbones. That inspired him to sort of forget about the sleeping part when they got to Laredo. A man could always sleep another time. Life didn't offer many nights with such pleasant company.

Petunia started chewing the edge of the pillow she held in one hand as she pounded her other fist on the mattress and sobbed, "Oh, harder, darling!" So Longarm did his best to please as he decided it didn't hardly matter whether she was a good cook or not.

Chapter 3

Petunia's two-story frame house, on a dark and silent sidestreet in Laredo, was a surprise. He didn't know exactly what it looked like on the outside, since Laredo had no streetlamps away from the main drag near the depot. It was a pure mystery to Longarm how the Mexican coachman they'd hired had found the place, even after Petunia gave him the address.

As he'd hoped, nobody but a few Mex baggage-smashers and drivers-for-hire had been up and about near the depot when their train pulled in a little after three. The conductor had seemed astonished to see Longarm helping the once-more-brunette Petunia down the steps. But he hadn't asked where Longarm had been all that time. He'd only figured that any man who detrained in the hometown of a man he'd just shot ought to have his head examined by a team of physicians. A few other passengers had gotten off down the line, but they hadn't been near enough to be of interest, and, so, save for Petunia and the conductor, nobody important could know he was in Laredo.

The surprising thing about Petunia's house was how sedate

and lived-in it appeared. She'd told him she meant to have a more respectable parlor house than most, so he hadn't expected a red lantern over the door or naked ladies in gilt frames over the bar. But there wasn't even a bar. The downstairs looked as though some decent family lived there. As Petunia showed him around, he noticed a Boston fern in the bay window of the sitting room, and there was a bookcase on either side of the fireplace. As Petunia took his hat, he said, "I know you can buy furnishings by mail, honey, but your plants have been watered recent."

"I know. I forgot to tell you, my lawyer in town didn't buy me an empty house and stock it. There was an elderly doctor living here until a few weeks ago. He died intestate and alone, so my lawyer took it from the county for this year's taxes, which they'd never get any other way."

Longarm grimaced. "Lawyers are good at doing things like that. He's a paid-up member of the courthouse gang, right?"

"Of course. What other kind of lawyer would a woman in my profession want? He said the kitchen was stocked. Would you like me to fix you some ham and eggs before we get undressed again, or would you like to get undressed now and eat later?"

He laughed lightly and replied, "Let's study on that. I don't have to get up early. How about yourself?"

"Well, with the weekend coming, it's small use starting to set up shop. If there's one thing I learned from Madam Ruth, it was to know better than to even interview a girl until I made sure of the local law, and the big shots will be home with their families until Monday or so."

He nodded, seeing some advantages to himself as well. "In that case, let's say we eat something and coffee up afore we crawl back betwixt the sheets. I ain't tired yet, but it's sort of unromantic to kiss a pretty gal with a growling stomach."

"All right," she agreed, laughing. "But I mean to get comfortable first. This corset's bad enough when a girl's just sitting demure. I think you may have broken my floating ribs back there on the train, and if I don't get out of the thing right now, I'll swoon at the smell of frying eggs and such."

He walked back to the steamer trunk the Mexican had left with his own gear in the vestibule, and when she unlocked it again, he pried it open for her. She took out a frilly housecoat and said, "A little dramatic to cook a late supper or early breakfast in, but I don't own an apron. Hold it while I get out of this dress, will you?"

"Here in the vestibule? Don't you have bedrooms in this house?"

"Silly, why go all the way upstairs if we're coming right back down? What's the matter with you? We're all alone in the house, and you certainly weren't shy when we were on the train a little while back."

So he stood there, feeling sort of foolish, as Petunia took off her hat and wig again and proceeded to shuck her duds by the front door. It was fairly dark, since the only lamps she'd lit were in the other room off the hall, and he doubted that anyone on the street out front could see much through the heavy drapes over the glass panels on either side of the door.

She stripped down to her familiar corset, shoes, and stockings, and it was surprising how good it all looked a second time, considering. She turned around and asked him, "Would you unlace me, darling? I assume you know how, you brute."

He hooked her filmy housecoat over his forearm as he stepped in close and untied the knot at the base of her spine, asking, "How did you get into this contraption, if you've been a good gal all this time like you said?"

She heaved a contented sigh as he started to unlace her and explained, "The maid at my last hotel helped me, if you must know. You certainly have a suspicious mind, considering I told you I was a bad girl before we both proved it."

He didn't answer. It was sort of interesting to watch her expand like that as he released the pressure around her middle. He'd been right about her having a normal waistline of twenty-four inches or so, and as her nicely formed body fell back into its natural curves, it looked like he was meeting up with another woman altogether. The fatty rolls at either end of the whalebone flattened out, and as her spine emerged, he saw that her back was prettier than he'd imagined, and he'd imagined it would look right nice. As he finished, she let the corset fall to the floor at their feet and turned to him with a relieved smile, stark naked except for her stockings and high-button, high-heeled shoes. She faced him boldly and placed her hand on her hips as she asked, "How do you like it so far?"

The face was the same. The rest was all new. Her breasts

hung a mite lower and looked softer. Her belly, above the patch of blond pubic hair, was flatter and her curves flowed more smoothly if less dramatically. He said, "You're pretty enough to carve out of marble and set in some museum with the other Greek ladies. How come you gals gussy up in those infernal instruments of torture, anyway?"

She rubbed her still-numb midsection and sighed, "Lord only knows. I suppose if the fashions called for Levi's, we'd be foolish enough to wear them. Kiss me, Custis. Getting out of that silly thing has made me hot again."

So he kissed her, and eating suddenly seemed less important. He wondered what the effect on her innards might be, with all her curves redistributed, so he asked, "Did you say the bedroom was upstairs, honey?"

She nodded, but said, "Never mind all that. There's a sofa in the sitting room that's never been christened yet."

"Jesus Christ, in the sitting room, Petunia?"

"Why not? It's my house, and I told you we have it all to ourselves." She giggled and added roguishly, "I just had a wonderful idea, seeing we have the weekend ahead of us. What say we do it at least once in every room in the house? It'll seem more homey after you've had me on every stick of furniture I own. Have you ever done it on a kitchen table?"

He had, and he suspected that she had too, but he didn't want to jaw about the past again, so he picked her up and carried her into the sitting room. He lowered her to the sofa near the cold fireplace and broke some records getting out of his own duds, for she did look like a new experience to be had, and, when he had her, she was.

She even felt different inside; as he'd suspected, the tight corseting had distorted her abdomen the last time they'd done this. But he had no complaints. The new Petunia didn't feel better or worse; she just felt different, like her naughty twin sister, maybe.

That reminded him of a couple of real twins he'd met aboard a steamboat on the Big Muddy a spell back, and that inspired him to new heights. He sure wished he could have a party with all three of them and maybe that Chinese gal he'd been so friendly with a while back...."

"Not so wild, lover!" Petunia protested as Longarm sort of lost control. Then, as he slowed down and put more weight on his elbows to be polite, she giggled and said, "This is crazy, but it feels like a new strange man inside me, and it takes some getting used to."

He laughed too, and then, as she started arching her spine in new-found freedom, she crooned, "Oh, forget what I just said and love me right."

So he did and they enjoyed it, but the next time they came, they both realized they were getting past passion into showing off, so Petunia said, "Save some of that for later, dear. I'll just run in the kitchen and rustle us up some grub while you get your breath back. I think it would be nice to finish upstairs after we eat. I'm looking forward to falling asleep in your arms with my tummy filled, from both ends."

He let her up and she scampered off to the kitchen in her shoes and stockings as he watched her hindquarters fondly. He reclined on one elbow for a time, considering whether reaching for a smoke in his rumpled duds down at the far end was worth the effort. He decided he'd been smoking too much lately, in any case. It was an expensive habit, and he'd been trying to cut down. He'd cut down a hundred times or so that very year. On the other hand, as long as he was going to be decadent, he reckoned he might as well go whole hog.

He rolled off the sofa, picked up his hickory shirt, and fished out a cheroot and a sulfur match. He lit up, and as he heard the tinkle of pots and pans from the kitchen at the back of the house, he decided to do some exploring, since he was on his feet in any case. He tossed the match stem in the fireplace and moseyed over to the bookcases, feeling more naked than usual since he'd seldom poked around a downstairs sitting room dressed like this. The carpet felt downright lewd under his bare feet. Longarm had other secret vices. Reading books was one of them. He was farm-bred and self-educated, so he sometimes didn't realize how well he'd educated himself, and was a little bashful about the odd facts that popped out of his weatherbeaten face at the damnedest times. But what the hell, an unmarried lawman spent a lot of nights alone in strange towns, and reading books was no worse than getting drunk alone, was it?

The books to the left were mostly novels and a cookbook tucked between two children's books. He supposed an old doctor living alone might have some use for a cookbook, but what had he been doing with kids' fairy tale books?

Longarm wasn't sure when the Brothers Grimm had been in business, so he took a book out and looked at the publication date on the flyleaf. It was a reprinted edition, run off the press less than three years back.

"Grandchildren?" He mused, putting the book carefully back in place. Petunia had said the old man had died intestate, meaning no will or next of kin worth mention. Of course, some old folks might read kid's fairy tales. He'd read some himself, and they were sort of interesting. He couldn't see himself buying expensively bound kids' books new, though.

Longarm moved over to the other bookshelf, where he saw matching sets of textbooks. That made more sense; a doctor would have books like that on tap. But they weren't medical books. They were lawbooks. He picked one off the shelf at random and read the title: *Torts and Damages, Webb County, Texas*.

That was esoteric reading indeed for a small-town sawbones. He could see a doctor having some general lawbooks on his shelves, but Webb was the county Laredo was in, so this book was a private printing that would cost a heap of money and wouldn't be all that interesting to anybody but a lawyer. He put the book back, scanned the shelf, and found a couple of books in Spanish. He spoke a little of the lingo, and anyone with a lick of sense could see they were on general Mexican law and specific Chihuahua and Sonora legal codes. Longarm knew the Mexican states just to the south were Tamaulipas and Nuevo Leon. So what the hell was a Laredo M.D. doing with lawbooks that would be of scant use to anybody in these parts?

He looked for the Mexican lawbooks a local man might have some use for. They weren't there. But he saw another book that was more interesting. He took the leatherbound folder out and whistled softly to himself as he read the title page: *Cattle Brands and Markings: Office of the County Clerk, Webb County, Texas*.

He was still holding the brand registry when Petunia came in, still naked but carrying a tray. She smiled prettily and said, "I thought we'd eat in here, Custis. What's that you're reading?"

He put the folder back with a casual smile and said, "I was just browsing through the old doc's books. You did say he was a doc, didn't you?"

Petunia put the tray down on a rosewood table near the sofa, and he admired the view as she bent over. "That's what they told me he was," she said. "I never met him, of course. Come on, eat your ham and eggs before they get cold. You can read later, if you don't feel up to other fun with me."

"That don't seem likely," he said as he sat down beside her. She looked relieved and moved her naked hip against his as they dove into the ham and eggs she'd fixed. Longarm was hungrier than he'd imagined and, wonder of wonders, Petunia cooked decently, too. He didn't think he'd better ask her if these were the limits of her talents. As a garden-variety whore, Petunia was making less sense by the minute. He wondered what and who she really was. But he'd watched her eyes when he asked about the old doc, and she was either as ignorant as she seemed or a better actress than most, whatever the hell she might be. He figured his best bet was to play along with her for now. It was black outside and he didn't even know what part of town he was in. Come sunrise, he'd just drift over to the stockyards innocently and play it by ear. He didn't know why the lawyer she said she'd contacted here in town had hired his own house to a would-be madam. It made no sense, no matter how he read it. Neither a doctor's nor a lawyer's house made any sense as a spanking new bordello. He didn't know Laredo all that well, but he knew many a cow town like it, and he'd never ridden through one yet where the whores and gamblers lived on the same side of Main Street as the doctors and lawyers.

He finished his ham and eggs and washed them down with some mighty fine coffee while he considered his next move. He knew what Billy Vail would tell him to do. Old Billy would tell him to lay low, like Br'er Fox, and say no more about it. Petunia undoubtedly had her own good reasons for going around telling everybody she was a whore. She'd sure as hell tried to convince him she was one, and he sort of felt he owed her for her dedication to her role.

As she drained her own cup, she sighed and said, "Oh, I'm starting to feel human again. Do you want some more, or shall we go upstairs and make love?"

"Neither, just now. I ain't sure there's time."

She looked puzzled as she answered, "We've plenty of time, dear. It's only five or so, and even when the sun comes up..."

Then she saw he was pulling on his longjohns and added, "Oh? Just like that? I'd heard you were a love-'em-and-leave-'em sort, but this is sort of abrupt, even for you, isn't it?"

He stopped and looked her in the eye. "I figured you know who I really was all the time, Petunia. You made up that story about seeing me in a Denver cathouse after you went and blurted too much on the train when that dumb cuss started with me."

"I don't know what you're talking about!" she lied.

He pulled on his pants and started hauling on his boots as he said, "We'd best cut this bullshit, Petunia. I suspicion they're onto *you*, too. Who do you work for, the Pinks or the Cattlemen's Protective Association?"

Slackjawed, she stared at him as he stomped into his boots and strapped on his gun rig, leaving himself naked from the waist up for now, as he moved over to the lamp, snuffed it out, and strode to the window. He hadn't really expected her to answer; he'd just been thinking aloud.

He knew better than to move the curtains. He peered out through the slit and said, "It's getting gray out. We're all right for now. I reckon they figured on letting you settle in for a spell before they sent anybody. That lawyer fellow is expecting you to contact him once you're set up in Laredo, right?"

"Of course. But what's this all about? You're acting like a maniac and talking even wilder, darling."

He saw there was little to fear now. He could see an old Mex leading a burro laden with firewood down the street outside in the wan light. He opened the curtains to let some of the light in before he rejoined Petunia on the sofa. She looked silver in the dim light and he kissed her gently before he said, "They might not know I'm here yet. But like I said, they're on to you, Petunia. Sure, you went to a heap of trouble setting up your cover story, but somehow they found out."

"What on earth are you accusing me of, Custis? I've admitted everything to you there is to know. Do you think I'm proud of my past?"

He chuckled and said, "Yeah, I think you've been enjoying yourself pretending to be a bad gal. I enjoyed it too. That old yarn about me fixing up Madam Ruth with those tokens has got around some. My boss gave me pure hell when he heard I'd corrupted a fellow federal employee like that. So spare me the details of how you found out who and what I am. When you spied me on the train, you came over to pump me and find out what Uncle Sam's part in the action was. Either that or you followed me aboard. You slipped up and let me know you knew something about me. I admire the way you covered up with that wild tale of meeting me in a whorehouse, but you don't know as much about the business as I do, and I've never worked in a crib yet."

"I guess I should feel flattered, if you mean to imply I'm not really a prostitute. But let me see if I understand you. Are you saying you are not a notorious counterfeiter?"

"Oh, hell, honey, you knew all the time I was law. But I'm dumber than you are, so it took me till just now to figure out you were law too." He grimaced and added, "I should be tied and horsewhipped. It's just starting to hit me how stupid we've been acting. Have you any notion how they'd have laughed at us if they'd come gunning for us just now and caught us on this fool sofa, going at it like infernal rabbits?"

Petunia started to protest some more. Then her shoulders sagged and she said, "They told me you were good. I never should have picked you up on that train. But you know what they say about female curiosity, and, damn it, I did enjoy having sex with you."

He put an arm around her naked shoulder and said, "That wasn't what gave your show away, even though you do enjoy nature study too much for a gal who sells it regular. We may have time to say good-bye right, once we get some things sorted out. There's a train heading north this afternoon. It ought to be safe for me to put you aboard her in broad daylight. They won't be expecting you to light out, and it's likely that nobody important knows I'm even here. First things first, though. I'd like you to give me the names of all the shady gents you contacted here in Laredo. I'll need the lawyer up north, too. He's the one who set you up, you know."

"Set me up for what, for God's sake?"

"A killing, most likely. It only took me one night to figure out you were a private dickess. They've been expecting you for some time, and now here you are, all alone, they think, in a house they control along with the patrolman on this beat and likely the neighbors on both sides. So who are you working for?"

"Cattleman's Protective," she replied, sighing. "Are you down here about the Laredo Loop too, Custis Longarm Long?"

"I'll ask the questions for now. I've got a notebook and pencil stub in my coat, on the floor, and we'd best get some names down. You can scribble 'em in for me."

He let go of her and bent to get his pad and pencil as she shivered and said, "It's getting sort of chilly, this close to dawn. You can't mean it that Thayer would set me up for a murder in his very own house!"

He jotted the name down and handed her the pad, taking her in his arms to warm her a bit as he asked, "Where would *you* murder a stranger, in some *other* gent's house? I just told you how easy it would be, Petunia. Seeing that you're a female, they might not figure on using a gun on you. Even if they had to shoot you once or twice, who's about to bust into a respected local politico's domicile after hearing shots somewhere in the night? Hell, if push comes to shove and they catch the bastard standing over you with a smoking gun, he can always say he surprised you and thought you were a burglar or something. It's his house. This is his town. You'd be put down as a passing-through fancy gal who likely went crazy and busted in to steal his books or something."

Her eyes filled with tears as she said tremulously, "Damn, this was an important case to me! They told me it might be dangerous, but Jesus, to be unmasked like this before I found out anything..."

He stroked her hair and said, "Now you just hush, pretty lady. Think how lucky things turned out. Had we not met and got to be pards, they would have made you vanish like magic and nobody on our side would know as much as the two of us just figured out between us."

"We figured something out, dear?"

"Hell, yes, we did. We know now that the local courthouse gang is in on the racket, which will relieve Uncle Sam some about his local marshal's office. We got us some names. We know that at least one member of the Cattleman's Protective is a crook working for both sides. Most important, we get to keep you alive and on your way home as pretty as ever, if a mite wiser. One thing, though. I'm going to have to swear you to secrecy for now. One of your sidekicks is a crook. We don't know which one. So when you get home, you're to tell 'em you lit out 'cause you suspicioned the crooks were onto you, period. I'd give you the story to make up, but I noticed you like to make up your own fibs, and you're good at it too."

She laughed softly and said, "I'm not really named Petunia. You may as well call me Molly, as long as we're putting all our cards on the table."

"Molly's a pretty name too."

"Really? I always felt it was sort of common. I think the thing I like most about this job is that I get to play such interesting parts and use such pretty names."

"A rose by any other name would likely kiss no better," he said, and then, suiting actions to words, he kissed her. She shuddered in his arms and said, "This is silly, but now that you know I'm not a bad girl I feel so naked and, well, bashful!"

"Finish writing the names you know and we'll go up and get to know each other better," he told her softly.

"Are you sure it would be proper? I mean, it's one thing to do bawdy things playing a part, but to go wild like that with a man who knows who I really am..."

"I understand. We'll just put your duds back on and say no more about it if it seems ugly to you, uh...Molly."

She hesitated, snuggled closer, and murmured, "I never said it seemed ugly to me, Custis. I just said it made me feel funny. Let me finish this damned scribble and see what it's like, now that I feel free to really let myself go!"

Chapter 4

They parted regretfully, with Petunia, or Molly, blowing tearful kisses at him from the train as it pulled out of the depot. The sun was almost directly overhead and the streets of Laredo were hot enough that the alley cats were walking on tiptoes. He was glad they'd had a bath together before sneaking her out of that house. He was starting to sweat, even with his frock coat thrown over his left arm, by the time he'd walked a block. But it was clean sweat and he had on a fresh shirt from his bag. Before they'd left the house he'd taken it from his gear, which now reposed under lock and key back at the depot. He figured he'd send for it when and if he found a safer place to stay in town. The house the crooks had offered Molly was a sure deathtrap and the hotel didn't sound much safer.

The way you found your way about most small towns was to get a haircut, whether you needed one or not. So, after he sent a coded wire to Billy Vail at the marshal's home address in Denver, Longarm found a barbershop and went in to sit a spell with his mouth shut and his ears open. The barber had another customer in his chair and others were waiting, so Longarm sat down, picked up a *Police Gazette*, and pretended he hadn't read last month's issue already. That nice-looking circus gal in tights was on the same page and he still admired her form, although he'd recently explored the possibilities of eighteen-inch whalebone waists, so if he ever met up with that circus gal, he meant to undress her first.

Another man came in and sat down, saying howdy to some of the others he knew. Longarm kept his face buried in the *Police Gazette* as the newcomer announced, "Well, they say he's in town, boys."

When another man asked who he was talking about, the gossipy gent added, "The man who shot Pecos McGraw. A whiskey drummer who was on the train and seed it happen was talking about it over to Rosie's just now. He said the gent as done the deed got off the train last night when he did, with a fancy-looking gal in a big hat. Drummer said he got the impression he might have shot some other gents in the past. Said he did old Pecos slick as hell, like he'd had practice."

Another man chimed in, "McGraw was supposed to be good. Did this here drummer say if it was done fair and square?"

"Oh, they went at each other decent and proper enough for a fight over a gal. That's what they had words about—the fancy gal in the big hat. Old Pecos insulted her or something, and when the gent with her called him on it, old Pecos slapped leather. Only he didn't slap fast enough, this time."

There was a general murmur of uninformed opinion, then someone said, "Well, it's no never-mind of mine, since it wasn't my gal and I'd be a liar if I said I admired McGraw's manners all that much. Man who done it must not have knowed McGraw hailed from here, if he got off at Laredo. There's many a man in town who just might want to buy him a drink for what he done, but when the boys Pecos drank with hear tell of their pal's killer being in town, they might not be so understanding!"

The man who'd brought the news laughed and said, "They already have. Old Jimbo Thorne and the Dobkins brothers are out looking for him this minute. I misdoubt they aims to buy him no drink."

Longarm made mental notes of the names as someone asked, "What's this poor pilgrim supposed to look like, Windy?" and the crier said, "I can't rightly say. Drummer said he was just a tall galoot with a mustache, like half the boys in town. Said he favored a cross-draw rig and that the war-talk leading up to the shootout had involved some discussion of him having a rep. Pecos McGraw had a rep too, now that I study on it. Can't say as it did him much good when it come time to back his brag."

The man getting his hair cut put in, "That new gent must be some punkins if he gunned old Pecos whilst his back was up and they was face to face with a gal watching. I was there the time Pecos gunned the Waco Kid in the Manhattan House. Waco was wanted for sudden deaths in other parts, too. Pecos put him in the box like a mean little kid stepping on a pissant. I am purely glad Pecos was no friend of mine, for the stranger who put old Pecos in the box must be another Hickok."

There was another murmur of agreement and somebody said, "Shoot, Pecos could have took old Hickok. This new boy must be mean enough to curdle milk."

Longarm concentrated on looking as pleasant as he knew how; he was aware that some of the others were glancing his way from time to time, and while none of them were looking ornery, that didn't mean much. Damned few townies looked ornery at a man, whether they figured he was a killer or not. He considered the choices he had. If he left without waiting his turn, it might look funny. If one of the men who were looking thoughtfully at him left ahead of him, as a couple of them would if he waited his turn, he'd likely find himself sitting in a barber's chair when at least three pissed-off gents came in to discuss his future with him. Longarm had survived being shot at in a barber's chair in his time, but it made more sense not to get shot at at all, if it could be avoided.

Taking out his pocket watch, Longarm made an elaborate show of checking the time before he rose with a weary smile and muttered something about coming back later. As he walked outside, not looking back, he tried to drape his coat on his arm over the .44 riding his left hip. But he heard the sudden silence you could cut with a knife, and as he got nearer the edge of earshot, he heard someone whisper, "Jesus, did you see the cross-draw rig and the cold way them steel-gray eyes looked through a man?"

Longarm grimaced as he turned a corner chosen without forethought and wondered what he was supposed to do now.

Laredo sure was turning out to be one unfriendly little town. Poor old Petunia-Molly had been sent packing before she'd gotten to see a thing, and now, if he had any sense, he'd be on his way, pronto.

If he went to the law and identified himself, he'd get some help and likely live. But he wouldn't find out anything they didn't already know, since some of the local law were crooked. Turning in the lawyer, Thayer, even if he could find an honest lawman, would be an exercise in pure futility. What could he charge Thayer with, renting his house to a lady for a night? No, the only edge he had on the few named suspects they had was that they didn't know yet that they were suspects. The minute he sent up the balloon, it would be all over. The gang would simply pull in its horns and wait him out. He couldn't hang around here forever, and they'd know that. Maybe if he lit out and made sure the names, at least, got to other honest lawmen... But that didn't set right with a born hunter like Longarm. It was his infernal case, goddammit. He didn't care who got the credit for cracking it, but he aimed to have the pleasure of being there when it was cracked.

Hell, all he had to do was stay alive some way, until one or more of these slick-as-a-whistle crooks made his move. He'd made his own, getting suckered into that damned gunfight like a green kid on a Saturday night. He crossed to the shady side of the street as he noticed that he seemed to have wandered into a Mexican neighborhood in his aimless departure from the neighborhood of the barber shop.

He saw a sign running the length of a two story adobe across the way. It read, POSADA Y CANTINA DE LOS VAQUEROS, which translated as the Drover's Hotel, since Spanish-speaking folk took longer to get to the point. He doubted he'd be welcome as a guest in the inn part, but wetting his whistle in the shade sure beat walking in circles under the noonday sun until he started frothing at the mouth. So he crossed over and went inside.

He could see right off that he might have made another bad move. Some other old boys had gotten the same notion about the noonday sun, and the cantina was full of Mexicans in *charro* outfits. The sign outside had said *vaqueros* hung out here, dammit, but it hadn't said how many.

They'd been talking about something when he came in. But

as he stood in the doorway, adjusting his sun-baked eyes to the shade, it got quiet as a tomb at midnight.

He nodded to nobody in particular and made his way to an unoccupied corner table. He felt a lot better as he sat down and got his back to the plastered adobe walls. Off in the gloom, a low voice muttered something about "gringo mother lovers," which was only to be expected. Then another voice said *"Esparcimientos, muchachos,"* and Longarm saw a tall figure in silver and black uncoil to rise and head his way with a sleepy expression. Longarm knew the black-clad *vaquero* had told the others to take it easy, but he'd seen that expression on a Mexican face before. Longarm got along better with Mexicans than most Anglos did, because he paid attention to them. He knew you seldom had to worry about a Border Mex who was scowling or yelling at you. When a man in these parts had some Indian blood and was really serious about something, he started moving and talking so slowly you'd think he was having trouble staying awake. Longarm had seen some ugly misunderstandings take place between his own kind and Spanish-speaking gents they didn't savvy. Most Mexicans *started* to argue just like anyone else. As long as they were waving their arms and making noise back at you, there was little to worry about. But when a Border Mex went soft and sleepy in the middle of a heated discussion, it was time to make up with him or keep one eye on his hands, for, like some Indians, a Border Mex was never more quiet than when he felt like killing somebody in the near future.

The man in the black, silver-spangled outfit stopped by Longarm's table, stared sort of sleepily down at the empty chair across from Longarm, and softly asked, *"Permiso, Señor?"*

Longarm nodded pleasantly. "Sit down if that's your pleasure, amigo. I don't savvy much of your lingo, no offense."

The *vaquero* smiled crookedly as he seated himself across from Longarm and said softly, "I mean no offense either, but last night you spoke quite good Spanish to the driver who picked you up at the depot, no?"

Before Longarm could answer, the Mexican added quickly, "I do that too, around *your* kind. Sometimes it can be most interesting to hear what people have to say about you, when they do not think you understand their language."

Longarm grinned sheepishly and said, "Well, you caught me fair and square. My handle is Custis Crawford, and I only came in here to cool off around some *cerveza*. If you think I'm more likely to catch flying furniture with my head, I'll just move it on up the road."

The *vaquero* turned in his chair and held up two fingers before turning back and saying, "I am called El Gato. I have made you welcome here. I did not think you would wish for me to tell the others why, but if they see we are *simpático*, nobody will trifle with you, eh?"

"That sounds reasonable, Gato. I hope this won't sound rude, but I don't seem to be able to place you."

El Gato nodded and said, "We have never met before. But I know who you are. Perhaps you will feel more relaxed with me if I place my own cards, how you say, on the *mesa*? I, El Gato, am a famous *bandito* and killer of unpleasant people. I am like your own good *ladrone*, what's his name, Roberto Hood?"

A young woman in a low-cut blouse came over and placed two beers between them with a shy smile. Longarm waited until she'd left before he said, "You're sort of a trusting cuss too, considering. You say the driver who picked me up at the depot last night told you I speak Spanish. That hardly qualifies me as your father confessor, does it?"

El Gato laughed boyishly as he started to relax, and said, "Ah, but you see, I know more about you than that. I am not an educated person, but I can put *uno y uno* together, no? It is known that the man who shot Pecos McGraw got off the train with a woman. You are the only person who got off the train with a woman. *Uno y uno* adds up to the fact that I wish for to be your friend."

Longarm picked up his glass and clinked it against El Gato's. "That sounds safer than being your enemy in this part of town. I take it you were not too fond of old Pecos, eh?"

"He shot my brother," said El Gato simply. He took a sip of his own beer, sighed, and added, "I will tell you something in confidence. I was, how you say, gunning for Pecos McGraw. I jumped the border a week ago, when I learned he had gunned my poor little brother over by the stockyards. I did not do this lightly, for the Texas Rangers are very unreasonable about one who robs the rich to help the poor. I arrived to find Pecos had gone up to Fort Worth on business. I was waiting for him on a rooftop across from the depot last night, but of course he did not get off as I expected."

Longarm repressed a shudder as he pondered having helped Petunia-Molly into that surrey with an armed ambusher watching. As if he'd read his mind, El Gato said, "I saw you and the others leave. I saw Pecos McGraw leave on a plank, wrapped in canvas, too, but of course I did not know what they were unloading up the line until later. I spoke to your driver, a distant relation. He too knows the trick of pretending to understand little of another language. He told me that when you were not kissing the pretty *señorita*, the two of you discussed the events on the train. We would not have met, had you not come here by chance this afternoon. I have no need, now, to risk my life on this side of the border. I am riding back to Mexico tonight, in the dark of the moon. I am most pleased that Chance has allowed me to thank you. My brother was a *pobrecito*, but he was, after all, my brother."

"I follow your drift," Longarm told him. "How come Pecos McGraw gunned your kid brother, El Gato? Was he an outlaw too?"

El Gato grimaced. "No. I told you he was a *pobrecito*. A poor, honest peon who thought the world was run according to the divine justice. He was working as a *vaquero* south of the border when he agreed to help drive some cattle up here for to sell. When this Pecos was not behaving as the bully of the town, he dealt in cattle. He accused my younger brother of being a cow thief. When my *pobrecito* brother demanded that he explain his accusations, Pecos shot him. He shot him down like a dog. My brother was not wearing a gun. At the coroner's hearing, Pecos and his friends said my brother had made a move for his knife. He did have a knife, a small one, in his pocket when they rolled him over. But I ask you, *Señor*, does it seem reasonable that a nineteen-year-old boy would draw a knife in the face of more than one armed Anglo?"

"Not hardly, but coroners inquests can be like that, when it's a man's own town. I hope you won't take this unfriendly, but I've got a reason to ask. Is there any chance the cows they were discussing might have been sort of...informally acquired?"

El Gato shook his head emphatically. "No. I am not in the

cattle business anymore, but my brother would not have dealt in stolen cows. I told you he was retarded about such matters. He even thought our *Presidente* Díaz was an honest man. You are aware, of course, of the political situation in my country, *Señor*?"

"I reckon your brother *did* think the world was run like the newspapers say. Even I know how old Porfirio Díaz stole the job of running Mexico from Juarez, dealing from the bottom of the deck."

El Gato made the sign of the cross and sighed. "Ah, Juarez *was* Mexico, may he rest in peace! I would not have to be a bandit if our Benito had managed to put things right, as he intended. It was the, how you say, big shots on both sides of the border who were frightened by Juarez. The little people loved him and he loved the little people. Men of property are always afraid of people like Juarez. His land reforms would not have hurt any honest people. But what is the use of talking? Juarez is dead, Díaz is *Presidente*, and my people are still poor. One does what one can, with pistol and torch, to ease the situation."

El Gato took another sip of his drink before he added, "As I said, I ride for safety as soon as the moon sets tonight. Your money is no good in this place, since the owners are my kinsmen and you are my friend. But this seems too small a reward for the man who avenged my brother's killing. I wish there were something else I could do for you, *Señor* Crawford."

Longarm started to tell El Gato he'd settle for the friendship. Then he reconsidered and said, "I do have a favor to ask, now that I study on it. I've been looking for a place in town to hole up. You ain't the only gent who knows I gunned old Pecos, and I ain't sure the Drover's or the Manhattan House would be places where a man could sleep in comfort."

"Un momento," El Gato cut in, rising from the table to make his way over to the motherly-looking lady behind the bar. Longarm finished his beer and lit a cheroot while he waited. The pretty little *señorita* ran over and slammed down another *cerveza* without being asked. He tried to thank her, but she lit out, blushing, before he could get the words out.

Longarm had the beer in one hand and the lighted cheroot in the other when El Gato came back and sat down again. El Gato said, "It is all, how you say, set? You have a corner room in the *posada* upstairs. I told Mama Felicidad not to tell anyone you would be staying here. There is a back entrance to this building. When you wish for to 'hole up,' as you say, you will enter by way of the kitchen and ask for Mama Felicidad. She will see that you get to your room unobserved."

"I see you *do* know your way across the border, El Gato. How much is this all going to cost me?"

"You make the joke, no? I knew Mama Felicidad did not like you Anglos very much, so I had to tell her for why you are the guest of our family. Please do not offend Mama Felicidad by offering her anything. My late brother's mother, who was of course also mine, was the cousin of Mama Felicidad. More important, she was fond of our mother, and the day before he died, my brother came here with a gift for to pay his respects to his elders, eh?"

Longarm nodded gravely and said, "I savvy your ways, amigo. I mean to take you up on your offer too, it's the best I've had in some time. I don't figure on bedding down before nightfall, but I'd like to leave this frock coat somewhere and I've got some stuff over at the railroad depot I'd feel better about if I had it in a friendlier place."

"Come," El Gato said, "I will introduce you to my kinswoman, and the two of you can work out the details."

Longarm rose to follow El Gato as the latter got up and headed for the bar. Longarm noticed that the other Mexicans had gone back to arguing about cockfights and women as though he belonged there. But the fat woman behind the bar moved down to one end as she spied them approaching. She said something to some *vaqueros* down that way and they moved politely up the bar, out of earshot.

El Gato put a hand on Longarm's shoulder as he introduced him to Mama Felicidad, who stuck out her hand. Longarm didn't know just what the form was, but he saw that her hand was palm down, so he took it in one of his own and removed his hat as he kissed the back of her plump brown paw. Old Mama Felicidad tittered like a schoolgirl and said, "You are right, El Gato, *El Señor es muy caballero!*" Then she told Longarm, *"Me casa es su casa, Señor."* He knew that was just a formality, since she went on in English and spoke it pretty decently when she said, "Your coat will be safe behind the bar for now, *Señor*. You say there are other things at the depot?

I shall send a *muchacho* for them, if you wish."

"I'd best fetch the stuff myself, *Señora*. Stationmaster might ask all sorts of fool questions if anyone but me was to ask for the gear I left with him."

"You will need someone to carry for you, no?"

"Thanks, but I'll manage. It's just a couple of bags and a cased rifle. I usually bring along my own saddle, but this time I didn't."

Longarm saw no reason to tell his new friends that his usual army saddle might draw more attention than a federal agent working undercover really had much need for. He hadn't exactly lied to anybody yet, and if they wanted to think he was some sort of owlhoot on the dodge, it seemed only fair to let them. He wasn't sure his superiors would approve of his hanging out with a self-confessed Mexican bandit, but what Billy Vail didn't know wouldn't hurt him, and as long as El Gato did most of his banditing on the far side of the Rio Grande del Norte, it seemed sort of foolish to raise a fuss about it.

He took some things out of his coat pockets, stuffed his vest and pants with them, and handed the folded brown tweed coat across to Mama Felicidad. He knew his cross-draw rig would be more noticeable now that he was wearing only his vest and shirt, but that couldn't be helped. He'd already considered switching his holster around to ride on his right hip, the way most Texans favored, but he'd decided against it. It was a lousy time to start practicing a side draw. He started to put his hat back on, but checked himself and put his free hand inside and pushed out the crown of his Colorado crush.

El Gato was a pro who didn't have to have things explained to him. He smiled and said, "It won't work. You can still see the line where it was folded down, like a North Plains rider's. If you wish for to pass as a Texan, you must start by buying a bigger hat and get some spurs that jingle when you walk. Those low-heeled boots you wear are U.S. Army issue, no? I have met few Texas Anglos who favor walking heels. Most of them are tall men to begin with, but they feel more comfortable in two-inch heels for some reason."

"You're right," Longarm agreed. "It's a waste of time." He folded the hat right again and added, "If they spot me, they spot me. You've just showed me it ain't all that hard to spot a stranger who fits my description in a town this size. What are the rules on shooting folks in Laredo? I mean, in broad daylight out on the street?"

"It depends on who one knows. Pecos McGraw killed my brother in broad daylight, with many townsmen as witnesses. As I told you, they called it self-defense. Had my brother killed Pecos McGraw, no doubt they would have hanged him for murder. One hand washes the other here. Laredo is like most small cow towns in this respect, eh?"

Longarm nodded, taking out his watch. It was midafternoon. He'd be as safe going over to the depot now as he would at any other time. If he met the three men who were looking for him, the fat would be in the fire. If they killed him, the local law would likely chide them gently and they'd be the men who got the man who killed Pecos McGraw.

If he managed to win at those odds, he'd either have to identify himself as a U.S. deputy or hang for the murder of three poor, innocent lads.

He didn't favor either choice very much.

He made it. Hardly anybody with any sense was about to wander about in summertime under a Texas sun, so Longarm didn't see anybody important on his way to the depot. He cut the odds by walking on the sunny side of the street. It damned near fried him alive, but it turned out to be a better move than he'd expected when he passed a florist's shop near the depot that he'd never have noticed, otherwise.

He found a hot and sleepy-looking gent he'd never seen before in charge of the railroad baggage room. He gave the attendant his stub and tipped him a dime for handing the gear over. Then he headed back the way he'd come.

Longarm traveled light in the field. He managed to pack the possibles and his booted Winchester on his left side, in case his right side was called upon to do something more important.

When he got to the florist again, he went in and bought a bunch of red roses wrapped in green paper. He figured he could always let go of the light bouquet if he had to slap leather.

But he didn't. He got off the main drag pronto and made his way back to the *posada*, checking to make sure he wasn't being followed. When he got there, El Gato had lit out somewhere and the crowd was starting to thin out. He wondered if maybe some of the other riders had been El Gato's followers.

It was a thing you didn't ask a friendly Mexican bandit about.

You didn't ask his relations, either. Longarm found Mama Felicidad right where he'd left her, behind the bar. She smiled and he went over and put the rifle and possibles on the bar. Then he handed her the flowers and said, *"Para usted, me dama afable."*

The friendly old gal looked more surprised than he'd expected, considering he owed her some show of appreciation. She unwrapped the slightly wilted roses and gasped, *"Ay, qué linda!"* Then she blushed and ran back to the kitchen with them probably to put them in some water. A Mexican at a nearby table murmured something sly to the man with him and they both chuckled. Longarm didn't turn their way when he caught the word *gorda*, meaning fat. He'd already noticed that Mama Felicidad was sort of plump, and old enough to be his mother besides. He sure hoped they didn't think he was courting old Felicidad. That was the trouble with folks down this way; a man was either supposed to ignore a woman totally or bat his eyelashes at her like he thought he was Antony and she was Cleopatra.

The younger and prettier gal who'd been serving him before came out from the rear and started moving his gear down behind the bar. She said, "Tía Felicidad is overcome, *Señor*. It has been some time since a *caballero* brought her roses."

That sounded like it might be true. Longarm had surmised that Felicidad might have been pretty, twenty years and maybe a hundred pounds ago. He started to explain that he was just trying to be polite to the little gal's old aunt, but that could be taken the wrong way too, so he decided to quit while he was ahead. The gal asked if he wanted another *cerveza*, and he told her he'd had enough for now. He had to mosey out some more for a look-see, now that he had a base of operations. A man his size couldn't get too fuzzy on beer, but it didn't pay to be fuzzy at all, with three men gunning for you.

Chapter 5

Longarm knew the late Pecos McGraw had hung out in the Manhattan House and around the stockyards. Avoiding the Manhattan House was no problem, but he didn't see how he could learn much about the local cattle industry if he stayed away from the stockyards, so that's where he went.

Finding the yards was no problem. He already knew where the railroad tracks were, and you could smell cows some distance away on a hot day. The Laredo yards looked like most others. Holding corrals and some loading chutes ramped up to where the cattle cars would be if a train was on the siding. There wasn't any train just now. It seemed even hotter and dustier in this part of town, and hardly anybody seemed interested in the forlorn-looking critters in the yards. Longarm made a rapid tally and estimated that a couple hundred longhorns were baking there in the sun, waiting to become beefsteaks. Longarm didn't consider himself sentimental about livestock. He'd stuck hogs on his folks' farm back in West Virginia, and when he fought Indians he knew enough to aim at their ponies. He'd worked as a cowhand in his time, and he knew the penned-up critters weren't pets. But he saw no reason to be cruel to dumb animals when there was no need for it. Some of the cows were down, and others stood listlessly, with their tongues hanging halfway to the ground. He moseyed over and checked the water troughs running along the rear rails of the holding pens. As he'd expected, the boards were barely damp. He looked about for somebody to cuss. Then he moved up to the water tower at the far end. It was a smaller version of the taller one closer to the tracks, meant to fill the locomotive boilers when the trains stopped here. A pipe ran from the big tower to the little one. He found a valve on another pipe running down to the cattle troughs, and turned it. Nothing happened.

He took out a cheroot and lit up, muttering, "Cow water's run dry and you don't work here, old son."

Then a thirsty calico cow lowed wistfully and Longarm said, "Oh, hell, as long as we're here..."

He gripped the smoke between his teeth and climbed up the wooden ladder to peer over the open rim of the tank. There was nothing wrong with the valve he'd turned down there. The tank was empty, save for a drowned rat in a puddle at the bottom. He started to tell the cows downstairs that he was sorry, but then he saw that there was another valve within reach. So he gave it a turn and, sure enough, railroad water from the higher tower started running down into the dried-out shorter tank. He knew locomotives got thirsty too, so he stayed where he was for now. The view from up here was sort of interesting. He could see clear across the rooftops of Laredo. That wide ribbon of bean soup to the southwest had to be the Rio Grande, so everything on the far side was Mexico. He saw that the riverbanks were lined with crackwillow and other scrub. Moving either way at night was no big deal if you had something to ride or just took off your socks. He looked down and saw that the water he'd released was running across the dry bottom of the tank and down into the cattle troughs. The cows didn't wait to be told to belly up to the bar. They acted sort of anxious, and the ones crowded back by those at the front started bawling fit to bust. He didn't want to bloat other folk's cows, so he let a little more water run and then shut off the flow. He didn't think he'd cost the railroad enough to matter, and he might have saved some lazy yardman's job, for some of those cows wouldn't have made it till he came back from his siesta.

As he climbed back down, a wary-looking old gent in faded denim and a brass badge was standing there, looking thoughtful. Longarm nodded at him and said, "Howdy. Hot day, ain't it?"

The other said, "I noticed. What was you just up to, young feller?"

"I was watering the cows, of course."

"You work for Boss O'Brian?"

"Nope. Can't say as I ever heard of him. Who might Boss O'Brian be, and what's he the boss of?"

The older man shifted his cud, spat, and replied, "O'Brian is in charge of these yards. I ain't sure what you just done is legal."

"I never heard of anybody being arrested for watering cows, ranger."

"Hell, I ain't no ranger, I'm a railroad dick. My job is to keep law and order along the right-of-way."

"We're on the same side, then. I don't know what happened to the boy who's supposed to be looking after this stock, but he's sure piss-poor at it. I still can't vouch for all of 'em making it aboard the next train alive and kicking. It's been nice talking to you, but if I make you nervous, trespassing, I'll just move on."

The older man spat again and said, "Mebbe. You got some sort of ID you'd like to show me, stranger?"

Longarm had more than ID. He had a federal badge inside the wallet he was packing at the moment on his hip. But he said, "My name is Crawford, and unless you aim to arrest me on some charge, you can just hope I'm telling you true."

The railroad dick frowned and said, "You got piss-poor manners, friend." Then his eyes went opaque and he looked a trifle ill at ease as he hesitated and then said, "Crawford? The Crawford who got off the Missouri Pacific last night around three?"

"What if I am?"

"I got to patrol on down the line, Mr. Crawford. You just water all the cows you want and we'll say no more about it, hear?"

The scared old railroad dick lit out, not looking back, and Longarm shrugged and headed the other way. He could see why gents like John Wesley Hardin enjoyed this game, risky as it might be. Longarm didn't get a kick out of scaring folks, but he could see how much fun it could be for a bully who did. He knew his real rep only scared bad folks, since even a tough lawman seldom gunned anyone just for the hell of it. But the mysterious drifter who'd gunned Pecos McGraw must strike the locals differently. One never knew what a plain old ornery cuss might do. He knew the railroad dick would tell folks that the man who'd gunned the bully of the town liked animals. Longarm had to chuckle as he considered how crazy that would sound. Maybe if they thought he was crazy, they wouldn't ask too many questions. He knew he was walking a mighty thin line between the horns of legality. As long as he didn't come right out and *say* he was a wanted desperado, no slick lawyer could get a client off on entrapment when it came time to charge the son of a bitch. A lawman working undercover was allowed to tell a few fibs about his right name and such, but once he out-and-out broke the law himself, all bets were off in court.

There was nobody around to question casually about the brands and markings of the cows, so he figured his next best move would be to get out of the sun. He heard the distant tinkle of a piano, so he headed for it, and sure enough, it led him to a corner saloon. He moved through the swinging doors and almost gasped with relief as he felt the coolness inside and smelled the beer. The Texas air was too dry to hold much heat in the shade, and it had to be ten degrees safer in here. He noticed some gents playing cards at a table in one corner, and a man sitting at the upright piano, playing a showboat tune with more enthusiasm than the crowd called for. Nobody seemed interested in him, so Longarm bellied up to the bar and told the man behind it he'd take anything wet, but if they had it, some Maryland rye would be even better.

The barkeep slid a shotglass and a bottle across the mahogany at him, but kept his hand on the bottle until Longarm placed a four-bit piece on the bar. The barkeep nodded and went off to wipe the mahogany some more while Longarm stood with his back to the room, watching it in the mirror over the bar.

Usually, when a total stranger entered a neighborhood joint off the beaten path, some local came up sooner or later, to size him up with some casual talk about the weather or something. But he'd already noticed that Laredo was an unfriendlier town than most. After a time, a couple of the men at the table got up and left, passing him with the elaborate lack of interest that spelled trouble in the offing.

Longarm knew the game. He didn't look directly at the braver souls who'd stayed at the table, not even in the mirror. But he sized them up, as he knew they were doing for him. One wore clean stock worker's duds. His ten-gallon hat was clean and he hadn't been dragged or stomped since he'd put on those faded jeans. He was a mite thick-waisted for a working cowboy, too. The other man wore the business rig of a townsman. His hatbrim was wider than you'd see on a fashionable gent east of Chicago, and he wore riding boots under his freshly pressed pants. He looked like a gambling man with better luck and taste than most.

Longarm decided this just wasn't his saloon. Had he been off duty and just looking for action, he'd have downed his drink and lit out. No one but a fool wasted time in unfriendly places when the world was filled with better things. On the other hand, he figured he might as well get it over with here as anywhere else, and it was hot outside.

One of the men who'd ducked out came back, not looking at Longarm, and moved over to the two men at the table. He said something soft and low. Then he left again, by way of the back door. He hadn't even looked the barkeep's way, but as Longarm had figured, the barkeep was an old pro. He moved casually over to Longarm's end of the bar and started to take the mirror down. Longarm's voice was casual too, as he said quietly, "Leave it. I'll pay for any busted glass."

"Ain't we being a mite optimistic, stranger?"

"Leave it anyway. I ain't asking you. I'm telling you."

The barkeep leaned forward so they couldn't be overheard as he said, "I can see you are a man who reads the weather signs good. This ain't my fight, but it *is* my saloon. If you was to go out the back way, it might give you an edge. It's a blind alley with plenty of cover. There's only one way they could get at you, and if you was behind some ash barrels, the odds wouldn't be so awesome."

"I thank you for the neighborly advice on tactics," Longarm said. "But, no offense, I like to plan my own campaigns. Since you are concerned about your furnishings, suppose you tell me where those gents behind me stand."

"They're like me. It ain't our fight."

"Just curious, huh? Well, you go on and wipe that rag on something and we shall see what we shall see."

The barkeep nodded down at the bottle and said, "The rest of that is on the house, and I am going back to the privy to read the catalogue for a spell. I am holding you to your word about that mirror."

He moved off, a mite faster than most folks headed for the convenience. Longarm put a foot up on the brass rail to shift his position so he could see the front door in the mirror as he poured himself another shot. He didn't drink it. He knew how dangerous it could be to keep sipping nervously at a time like this.

The man in the ten-gallon hat and jeans got up and walked over, slow and thoughtful. He was wearing a Walker conversion low on his right hip. He placed his hands politely on the bar next to Longarm. "Howdy, they calls me Boss O'Brian," he introduced himself.

"You ought to be ashamed of yourself, then. I just came over from the stock pens, and those cows are in piss-poor shape. I watered them some, but maybe you ought to go take a look at them."

"I admire a man who knows how to make friends so easy," O'Brian said. "I was about to say that if your name be Crawford, a sudden vacation of the premises might be in order. Old Jimbo Thorne is headed this way with the Dobkins brothers. Somebody else you was so polite to must have told them you was here."

Longarm nodded and said, "Somehow I had that part figured out. The barkeep says he'd just as soon sit this out. How about you and that dude over yonder?"

"We ain't in the game," O'Brian replied. "Pecos McGraw and me was on fair terms, but I'll allow he could be a moody cuss, and they say you took him on the square. I will tell you true that I don't give two hoots or a holler about you, but old Jimbo is a tolerable worker when he's sober, and I'd rather see him over to the yards, where he belongs, than in jail."

Longarm smiled crookedly. "Now I know who was supposed to be tending them cows. What about the Dobkins brothers?"

O'Brian's mouth twisted distastefully. "White trash. But

mean white trash. If I was you, I'd use the back door some."

"I thank you for the advice, but I went into an alley one time. Her name was Maria and she said she loved me, too."

He nodded at the mirror and added, "If you aim to sit this one out, you'd best move clear, for I see we are about to receive visitors."

O'Brian turned, spied the men coming along the street outside, and went back to his table without another word. He sat down, talking low to the man in the gray suit.

There were two men out there. One seemed to be missing. Longarm sighed and muttered, "Jesus H. Christ, don't anybody know another way to do it?"

He turned his back to the bar and hooked his elbows over it, planting a heel on the brass rail. The man in the suit across the room frowned and looked pointedly at the sixgun hanging on Longarm's hip, one hell of a ways from his right hand. Longarm knew he looked vulnerable. A man had to use any edge he could.

The Dobkins brothers came in. Longarm knew they were brothers, since ugliness of such an extreme sort tended to run in families. Neither of them looked too bright, even sober—which they weren't. They wore the same dirty work clothes and packed similar gun rigs. Lefthandedness ran in families too. They stopped just inside the door, like Tweedledum and Tweedledee, staring at him owlishly. The one on the right licked his lips and asked, "Is your name Crawford, stranger?"

Longarm smiled and answered pleasantly, "Close enough. Let it be known to one and all that I am offering you boys a drink, if a drink be your pleasure. I hope it is, for I am a purehearted pilgrim who bears no ill will to any man I've heard tell of in these parts."

The one on the left said, "We is friends of Pecos McGraw, you bastard."

"Correction, neighbor. You *were* friends of Pecos McGraw. Past tense. I was trying to be peaceful with him too, but some old boys just don't know enough to quit while they're ahead."

"I'd drop it, if I was you boys," O'Brian said quietly from across the room. "The man says he wants to be neighborly."

The brother on the right kept his eyes fixed on Longarm as he said, "Stay outta this, O'Brian, 'lessen you wants *in*."

"Son," O'Brian replied, "it's your good fortune I don't. I

am advising you fatherly that you are biting off more bear than you might be able to chaw."

The other brother growled, "Shit, are we gonna jaw about it, or are we gonna settle up?"

His opposite number nodded and said, "Fill your fist, Crawford."

Longarm grimaced at this weary cliche; every owlhoot he met these days seemed to have read Buntline. "Not hardly," he said. "I came in here to shade and drink some redeye, not to molest children. I don't draw on invitation. I am also trying to be a friend to you, and I sure hope you are paying me some mind. Explaining these matters to the coroner gets tedious, and you can all plainly see I am not looking for a fight."

The brothers hesitated; this wasn't going according to plan. Then the one on the left said, "All right, I am going to count to ten, and then I am going to slap leather. You do as you've a mind to, Crawford."

Longarm didn't answer. Dobkins started counting slowly. Longarm listened with polite interest; he wondered if the moron was going to be able to count that high without using notes....

As Dobkins got to eight, the two men sitting across the room rose and moved farther away. He reached nine, took a deep breath, and blurted, "Ten! Goddamn your eyes!"

The Dobkins boys both went for their guns, and Longarm fired both barrels of the two-shot derringer he'd been palming in his right hand; after that, things started to get really noisy.

Longarm dropped the empty derringer and kicked himself away from the bar to drop on one knee, his back to the Dobkins brothers as they both went down, looking surprised. Longarm had drawn his more serious sixgun as he moved, and sure enough, a husky gent in a red-checked shirt came out of the back with a .45 in each fist and a vicious scowl on his red face. He peered through the smoke in the general direction of the sounds he'd heard. By the time he spotted Longarm in the middle of the floor and lower than he'd expected, he was on his own way to Boot Hill.

Longarm saw no need for formalities under these conditions, and simply put three rounds into the man, folding him like a jackknife and putting him on the floor, with his unfired guns sliding every which way. Longarm pivoted on his knee to cover O'Brian and the other man, but they were pressed against the far wall, their hands out to the sides, polite as hell. He nodded and rose, glancing at the two bodies near the doorway. Then he backed to the bar and knelt, still covering them, and picked up his empty derringer. He put it in his pants and said, "Well, the law ought to be along soon. You do have *some* law in Laredo, don't you?"

Gray Suit laughed and said, "We do, and right now you need a lawyer. Let me introduce myself. My name is Thayer, and I am a member of the local bar. I charge five dollars for a consultation."

Longarm said, "I can't spare five dollars. If you boys want to leave, I ain't stopping you."

He waited with interest for the answer. This was the lawyer that Petunia-Molly said she was supposed to be working with.

Boss O'Brian looked at Thayer with interest, too. The lawyer shrugged and said, "As an officer of the court, I'd better hang around." So O'Brian said he'd stay too. Longarm sighed and began to reload. It sure looked as though he was going to have to show his federal ID, if he didn't aim to be hanged by the county.

The barkeep came in, asking if it was over. Then he spied the three bodies spread across his floor and marveled, "Sweet Jesus!"

Thayer said, "Yeah, everybody knew Crawford here was a gunslick. Some kids just never listen."

Longarm moved back to the bar to have another drink. Thayer came over to join him, saying, "That trick with the palmed derringer was mighty slick. I wouldn't mention it when the marshal gets here, if I was you."

"I don't remember hiring you, lawyer Thayer."

"It's on the house. Oh-oh, here they come."

Longarm looked up as two men came in with drawn pistols. One wore a town marshal's star. The other had on a white shirt and wore the badge of a captain in the Texas Rangers. His eyes met Longarm's and his face went wooden-Indian. The town marshal stepped around one of the Dobkins boys and lowered the muzzle of his gun when he saw that nobody was pointing anything unfriendly at him. The Ranger captain holstered his own .45.

"Afternoon, Jim," Thayer said. "I can see you are curious as to the distressful sounds coming from this place. In case you're wondering what it's all about, this tall gent just had a fight forced on him by the lads you see spread out for your perusal. As a lawyer, I would say it was pure self-defense. As a witness, I can say that Crawford here tried to avoid the fight and only fired when they slapped leather on him."

The town marshal looked at the other men in the room. The barkeep said, "I didn't see it. I was out back."

O'Brian hesitated, shrugged, and said, "I was here. Thayer is calling it like it happened, Jim. I tried to tell the Dobkins boys to back off graceful, but you know they never had a lick of sense."

The marshal turned to the Ranger, who shrugged and said, "I'd say it would be a waste of time. But you go on and arrest him if you've a mind to. I only came to town on that tip about El Gato we was jawing about when the shots rang out."

The marshal nodded at Longarm and said, "I heard about you being in town, Crawford. I meant to advise you to ride out as soon as we met up."

"I don't have a horse," Longarm replied. "But what the hell, nobody's gunning for me now, right?"

Thayer laughed loudly. "That's for damned sure. You should have seen it, Jim. It was three to one, and this jasper made it look *easy*! I'd put him up against John Wesley Hardin, with Clay Allison thrown in for good measure. The damned fools knew he'd taken Pecos McGraw, too. If you're going to insist on taking this before the grand jury, I'm going to have to say these three idiots committed suicide, and my client was within his rights when he helped them shuffle off this mortal coil, too!"

The town marshal eyed Longarm warily and said, "Well, I see no need to get huffy about it. But, no offense, I sure wish you'd come with me to make a statement for the coroner, Mr. Crawford."

Longarm allowed that that sounded fair. Thayer offered to come along. When Longarm said he still didn't want to hire him, the lawyer gave him his card and said, "Look me up later. I may want to hire *you*."

Longarm left with the two lawmen while a crowd started to gather out front. Somebody whispered, "That's him, the tall one in the brown vest. They say he kilt a man in Oklahoma just for asking which side he rid on in the War."

74

The three of them went to the private home of the doctor who acted as the county coroner, a couple of blocks away. The doctor's wife let them in and said her husband was out on a house call, but she'd be proud to coffee them in the sitting room until he got back. The marshal looked at his watch and said he had to check in at his office about a wire he'd sent. He said he'd be back directly. So Longarm and the Ranger captain were left alone together for a few minutes while the doctor's wife went out to her kitchen to put the Arbuckle on.

The Ranger captain's wooden-Indian look softened a bit and he said, "I sure hope you aim to tell me what the hell is going on, Longarm."

Longarm smiled and said, "Howdy, Tom. Long time no see. I'm glad you got the promotion you were expecting the last time we worked together."

The captain said, "Never mind all that. What's this about you being named Crawford. I damn near shit when I saw it was *you* they had down as the big bad man from wherever."

"I've been trying to get used to it, too. I reckon you can guess why I'm really here."

"Sure, the Laredo Loop's no mystery, save for who's behind it all. Where'd you come up with Crawford for a name?"

"Ain't you ever heard of Crawford Long? I don't know if we're really kin, but I've always been sort of proud about Dr. Crawford Long. When I make up new names, I try to come up with one I'll remember. Crawford Long was the doc who invented anesthesia, and I'm trying to keep folks in the dark too, so..."

"I don't know any Doc Long, but you're in a real mess, Longarm. Don't you know how dangerous it is to go around pretending to be a famous gun? You're likely to have half the asshole kids in Texas out to gun you for a rep."

"Yeah, I noticed that back at the saloon. But you can see nobody wants to talk to paid-up lawmen about the Laredo Loop. Who's this gent you're down here after? Mex outlaw?"

"I never met an Anglo called El Gato. He's wanted for a killing up on the Big Bend. They say he don't like Texicans much. Fair is fair, and the cowhand he shot called him a greaser, but we've got rules in this state about shooting folks and then just riding off laughing. Austin wants me to bring him in, and that's what I mean to do."

Longarm considered where his loyalties lay. Old Tom was a friend, and an outlaw was an outlaw. He asked, "Do you reckon this El Gato gent is mixed up in the cow business I'm working on?"

"Not hardly. We figure the thieves working the Laredo Loop are in with the Mexican government. Last we heard, *El Presidente* Díaz has his *rurales* out looking for El Gato too. El Gato's some sort of hero to the *pobrecitos* down that way. When he ain't smoking up Texas hands, he shoots *rurales* on sight."

"Well, a man who shoots *rurales* can't be all bad. I've been holding out on you, Tom. I met El Gato a while back. He ain't in Laredo. He's ridden back to Mexico."

The Ranger looked surprised. "Damn, you do get around, don't you? You met up with El Gato and the two of you are still alive? Hell, put me on his trail, old son. Where in Laredo did you meet him and how do you know so much about him?"

"Don't press me, Tom," Longarm said. "I am telling you the truth to save you barking up some wrong trees at the taxpayers' expense. I give you my word he's not in Texas anymore. I really don't know where in Mexico he is right now. If I told you where and when I met him, you'd just naturally mess up a good thing I have going for my own case. You see, El Gato and me were sharing the same hideout, and I ain't sure I've done with it yet."

Tom didn't look too happy, but he nodded and said, "Well, I know no Mex would tell a Ranger much, no matter how polite he asked. How the hell do you get in so thick with greasers, Longarm?"

"I dunno. Maybe, for openers, I don't call 'em greasers. I never had a granddaddy at the Alamo, so it likely gives me a more objective view. You don't like Spanish-speaking folks much, do you?"

"Oh, hell, I ain't *mean* to 'em. I never call a greaser a greaser to his face."

"I reckon they just have to guess how you feel about them, then. But let's get back to the Laredo Loop, Tom. To pay you back for being so coy about El Gato, I'll tell you something I ain't supposed to. Uncle Sam thinks some local, state, and maybe even federal lawmen are working with the thieves. An awful lot of beef keeps turning up missing along the border, and somebody down here ain't doing his job right, according to Billy Vail."

Tom shrugged and said, "Old Billy is wrong, even if he *was* a Ranger one time. Give us credit for some casual interest in crime, Longarm. We've traced more than one stolen cow in our time. We have our own informants and we know pretty much what's going on. Have you checked any brands since you came to town?"

"Saw some thirsty stock over to the yards. Didn't have time to study all their brands."

"Save yourself the effort. We have a man spot-checking. I'll bet you two to one you won't find a cow over there that ain't branded legal."

"Shoot, it ain't all that hard to run a brand, Tom."

The Ranger nodded and said, "No argument. We know a lot of stolen cows are coming in from Mexico. The horns give that away."

Longarm started to ask what Tom meant. Then the light dawned. "Right," he said. "American steers are castrated as calves, so their horns grow monstrous along with the rest of them. Mexicans castrate full-growed critters, so a Mex steer has the same kind of horns as a bull."

"Right," the Ranger said. "It *do* make one thoughtful when a steer wearing a registered Mex rancher's brand comes across the border with a ten-foot spread of horn, but try and get a jury to savvy that."

"Then Texas agrees with Uncle Sam that the loopers are selling American cows as Mex?"

"Hell, everybody knows that," Tom snorted. "But what can we do? We *do* check for old brands, and if a cow's been stole in Texas we'd have the brand on file. But they sell stolen Arizona beef here and likely Texas cows in Yuma, so..."

"I know how the Laredo Loop works, Tom. What I'm having trouble with is why nobody seems able to stop it. The Laredo Loop is an open secret, like the Tenderloin in Dodge. You know, of course, that to run a whorehouse anywhere, you have to have the local law paid off?"

The Ranger took a deep breath and let it out slowly. "I'm pretending I didn't hear that, Longarm. You know goddamned well the Texas Rangers are not for sale."

Longarm held up a cautionary hand. "Don't get your bowels

in an uproar, old son. We ain't accusing, we're just thoughtful. *Some* damned lawman has to be bought off around here!"

Tom said, "That's no mystery, neither. Everybody knows who the thieves pay off. It's the damned greaser *rurales*, south of the border. What the hell do you expect us to do about it? Texas ain't allowed to invade Mexico no more. Give me ten good Rangers and a hunting permit south of the border, and I'd clean up the Laredo Loop in six weeks or less. Trying to put a stop to it from this side of the Rio is a waste of time. You got to catch a man with a stolen herd *before* he's had time to run the brands and let 'em heal on a greaser ranch. Once they ship 'em north with legal brands and papers, it gets impossible to prove anything in court."

"Haven't you caught anybody selling stolen cows, Tom? We know about the razzle-dazzle down in Mexico, but they have to *sell* them on our side of the line, and—"

"We arrest folks all the time," the Ranger cut in. "I told you proving it in court was the tedious part. I personally collared a cow buyer in San Antone last month, with some cows wearing New Mexico brands listed as stolen. It takes time to check every damn wanted flier, but we do our damn homework when there's a few spare minutes. This dealer had some Long Rail–branded critters, and that ain't an easy brand to cover up. So I took him in to discuss his bill of sale with the judge. The goddamn judge let him go. There was no argument about the cows being stolen off the Long Rail spread a while back. Trouble was, the son of a bitch had bought 'em legal off a Mex outfit and had the papers to prove it."

"What did the Mexican dealer have to say about the older brands, Tom?"

"Don't know. It's hard as hell to question a man in Mexico from San Antone. All we could do was write him a letter. He never saw fit to answer."

"Can't anybody complain to the Mexican government?"

"Sure. We do it a lot. *Presidente* Díaz says we're just acting surly about the Alamo and complains to the U.S. State Department about our harassing honest Mexican *rancheros*. Austin's told us not to pester the greasers no more unless we have something we can prove in court. They won't let us ride down there to prove it, neither."

The doctor's wife came in with coffee and cakes, so they

had to pretend they didn't know each other some more. The infernal woman stayed with them; she likely figured they enjoyed her company.

A million years later, the town marshal came back. He nodded to Longarm and said, "Well, you just won another round. When I heard you was in my town, I sent some wires. You don't seem to be wanted noplace, Crawford. It beats me how this could be possible, considering how hard it is for you to get along with folks. I don't suppose you'd like to prove to me that your name is really Crawford, would you?"

Longarm didn't answer. His Ranger friend said, "I know him, Jim. His name is Custis Crawford, like he says. As we jawed while you was out, it came to me where I'd seen him before. I knowed him up in Forth Worth, afore he turned bad."

The town marshal said. "I wish you'd remembered sooner, Captain. Are you saying he's just mean and not an owlhoot?"

Tom grinned at Longarm as he elaborated, "Oh, we suspicion him of all sorts of things, but we was just talking about how hard it is to prove some suspicions in court."

The marshal nodded at Longarm and asked, "What do you do for a living when you ain't shooting folks, Crawford?"

"Oh, a little of this and a little of that," Longarm replied casually. "The captain and me were just discussing some missing cows. To tell the truth, I'm a mite hurt at his suggestion that I might know something about it. I ain't stole a single cow in recent memory, and the only reason I left my last honest job was a misunderstanding with the foreman."

"I trust they gave him a decent burial?"

"Shoot, I never killed him, just messed him up a mite. But the big boss fired me anyway. As I was just telling the captain here, I came down to Laredo looking for honest employment."

Before the town marshal could question him further, the doctor came home. So they told him about the fight at the saloon and he said, "I'm ahead of you gents. I was just at the undertaker's, and I talked to lawyer Thayer. He was arranging for the boxes and such. He told me all about it. I'll just fill out the papers when I find the time. I see no need to convene a jury on an open-and-shut case like this. But it was kind of you all to drop by."

As they all stood up, Longarm asked the doctor, "How come Thayer takes such an interest in folks who commit suicide, doc?" and the doctor said, "Oh, the Dobkins brothers were just thrown in extra, as long as he had to bury old Jimbo Thorne. Jimbo worked for Thayer."

Longarm's eyebrows rose a notch. "Do tell? I never got to talk much to Thorne, but he sure didn't look like a law clerk to me."

The doctor smiled and replied, "He wasn't a law clerk. He was a security man at the stockyards."

"Oh? I thought Boss O'Brian ran the stockyards."

"Sure he does. But he don't *own* 'em. Lawyer Thayer is the owner of the stockyards. It's a sideline to his law business. He wound up owning them a while back when a client couldn't pay."

The town marshal said, "I remember that. Thayer was the defense attorney in the case. They say he put up a good fight in court, but his client went to prison anyway. Something about crooked cow dealings, wasn't it, doc?"

"Yep. Thayer got him off with five years instead of the twenty he had coming. Even doing five, a man can't pay enough to matter, so Thayer wound up with everything he owned."

Longarm felt in his pocket for the card the lawyer had given him. He knew what kind of job they were talking about now. The late Jimbo Thorne had been Thayer's hired gun. So now the lawyer was in the market for a new one. As they all started filing outside, Longarm nodded to himself and tried not to grin.

Outside, the town marshal stopped him on the plank walk and said, "I sure hope the sun don't set on you in my town, Crawford. No offense, but Laredo has a vagrancy ordinance, and you are one sinister cuss with no visible means of support."

"Don't get your bowels in an uproar," Longarm told him. "I think I've got me a job."

Chapter 6

Thayer's card said his office was above the Manhattan House, which was a big saloon downstairs with offices and such on the second floor, reached by an outside staircase. A prissy clerk inside said Thayer had left for the day. So Longarm went downstairs, saw that the saloon was much the same as any other, except a mite bigger than most, and nobody there knew where the rascal was, either. Longarm considered asking his way to the undertaker's or going back to the saloon by the stockyards, but neither notion struck his fancy. It was getting tedious, meeting up with the friends of folks he'd just shot.

The town law had warned him not to let the sun set on him on the streets of Laredo, and it was getting late enough to study on that. He figured he could find the house he and Petunia-Molly had been to last night, but that wouldn't be such a smart move, either. He'd hole up and look for Thayer in the morning.

He want to the Alhambra Baths and hired himself a private tub in a room with a door that locked on the inside. The tap water was the color as well as the temperature of weak tea, but the naphtha soap would cut the grease he'd built up on his hide under the Texas sun. He decided that as long as he was going to wash all over, he might as well spring for some toilet water. It smelled sort of sissy, but it helped when he had to put his shirt back on. When he got back outside, the sun was setting and the town was coming to life again. Longarm had seen all the action he wanted to until he did something about that vagrancy regulation. So he went back to Mama Felicidad's *posada* and went through the business of getting cussed at softly, until the Mexicans in the place saw that the pretty waitress thought he was all right.

He asked her what they had for supper, and she said he could have tortillas and beans or beans and tortillas. He asked her which was best and she didn't get it, so he said he'd have tortillas and beans. It seemed a pure waste that a gal so pretty had no sense of humor, and he decided he'd best not josh her. Spanish-speaking folk were touchy about the way strangers spoke to their womenfolk, and the fool gal blushed and got all flustered if you so much as asked her what time it was.

She brought him his supper, and it was a good thing he'd made up his mind to act polite, for, while he liked his chili hot, this was ridiculous. He knew he had the border to thank for that, as he washed down every bite with beer. Up Denver way, they made the stuff a mite mild for his taste. In Santa Fe it was just right. As you got closer to the border they started trying to prove something. He knew the pepper tapered off the same way on the far side of the border. Border folks of both breeds kept trying to top one another on how much liquid fire they could swallow without sobbing in pain. The tortillas helped. Tortillas were supposed to be bread, though they looked like flapjacks and tasted like blotting paper. If you rolled some of Mama Felicidad's molten lava in a tortilla and washed it down fast with cold beer, you could just about manage to keep your eyes from watering.

He didn't see the fat old gal behind the bar this evening. Her place had been taken by a sulky-looking hombre who looked like a pissed-off Chinaman. Longarm saw that the little waitress was calming him down, or trying to, as they tried not to look his way.

The girl came over to ask if he wanted second helpings. Longarm said, "Not hardly. Where's your aunt this evening? I wanted to talk to her about the room I'm hiring upstairs."

The waitress said, "Tía Felicidad drove out to her *rancho*. I will show you to your room whenever you are ready for to go to bed."

He wasn't sure how to take that. She was blushing like a rose. He took another swallow of *cerveza* and said, "It's early yet. I didn't know your aunt was a *ranchera*. How many head does she have out wherever?"

"Oh, no more than a dozen *vacas*, *Señor*, but she keeps pigs too. That is for why she had to go out there. For to slop the hogs. The *chico* she hired to take care of her beasts has run off. We think he may have ridden away with El Gato. Tía Felicidad is very cross. She says it is not dignified for a woman of her position to slop hogs."

The girl droned on about livestock and runaway help as he listened just to be polite. He didn't give a hoot where the old gal had gone, as long as his room was waiting upstairs. It made sense for a lady who owned an eating place to keep some hogs. A dozen cows didn't sound all that interesting. He knew that lots of small holders kept a few head to keep the brush down on a little spread. But he was sort of annoyed with himself for not having stolen that brand book from Thayer's house. The Rangers didn't think El Gato was in the cattle business, but if El Gato was kin to these folks, it might be interesting to check old Felicidad's cows out. He'd know government beef brands if he spotted any under the fancy, curly designs Mexicans seemed to favor.

The waitress left to serve other customers. A man in a big black sombrero came over and sat down at Longarm's table, uninvited. He didn't have to say he was looking for trouble. No well-brought-up Mex ever sat down without asking permission first.

But Longarm hadn't come back to the *posada* to get in another fight. It had been his notion that this was the one likely place in town to avoid further bloodshed, so he touched his hatbrim politely and asked, "What are you drinking, amigo?"

The Mexican said, "I seldom drink with a *gringo*. It is said they carry the clap in their *mostachos*. No doubt they pick it up from eating their mother's pussies, eh?"

Longarm replied in Spanish, saying, "It is said the open mouth draws flies. But one must make allowances for youth. I am here as a guest of the family, *muchacho*."

"You call me a *muchacho*? You dare?"

"I'll call you an elephant if you want. If you want me to call you an *hombre*, suppose you start acting like one. You've no reason to pick a fight with me."

"No? Maybe I will be able to think of one if I put my mind to it. Is it true you *gringo* bastards sit down to pee, like a woman?"

"How come you're so interested in my cock, *muchacho*? You don't look like a *mariposa*."

The Mexican grinned, enjoying the way the conversation was going now.

He said, "I will bet you a Mexican butterfly can beat a *Yanqui* bull in a fair fight. Do you enjoy fair fights, *gringo*? I see you are alone in our *barrio* this evening. You must be very brave, or very stupid. What would you do if I pulled your *mostacho*, eh?"

"I don't know. You're not going to do it, so let's not worry about it."

"Hey, *gringo*, I like your style. What do you say we go outside and have a good fight, eh?"

Longarm shook his head wearily and said, "*Gracias*, no. But I'll still buy you a *cerveza*."

"*Ay, qué chihuahua!* Are you afraid of me, *gringo*?"

Longarm shrugged and said, "You can think so, if it makes you feel good. I usually have a reason when I get into a fight, and you haven't given me a sensible one so far. We're not after the same girl or the same job. If I didn't like most Mexican folk, I wouldn't be here, so why don't we drop it?"

The man in the black sombrero said, "Hey, please? I really wish for to fight you, *gringo*. Won't you do it as a personal favor to me?"

Longarm saw that the mean-looking barkeep was over the bar and headed their way with a stout-looking bottle in one hand. Longarm sighed. He'd been looking forward to that bed upstairs, but this was getting downright unfriendly.

The Chinese-looking bartender came to the table, looked soberly down at the offensive man in the black hat, and said, "Out."

The Mexican looked startled and said, "What do you mean, 'out'? Can't you see this *gringo* and me are having an important discussion?"

The barkeep said, "I have been listening to your discussion, and when I say out I mean outside, *muy pronto*, and I mean *you*, Garcia."

"Hey, for why you take this stranger's part against your own kind, Chino?"

"You are not my kind, Garcia, you are trouble. Mama Felicidad has told you what would happen if you started any more fights in here. The door is over that way. I shall not say this again."

"*Caramba*, nobody tells Garcia where he must go or stay!"

So Chino hit him, hard, with the bottle. The bottle didn't break, and since something had to give, it was Garcia's head. The bully keeled over in his chair and hit the floor, out like a light. Chino put the bottle on the table and said, "I *told* him I would not say it again." Then he bent down, took Garcia by the booted ankles, and dragged him across the floor and out the door as others in the room chuckled fondly.

Chino came back, picked up the bottle, and said, "I thank you for not letting him provoke you, *Señor*. The police have told us we must have fewer fights in here."

Longarm nodded soberly and said, "I think I owe you a drink, Chino."

The barkeep said, "You owe me nothing. I have a job to do. I do not like to be called Chino, by the way. I am called Tomás by my friends."

"Can I call you Tomás, then?"

"No. If you must call me anything, call me *Señor* Lopez. I do not know why Mama Felicidad has made you welcome. I don't care. I only work here. I don't make the rules. But one of the rules is that we are not to have any more fights in here. I did what I had to. I don't like Anglos, either."

He turned away before Longarm could ask him why. Longarm took out his watch. It was a mite early to turn in, but this place was sure moody. He finished his *cerveza* and tried to catch the eye of the waitress. But now the girl was talking to the sullen barkeep with her back to him. She had a sort of pretty back, but he wanted to pay up and get the hell out. Sooner or later, old Garcia had to wake up again and he'd likely be as safe in the Drover's Hotel after all.

The girl went in the back for somebody's order. The sullen-looking barkeep came around the end of the bar with a glass of beer and brought it over to Longarm's table. He put it down and said soberly, "I did not know you were a friend of El Gato. It is permitted that you call me Tomás after all."

Longarm smiled and said, "You can call me Custis, then. Do you expect that fellow you hit on the head to come back for second helpings?"

Tomás said, "Not if he knows what is good for him. Had I known you were here as a guest of El Gato, it would not have happened. I will tell this to Garcia the next time he mentions you."

"And if he still wants to fight me?"

"I will kill him, of course. El Gato is my cousin. The man you killed the other night murdered a kinsman of mine. He had many other relations in this *barrio*. Garcia will not be allowed to molest you further. Do not concern yourself with such stupid people."

So Longarm didn't. He finished his *cerveza* and the waitress brought him another, saying, "Those *caballeros* over in the corner told me to bring this to you, *Señor*."

Longarm raised the glass to the men at the other table and asked the girl, "Are they cousins too?"

"*Quién sabe?* It is hard to keep track when one comes from a large family."

"Well," he said, "you just give those boys a couple of drinks on me, and we'll say no more about it."

So she did, and when the others got their drinks, one of them stood up and came over. He asked, *"Permiso?"*

When Longarm answered, *"Por favor, Señor,"* he sat down.

"You have had a busy day, *Señor* Crawford. We heard about the fight with McGraw's friends."

"Oh, I take it they weren't popular with you folks, either?"

The man shurgged. "A *gringo* is a *gringo*, present company aside. We know something else about you. We knew you were questioned by a Texas Ranger this afternoon. We knew he came to Laredo looking for El Gato. We know you did not tell him about this place, for if you had, there would have been a posse of Rangers here by now. Palomina tells us there is nothing we can do for you, since you are already a guest of El Gato's, but if you have any other needs, you may count on us, eh?"

"That's right neighborly, *Señor* . . . ?"

86

"No names, *por favor*. Palomina knows how to get in touch with us if you need us."

The man rose to rejoin his sidekick at the other table. A few minutes later the two of them left, smiling at Longarm. So the little waitress was called Palomina, meaning "little dove," eh? That sounded reasonable. He couldn't think of anything he might want from the two *vaqueros*, but it was nice to know that at least somebody in town was on his side for a change.

Longarm decided he'd best quit while he was ahead. The place was starting to thin out, and the kitchen had closed for the night. From here on, the only customers would be serious drinkers, and he'd met enough of *them* for one day. He waited a spell to see if Palomina came back. When she didn't, he got up and went looking for her.

He found her in the kitchen, saying good night to another fat old gal. Now that he'd gotten used to them, he could see the family resemblance between little Palomina and both of the older fat women. It seemed a shame, but he knew she'd look like the cook or Mama Felicidad in a few years. It had nothing to do with her Spanish or Indian blood. Prosperous Mex gals stayed slim and young-looking as long as any others. *Peones* ate too much starch and admired meat on a woman, so you had to catch them under twenty-five if you liked trim figures.

When the cook left, he told Palomina he wanted to bed down. She blushed some more, lit a candle, and told him she'd show him the way.

He followed her up a narrow staircase and down a corridor. She took a key from her apron pocket and unlocked a stout oak door before handing him the key. She led the way inside. The room was small and smelled clean. He saw that his possibles and cased rifle were on the floor near the bed. She asked him if the room suited him, and he said it did. So she shut the door and asked him if he wanted to sit down and test the bedsprings.

He figured he was stuck with the bed for the night, even if it was full of rattlesnakes, but to be polite he sat down and bounced a couple of times, saying, "It's a grand old bed, Palomina."

She blew out the candle and said, "Oh, my candle has gone out."

He didn't answer. He wasn't sure what in thunder he was supposed to say. The next thing he knew, little Palomina was in his lap, saying, "Oh, forgive me, I seem to have tripped in the dark."

She didn't seem to be making any effort to rise, so he put an arm around her waist to steady her. She took his wrist, guided his hand up to one nicely rounded little breast, and gasped, "Oh, *Señor*, whatever are you doing?"

Her nipple felt nice against his palm, but he said, "Let's study on this, honey. You did say your old aunt had left for the night, didn't you?"

Palomina snuggled closer and replied, "She did not say she was coming back. Oh, *Señor*, you are so wicked. What kind of a girl do you think I am?"

He had a notion what kind of a girl she was, so he kissed her. She kissed back like a lovesick mink and twined her tongue with his for a spell as she lowered his hand to greener pastures. But when he managed to learn that she wore nothing under her skirt, she giggled and said, "Oh, this is terrible. I think you are trying for to seduce me, no?"

"That's a reasonable suspicion," he said. As he lowered her to the mattress, she moaned and spread her thighs, sighing, "It is no use, I can't resist you. You are too strong for me. But please let me take off my clothes before we wrinkle them, no?"

So he let go of her and she started shucking her duds, while he did the same. It sure sounded silly, the way she kept protesting that she wasn't the kind of girl he seemed to think she was.

By the time he'd shucked his boots and pants, Palomina was stark naked and had thoughtfully put a pillow under her hips. But as he entered her, she gasped, "Oh, no, never, I can't! Whatever will I tell the *padre* at confession?"

"That you enjoyed it?" He grinned, settling into the saddle and getting down to business. She moved her little rump like a saloon door on payday, and had she been doing this professionally, she'd likely have retired rich. But even as she bumped and ground against him and clawed his back with her nails, she was saying, "Oh, this is very wicked and you are far too big for me!"

He wondered if she was trying to compliment him or if she was a little embarrassed about her honey pot. It was a good thing he was well hung; Palomina wasn't the tightest virgin he'd ever seduced. She was a good lay. In fact she was a great lay, but he wouldn't have bitched if she'd been built as small as she looked with her duds on. He knew she didn't get to do this when her old aunt was home, but her aunt must have spent a lot of time away, for the little sass screwed like a gal who'd had plenty of practice. Her interior muscles were skilled at hanging on, but despite her maidenly ways, he knew she could have taken on a horse, if she put her mind to it. From the way she acted, he wasn't sure she hadn't tried that, at least one time. He started gently, aware that she was a small gal, on the outside at least. But she pulled and clawed him closer and wilder and couldn't seem to get enough of his weight aboard as she threatened the bedsprings with destruction.

Her surprising early looseness made it possible for him to hold back longer than usual on the first orgasm, but then, as she warmed to the task, she got more than tight enough and she came just ahead of him, moaning, "Oh, I feel so defiled!"

As she felt him coming, she sobbed, "Oh, no, you didn't come in me, did you?"

"What did you expect me do do?" he growled. "This is getting sort of tedious, honey. I'll take it out if you just can't stand any more, but if you want to make love, let's just do it."

She giggled and said, "I know I should make you stop, but it's too late. I am going to have to do penance in any case, so maybe we should sin some more, no?"

So they did. And it got better once she settled down to enjoy it with no further protests and a couple of wicked suggestions of her own about positions. A couple of her suggestions wouldn't have worked if she hadn't been built loose as well as athletic.

Longarm wanted to smoke and talk a bit afterwards, but Palomina said she was afraid of being caught and was out of bed and dressed before he could protest. He kissed her in the doorway and let her go, not really regretting it. He'd had enough for now, and the exertion had put him in shape to sleep, early as it was. So he flopped back down and tried. He had a big day ahead of him, and it wouldn't kill him to catch more winks than usual.

He was wearier than he'd thought, for he was soon sound asleep and having a real funny dream. Then he woke up, got his bearings in the dark, and discovered he wasn't really dreaming about a lady sucking him off. It was happening!

He hissed and muttered, "Jesus," as he placed his hand on the bobbing head in his lap. He was on his back in the pitch darkness, and she was on her knees beside the bed, giving him a skillful French lesson. He ran his hand down her cheek to a naked shoulder and said, "Hey, don't waste it, honey. Climb up here and let's do it right!"

So she giggled and slithered up into the bed with him. She was still gripping his erection with one hand as he took her in his arms and started to kiss her. Then, as he felt how much there was in his arms, he realized he wasn't holding little Palomina. This was the fattest woman he'd ever held against his own hide, naked. She was damned near as strong as he was, too, for she rolled him on his back and got on top, as he gasped, "Is that you, Mama?"

"Call me Felicidad, *querido mío*!" she replied as she lowered herself on his inspired shaft. He hissed in surprise and pleasure as the huge woman enveloped him in her tiny sex. It hardly seemed possible that a man could get close enough to matter between her huge and surprisingly firm thighs, but she wasn't fat between her legs. Had he not known better, he'd have thought he was abusing a child. "*Ay, qué maravillosa verga!*" she gasped.

"Am I hurting you?"

"Sí, a little, but I love it. But we must be very quiet, *querido*. My innocent little niece is sleeping just down the hall, and she would not understand that there are things a grown woman desires that the *padre* might not approve of."

"Yeah," he admitted, "the *padre* ought to find confession sort of interesting around here."

"*Ay, María*, I am coming and you are coming and . . . oh, what a lovely way to die!"

Neither one of them died, of course. And after he got his wind back, Longarm rolled her over on her back to do it right. It was a very odd position, considering how old-fashioned it was supposed to be. Mama Felicidad didn't need a pillow under her big behind. He was almost on his knees atop her, and it was interesting to ride her big breasts like he was swimming over waves of gelatin dessert. He was glad the light was out, for he knew he'd have burst out laughing if he'd been able to see himself in such a ridiculous position. But damn, she sure felt good where it counted. He'd never understood till now why some old boys liked fat women. He didn't know that he wanted a steady diet of this, but it sure was an experience to remember.

She liked it too. She raised her knees, got a thigh against his torso on either side, and proceeded to bounce him up and down as one might bounce a baby on one's knee. He came, went limp, and just let her go on solo. He didn't think she noticed he'd stopped pumping; Felicidad had him going in and out as hard and fast as he'd have managed, even trying his hardest. It took only a short time until he was back in action; even wet with love juices, she was almost painfully tight.

Felicidad gasped, shuddered under him like an earthquake, and went limp as he kept pounding. It felt like he was making love to a little girl who'd somehow found herself inside a friendly hippopotamus. He ejaculated hard and went limp atop her, and after a while he noticed she was crying softly.

He slid up her soft, moist mounds until he could kiss her gently and ask her what was wrong. She said, "You should not have brought me those beautiful roses, *querido*. I have behaved so silly."

He kissed her again and said, "I reckon I can get as silly as anybody, Felicidad."

"Oh, you men are like that, when you have the hard-on. But confess to me. Would you have approached me if I had not crept in here like a shameless *puta* for to seduce you?"

He knew there were times to tell the truth, but this wasn't one of them. "I don't reckon I would have. You're a right handsome woman, but I couldn't get up the nerve to say so."

"Oh, *querido*, is that really why you brought me the beautiful roses?"

"What other reason could there be, Felicidad?"

He'd meant it to cheer her up, but it seemed to make her bawl even harder. She sniffed and said, "Oh, you are such a gallant liar. I did not know you Anglos had such tender feelings."

He was still soaking in her, so he moved teasingly and said, "It sure does feel tender in there. You sure are built to pleasure a man, Felicidad."

"Pooh, do you not think I own a mirror? I am old and fat."

"Stop fishing for compliments, gal. You ain't much older

than me, and if I didn't like my gals pleasingly plump, I wouldn't be doing this, would I?"

"Oh, you *are* doing it, aren't you? How many times have we come?"

"Can't say. Who counts? Let's just do it till we can't anymore."

She started moving, and he was surprised to feel himself starting to enjoy it again. "Are you sure you're not just saying that to comfort me?" she asked.

"Honey," he said, "this is comforting as hell. You know us gent's ain't like you gals when somebody is fibbing. A gal can say she's enjoying it when she ain't, but I ask you, does what I got inside you feel like I'm faking?"

"Oh, you do feel a little something for me, no?"

"Well, I don't want to hurt you. So maybe we'd best stop for a while," he suggested.

"You are not hurting me, *querido*."

"I'd best be gentle anyway. You're too sweet to let on if you had enough."

He rolled off and started to reach for a smoke. Then he realized he'd have to light a match and decided to pass on the notion. Felicidad nestled against him and purred, "Oh, you are so understanding. I did not wish to deprive you, but in truth I may be a little sore in the morning if we do not stop. I have never done it so many times in one night, and I have been married three times."

He didn't answer. He hadn't thought she'd learned how to move like that in a convent. She asked, "Why does it have to happen to us all so soon? Only yesterday I was as young and little and pretty as my niece, Palomina. Of course, like she, I was too innocent to know what I was missing."

"Yeah, I noticed she acted sort of innocent."

"*Ay María*, such a waste when fate gives us such little time to be young and pretty. Think me wicked if you wish, but I have often told little Palomina she should get at least a lover if she cannot get a husband right now. But she says she could never be a bad girl. Tell me, *querido*, do you think what we have been doing is bad?"

He chuckled fondly and replied, "I thought it was right nice. But I don't reckon you have to worry about your niece. She'll likely get over her shy ways in time."

Felicidad sighed and said, "I fear she would be most upset if she had any idea I behaved so wantonly tonight, my *caballero*. I wish for to stay and sleep forever in your strong arms, but I must creep back to my own bed now. *Permiso?*"

"Oh, go ahead, I won't have any hard feelings."

She got it. She laughed and started to play with him some more. That was the trouble with women. They sometimes turned out innocent when you wanted 'em wicked, or smart when you'd as soon have 'em dumb. He started to tell her they'd best take no more chances. But then he noticed how nice she moved her lips on a man's tool, and he decided it was only polite to let her hang about a while longer. What the hell, it was her *posada*.

Chapter 7

Lawyer Thayer looked like he'd been sucking lemons when Longarm found him in his office the next morning. Longarm wasn't surprised to see how fancy the oak-paneled office was, considering it was over the biggest saloon for a country mile. He'd already checked out the fact that Thayer owned the saloon and just about everything else in town. Thayer was expensive, and when a client didn't have the cash in hand, he'd take a mortgage.

Longarm sat down across the desk from Thayer without waiting to be invited, and Thayer said, "If you want to work for me, you're going to have to improve your manners, Crawford."

Longarm took out a cheroot, thumbed a sulfur match, and lit up as he answered, "I ain't working for you yet. I've had time to sleep on your offer. To put the cards direct on the table, you boys told a few fibs yesterday."

Thayer smiled thinly and said, "I saw no need to mention the palmed derringer to the town law. You know, of course, that if anyone wanted to be picky about it, they could say you were waiting for those three boys with killing in mind."

Longarm nodded benignly. "I'd have been dumber than I look if I'd been standing there empty-handed. You folks had me set up before I ever got there. All the help around the yards had lit out, and they tell me you own the yards. Jimbo Thorne worked for you too, and his job wasn't watering the stock. He was your backup gun for anything Boss O'Brian couldn't take care of with his war talk and fists."

"No argument," Thayer said. "You know how surly some cowhands can get during a discussion of the price of beef. I knew Thorne and the Dobkins brothers were after you. I sent O'Brian over to warn you, too."

"Oh, him and the barkeep warned me neighborly as hell. They both told me to duck out the back, where Jimbo Thorne was set up with two guns covering the rear exit."

Thayer shrugged matter-of-factly. "Thorne worked for me. I told him to forget he used to drink with Pecos McGraw, but you know how muley some gents are. I didn't know how good you were, but I figured you had to be good to take McGraw. I needed Thorne, so, sure, we tried to give old Jimbo the edge. But that's all ancient history. Your slick gunplay created a vacancy in our organization, and I can't think of a better man to fill Thorne's boots than the man who blew him out of them. Officially, you'd be working as Boss O'Brian's segundo around the yards. I can see you've worked cows, and you're a yard puncher, should anyone ask. I've noticed you tend to be a mite surly too, so let's have it understood that you are not to go for the throat of anybody O'Brian or me don't sic you on. How do you get along with greasers?"

"Oh, I can savvy a little Spanish. Why?"

"We have a lot of dealings with Mexican drovers, since this is the legal crossing of the Rio Grande. We get a good price now and again on Mex beef. But as you likely know, some *vaqueros* can act sassy. They seem to think we expect it of them on our side of the line. I don't allow my hands to gun a Mex for the usual remarks about Texas motherhood. O'Brian will tell you if a Mex needs a gunning. You're not to do it on your own."

"What if one of 'em goes for me?"

"That's different, but I doubt it'll happen. Young Mex boys north of the border are just acting like young Texas boys south of the border. Kids sort of whistle and swagger, walking by a graveyard or any other place that makes them nervous. I expect men working for me to act grown up."

Longarm took a drag on his smoke and said, "I wouldn't want this to get about, but you may have noticed I don't start fights. I just finish 'em. What kind of money are we jawing about? You do *pay* folks who work for you, don't you?"

Thayer nodded and answered, "You'll start at a dollar a day and we'll see."

Longarm grimaced and said, "Forget it. I've rode as a top hand in my time, and right now a top hand can draw three dollars a day and all the beans he can eat."

"Maybe, but you're not working as a cowboy. You'll be working afoot about the yards."

He saw that Longarm wasn't grinning about that, so he added, "Look, I have to keep books. Suppose we put you down as a dollar-a-day puncher and I pay you a couple more under the table?"

"That's still only what I'd get working on some dumb ranch. You did say you wanted my gun working for you too, didn't you?"

"Yes, but we seldom have any trouble Boss O'Brian can't handle. Even during roundup, the odds are you'll never have to draw on anybody."

"Maybe. You hardly ever need a doctor or a lawyer, either. But when you do, you want a damned good one, and damned good comes damned expensive."

Thayer drummed his fingers on the desk blotter as he thought that over. Longarm obviously didn't care whether he got the job or not, since it offered some problems as well as opportunities for his investigation. He'd told the simple truth, and three dollars a day for a hired gun really was ridiculous. Thayer either didn't really want him to take the job, or he was tight as hell. The lawyer had that sleek, fat-cat look of the successful greedy man. But he could be playing chess, for he looked smart too.

Thayer finally exhaled loudly and said, "All right. I had you down as a moody cowboy, but I might have known you were a professional killer. How does the going rate of a hundred a week sound to you?"

"A lot better. Who do you want killed first?"

"I'll let you know when the time comes," Thayer laughed. "It's understood that at those rates I have your undivided attention, and there's to be no discussion if I want to sic you on somebody I find bothersome?"

"You just said you took me for a pro, uh...boss."

"All right. You're on the payroll as of noon. O'Brian will be expecting you over at the yards. While I've got you here, I'd like to clear up another matter that's been bothering me."

"What's that, boss?"

"You got off the train with a fancy gal called Petunia. The two of you went to a house I'd rented her. We had a business deal. Did she, ah, say anything about me to you?"

Longarm pretended to ponder, then brightened and said, "Oh, you must be the lawyer she mentioned. She said she'd hired somebody here in Laredo to put things right with the courthouse and such before she opened for business. I didn't know that was your house, though. She said it belonged to some old doc who died."

"I told her that," Thayer said. "It's really the house of a former business partner who's in state prison at the moment. I'm looking after it for him, and I figured he could use the rent money. Getting back to the whore, she never showed up here. They tell me you put her on the northbound train."

"I did. She asked me to help her with her things. You see, we were on sort of neighborly terms by then."

Thayer grinned lewdly. "I just said she was a whore. Was she any good?"

Longarm didn't like to talk about a lady behind her back, but since he'd likely saved old Petunia-Molly's life, he figured she'd forgive him if he grinned back sort of dirty. Then, since he'd played some chess in his time and knew Thayer might have a complete account of the female private detective in question, he said, "Funny thing, though. She wasn't brunette like I thought. You know all that inky black hair atop her head? Well, it was a wig. Ain't that a bitch?"

"Do tell? What color was her real hair, Crawford?"

"Blonde. All over. I asked her why she wore the wig, but she wouldn't say. She sure was a spooky sort of gal."

"That's interesting," Thayer said levelly. "Why did she say she was leaving without meeting anybody here?"

"She never said. I asked, of course. I was sort of looking

forward to a whorehouse run by such a saucy wench." He took another drag on his smoke and then added as an apparent afterthought, "Oh, she did get a message, now that I study back on her."

"What kind of a message? A telegram?"

Longarm knew that a man who controlled as much as Thayer did could check to see if a wire had been sent to his own house, so he shook his head and said, "Nope. Some jasper came to the back door with a note. I didn't see him, as I was in bed sort of nekked, and old Petunia went to the door in her shimmy. Before you ask, I didn't get to read it. She sure did a funny thing with that note, after she read it. You'll never guess what it was in a million years."

"Goddammit, Crawford, I'm not paying you to play spell-me-a-riddle."

"Well, you ain't gonna believe this, but she *et* it! She read what it said, went sort of green around the gills, and *swallowed* the damn note, ink and all. Ain't that a bitch? I tried to get her back in bed, but she said she had to catch the train, so, being polite, I put her aboard and she swore she'd write. I sort of doubt that. I've put gals on trains sudden before. You know what I think the note said? I think the law was after her for something more serious than selling her ring-dang-doo. You'll likely disbelieve this too, but I suspicion she wasn't a whore a-tall."

Thayer stared down at his desk as though he'd suddenly noticed how interesting a green blotter was, as he answered, "Oh? What made you think that?"

"Just a feeling I can't explain, like how you know when somebody's fixing to draw on you. I've met a few businesswomen in my time, and—I dunno—she didn't act like a whore in bed."

"Well, for God's sake, she let you screw her, didn't she?"

"Yep, and that was sort of spooky too. She never asked me for money. But she, uh, acted like she was dwelling in her mind on other matters all the time I was with her. You know what I think? I think I've been used and abused!"

Thayer laughed and asked, "What are you talking about, Crawford?"

"She was there when I had the shootout on the train. She knew I was good with my guns. I think she picked me up and brung me along as an unpaid bodyguard, and I'm a mite hurt about that. Oh, sure, I got free room and board and other favors a gent shouldn't dwell on, but when I consider how I might have been called on for a shootout with person or persons unknown, with no financial discussion first, it makes me feel a mite foolish."

Thayer muttered something obviously intended to be soothing, and Longarm saw he'd convinced him he wasn't all that bright. Thayer had him down as a cowhand gone wrong, whose wits were quick enough in a firefight, but not a thing a fancied-up dude with a law diploma had to worry about. Longarm reflected that it sure was funny how easy it was to make folks think you were dumber than they were, when you considered how hard it was to make 'em think you were smarter.

Then Thayer said something about having paperwork to do, so Longarm rose and said he'd attend to a few chores before heading over to the yards and reporting to O'Brian.

The first thing he did was to check into the Drover's Hotel, down the street. The room he hired wasn't as clean as the one at the *posada*, and he doubted it came with hot running *muchachitas*, but a hand working for you had to be staying *someplace*, and Longarm didn't want them to know he had made a few other friends in town.

He put the room key in a pocket and used some sidestreets to get back to Mama Felicidad's. He was aiming to get his things, of course, but when he spied a crowd out front, he stopped under the shade of a live oak and asked a Mex coming up the walk what was going on. The Mex said, "A killing, *Señor*. Some *hombre muy malo* just shot Chino, the boy who tends bar for Mama Felicidad!"

"Anybody see it happen?"

"No, *Señor*. Chino was alone out front, for to mop the floor, I think, and the killer picked him off from the doorway with a shotgun. The Anglo lawmen found the spent shotgun shell in the dust outside the doorway. Forgive me, I mean no offense, but they are questioning everyone in the *barrio* and I do not wish for to speak with them, since I know nothing and they are so impolite when one says he knows nothing."

His informant passed by, and left Longarm mulling it over under the live oak. There were a couple of ways he could play this. He could turn about and mosey off. There wasn't anything up in his *posada* room that he couldn't replace cheaper than his own hide. On the other hand, should anybody search the premises and find obvious Anglo gear...

He turned, found the entrance to the alley running behind the *posada*, and moseyed down it thoughtfully. He found the rear entrance of Mama Felicidad's, and since nobody seemed interested, he ducked inside. The kitchen was empty. Everybody seemed to be up front, talking to the law. Longarm headed for the stairs, only to meet Mama Felicidad coming down them, carrying his things in her fat arms. Her eyes were redrimmed and she looked surprised to see him. But she said, "Oh, thank God you came in the back way, *querido*. A terrible thing has happened!"

"Yeah, I just heard about Chino."

"Oh, *sí*, that happened too! We think it must have been Garcia. But I was talking about my *vacas*. Somebody stole my whole herd last night while we were ... you know."

"How many head are missing and what are you doing with my things, honey?"

"They took all thirteen of my poor *vacas*. I was of course about to hide your things in the pantry. None of our people ever tell the Anglo police anything, and they will probably search my *posada* for, how you say, clues?"

"Close enough. How come you don't tell the law that Garcia gunned Chino? It seems to me you'd save yourself some worry if the ornery rascal was locked up."

"Oh, no, *querido*, that is not the way of my people. Chino has many relations, and they would be most offended if the Anglo lawmen only put Garcia in a comfortable jail, eh?"

"I follow your drift and we'll say no more about it. I'll take my stuff and be on my way for now. But I'll be back this evening."

The fat woman blushed girlishly and said, "Oh, I wish we could, but I do not think you had better come back so soon, *querido*. It might not be safe for you. Garcia does not like you either."

"I noticed. I think I might have gotten Chino gunned. Is killing Garcia a private game, or can any number play?"

"As a friend, you have the right, of course, but do not concern yourself with Garcia. If he is not in Mexico by now, he is already dead, for some of Chino's brothers are watching the river crossings our people use when they do not wish for to discuss their travels with the Texas lawmen. There is no need for you to come back, alas. Go with God, and try for to remember me once in a while, eh?"

He took the things, placed them on a nearby table, and took the nice old gal in his arms to kiss her. It had to be a brotherly kiss, with the lights on, but she took it kindly and tried to inhale his mustache. He said, "Simmer down. I want you to listen to me tight. Make sure nobody messes up any sign your stolen cows might have left before I have me a look-see. I'm supposed to be somewhere else this afternoon, so I can't get back before sundown. By then, things should have gotten quiet around here again. We'll go out to your ranch and I'll see if I can cut some sign. You have a good cutting horse and saddle I can borrow?"

"I can get you one from my cousin Hernan. But what is the use, *querido*? By now my cows are in Mexico. Not even my relations would dare to follow cow thieves into Mexico. Everyone knows the people who do this thing have *los rurales* covering their trail, and any man trying for to recover my poor *vacas* would be shot as an outlaw by *los rurales*, eh?"

He let her go and said, "Look for me about sundown," and picked up his cased rifle and other gear. He slipped out without anyone seeming to notice, and made it back to the Drover's Hotel without incident.

It was after one, and Thayer had told him to report to Boss O'Brian at high noon. Maybe if he fucked up even more, they'd fire him without getting suspicious. The dumb job was a dead end, even if Thayer wasn't trying to slicker him. A man on an undercover investigation needed elbow room and a chance to snoop about. He couldn't ask enough questions to matter over by the yards without making the gang suspect his motives, assuming they were the gang he was after and they weren't already onto him.

He knew Thayer played a good game of double-bluff, and when he'd learned the Cattlemen's Protective was sending Petunia-Molly, he'd been slick enough to offer her help. Hiring a federal deputy as a gunslick wouldn't be Thayer's dumbest move, if he knew more than he was letting on. Longarm hadn't forgotten that suggestion about the back doorway at the saloon, and even if they weren't trying to get him gunned now, they had been then.

He got to the yards to find Boss O'Brian and some pokes loading beef aboard a string of cattle cars on the siding. A county brand inspector was seated on the rails of a chute, holding a clipboard Longarm knew was a list of brands reported missing. So he didn't have to worry about Felicidad's cows leaving town *this* way.

O'Brian scowled at Longarm and said, "It's about time you got here, Crawford. You're an hour later than you should be."

Longarm shrugged and said, "My watch must have stopped. What do you want me to do, boss?"

"Just stay the hell out of my way. There's nobody but us working the cows today. It's getting too infernal hot for anybody to start trouble with anybody, anyway."

Longarm shrugged and drifted over to the loading chute they were using at the moment. He picked up a spare poke leaning against the rails, forked a leg over, and got near the car door, across from the brand inspector. He nodded to a kid of about sixteen who was perched nearby and said, "Move down and dress up the line, pard. They don't bunch as bad in the doorway if you poke 'em up the ramp with a lot of little jabs instead of trying to make 'em leap aboard."

The youth started to say something, nodded, and moved down to the middle of the chute as Longarm had directed him. Longarm nodded to the inspector as he jabbed a ladino steer with the nail on the end of his broom handle and sent it into the car, cussing him out in cow-talk. There was no sense in trying to talk above the bawling of the cows and the rumble of their hooves on the boards of the ramp. Longarm figured a Texas man could already see how many of the so-called Mexican steers had an admirable Texas spread to their horns. The brands were the usual fancy ones they favored south of the Rio. He didn't see any that were out-and-out raw, but some of the Mex brands looked a lot more recent than the older ones on other parts of the critters' hides. Each old brand had been crossed out with a single line, as usual, but of course the brand inspector could see that, and while some of the old markings looked American, he apparently didn't see fit to cull any cows out.

They got the car loaded and one of the yard boys dropped the gate at ground level as Longarm rolled the car door shut. As he and the brand inspector climbed down to move up to the next chute, he introduced himself as O'Brian's segundo and said casually, "They sure have been stocking up down in Mexico with our kind of scrub, haven't they?"

"Not *Texas* scrub," the brand inspector replied. "I read horns too. But the tale they tell me is that some Mex dealers bought a mess of American cows during the dry spell we had the last couple of years."

"Do tell? I didn't know it rained more on their side of the border."

The inspector chuckled. "I'm ahead of you on that one, cowboy. It don't rain at all where some of these cows just come from. They irrigate the desert ranges, so it don't matter what the weather's like, one way or the other. They have proper bills of sale for past ownership, and you know beef was way down during the drought, too. Too many of our old boys figure on making a quick killing by raising cows. Them Mex fellows ranch as a way of life, like they been doing for a couple hundred years, so they can afford better to wait. What they seem to have done was slick business, but legal. They bought cheap beef off outfits going out of business, run 'em down to fatten 'em a mite on irrigated fodder, and now that beef's up again, they're shipping 'em to Chicago, New York, and other hungry places."

Longarm didn't think he'd better ask any more questions right now, so he climbed up to open another door on the side of an empty cattle car. But the old brand inspector liked to talk, so he climbed up right next to the tall deputy, and as Longarm signaled the kids to open the lower gate, the inspector stabbed his papers with a finger and said, "Here's an example of what I'm talking about. The outfit was the Bar Seven Slash, in New Mexico. I'd never heard of the brand, so I sent me a wire. I ain't so dumb."

"You can't be dumber than me," Longarm observed, "as you get to work with a pencil whilst I wave this poke. The Bar Seven Slash checked out, I take it?"

"Sure it did. You wouldn't be loading them old Bar Seven Slash critters if I didn't know for a fact there *was* a Bar Seven Slash spread, and that they sold out to a Don Fernando of the Spur and Hat brand, in Mexico, lawful and proper."

"New Mexico spread went busted, you say? How could they answer your wire if they ain't in business no more?"

"Hell, son, don't try to teach your granny to suck eggs. I

checked it with the county clerk. The folks who used to own the Bar Seven Slash went back East after they went bust, but the property deeds, brands, and such are a matter of public record."

The cows started coming up the ramp. Longarm saw that a walleyed white-blaze was going to hang his horns up, and poked the side of the critter's neck to steer him into the car. As Longarm poked a brindle in after him, the brand inspector pointed with his pencil and said, "See that Rocking K brand under the fancy Mex one? That critter first saw the light of day in Arizona Territory. Come off a small spread dusted by drought and hit tedious by Apache. Owners sold what was left of their herd to a Mex buyer about a year or so ago. You got to get up early to pull the wool over *my* eyes!"

"I can see that. You got a wire from Arizona saying it was all right for old Rocking K cows to live in Mexico for a spell, right?"

"Durn tootin'. You likely heard of the Laredo Loop, ain't you, son?"

"I did hear some mention of it, now that I study on it. What about it?"

"It *ain't*. It's just a notion, like the Sidehill Winder or the Big Blue Ox. We've been watching for stolen American stock coming in from Mexico. The rumors is exaggerated. There's no way it'd work like they say. Maybe one or two hot cows could slip by us now and again, but we do check out any American-looking brands we see regular. The home address has to be on the proper bill of sale. So it only takes a day to wire and get an answer, and no suspicious cows move until we do so."

Longarm poked another cow aboard and told the inspector he was mighty slick. But it was all so stupid he couldn't believe it. It was no wonder Billy Vail had sent him down here, if this was what the local law thought was a proper check on brands.

It was so simple it seemed childish. The damfool brand inspectors were checking the addresses listed on the Mexican bills of sale, so of course when they wired somebody there, they'd get a satisfactory answer. The older man had said the outfits he'd checked on were no longer in business. He was too dumb to see that they'd *never* been in business! The crooks just sent somebody to a county where they hadn't stolen any cows. It only took a few dollars and a day to register a "new" brand with the county clerk. They'd wait a while and then file that they were going out of business. So the county would have a record that, sure enough, there had been such an outfit in the county a spell back and . . . Jesus, couldn't anybody around here add that up? What cow thief was about to fake papers giving the true location of the spread he'd robbed? The real owners would have filed missing-cow reports in their own counties, and all the thieves would be breaking rocks by now.

He made a mental note on that Bar Seven Slash brand, since he noticed they were loading a mess of them. He didn't ask the brand inspector where the dummy spread in New Mexico was. He'd find out later where the *real* Bar Seven Slash was.

Boss O'Brian came over and leaned on the rail to observe grudgingly, "You're pretty good with that poke, Crawford. Reckon Thayer might have known what he was doing when he hired you, after all."

Longarm shrugged and said, "I think you're pretty, too." He knew he didn't dare ask the brand inspector anything else, but the man was an idiot, so it hardly mattered.

Boss O'Brian said, "Don't wise-ass me, Crawford or whomsoever. I never said nothing when you grabbed that name outta midair, but that don't mean I was birthed yesterday."

Longarm stared down at him thoughtfully and O'Brian nodded and said, "You heard me. I reckon I know Camp Crawford is just outside of town. Couldn't you have come up with something more original, seeing as you're so infernal smart?"

Longarm gave himself a good swift mental boot in the butt as O'Brian's words sank in. He'd made a godawful blunder when the name Crawford just popped into his mind on his way to Laredo. He'd really thought he was thinking of Dr. Crawford Long, but of course Camp Crawford had been the army post that Billy Vail and he had agreed he'd best stay away from this time, if and when he wanted to borrow one of Uncle Sam's horses!

He grinned sheepishly and said, "Some old boy from up Dodge way must have told you my real name, huh?"

He could see the little gears turning in O'Brian's eyes as he filed that remark about Dodge City away. Longarm had hoped he might. Anything to keep them from considering Denver. O'Brian shrugged and said, "Like I say, it's no never-mind to me, if Thayer hired you and you don't step on my toes."

The brand inspector had gone sort of quiet and pensive. For a man who wasn't looking for trouble, O'Brian had sure picked a funny place and time to mention names. Longarm grimaced and said, "If you don't want me on your toes, you'd best keep your feet out from under 'em."

"What's that supposed to mean, Dodge City boy?"

"If you don't know, you'd best go see a doctor, for you are purely talking an awful lot for a man whose brain never grew to match his size."

Boss O'Brian frowned and said, "I don't allow many folks to sass me like that, *muchacho*!"

Longarm shrugged, poked another Bar Seven Slash through the doorway, and said, "If my manners offend you, I'll be proud to meet you whenever and have it out. If you don't want to fight, you'll either have to let me be or fire me. I don't take much shit for my day wages, either."

O'Brian started to say something, reconsidered, and moved off, hitting a corral post a lick with his cattle poke and yelling something at one of the kids. Longarm smiled at the brand inspector and said, "He must have got up on the wrong side of the bed this morning."

The brand inspector didn't answer. He seemed interested as all hell in his clipboard just now, so Longarm let him be. He knew what the inspector was thinking. He was mulling over what Boss O'Brian had just "let slip," but what the hell, when he sent that wire to Dodge he wasn't going to get any interesting answers. Longarm knew O'Brian would likely tell Thayer he'd found out where their new hand hailed from. Longarm had picked Dodge with that in mind.

They finished loading the car and moved to the next one. It took until a quarter to three before they'd seen the last of the damned cows, and nobody waved good-bye as the train pulled out to the main line with them.

Longarm hung the cattle poke on its nail in a corral post, and took off his hat to dust off his pants. He was sweated by the heat, and his mouth tasted like it was full of mummy dust. The brand inspector had lit out like a scalded cat before the train had even started.

Boss O'Brian came over, calling out to everybody, "All

right, boys, let's rake the yards and pack her in for the day. But I'll expect you all early tomorrow, for there's a herd of Mex beef arriving with the cold gray dawn."

Longarm started to look around for something better than his hands to pick up cow turds with. Boss O'Brian said, "Not you, segundo. Rank has its privileges and I owe you a drink, over to the saloon."

Longarm raised an eyebrow. O'Brian nodded and said, "I was out of line and I admit it. I wasn't thinking about old Ned being law when I mentioned last names. He's been down here ticking off brands for so long that I get to feeling like *he* works for us too."

"Fair is fair, then," Longarm said. "I take back anything hasty I might've said, and we'll drink on it."

They left the yards and headed across the broad dirt road to the saloon he'd had the fight in. He mentioned that to O'Brian, and O'Brian said, "They ain't mad at you no more. No glass got broke and they wasn't closed down by the law. You hear about that shooting over to the Mex quarter, earlier today?"

"Heard there'd been a shootout. Didn't know where it was or what it was about."

"Well, one Mex gunned another and now the place it happened in has been shut down by the city until the coroner's jury holds its hearing. It's pure dangerous to serve hard likker to greasers. Most of 'em are really Injuns in the first place, and ornery enough cold sober. Our saloon is all right with the law, though, since they mostly serve white men and the boys you gunned wasn't served in there anyway. Lawyer Thayer told the law there was no way in hell the barkeep could be blamed for what happened, so it's all jake."

"Thayer sure volunteers his services a heap. Or does he own yonder saloon too?"

Boss O'Brian laughed and said, "There you go. You're starting to learn how this town works. Thayer don't own all of Laredo, just this end of it."

They were almost across the road when the short hairs on the back of Longarm's neck started prickling. As the two men clumped up the wooden steps, Longarm stood aside and said, "Age before beauty, boss."

"You go ahead, old son," O'Brian insisted.

So Longarm took a deep breath, drew his sixgun, and slammed through the batwings, crabbing to one side as he entered, and dropping to one knee behind a table he remembered.

The shotgun roared and blew a hole in one swinging batwing big enough to toss a cat through. Longarm fired at the Mexican holding the shotgun. The second barrel went off, shattering the window above Longarm's head as he fired again. He was set to put a third round into Garcia, but the Mex dropped the shotgun, stared at him sort of bewildered, and fell sideways from the bar like a sawed-off tree. Longarm knew he was dead when he hit the floor.

There didn't seem to be another soul in the place, and it was eerily quiet as the smoke slowly cleared. He stayed low and reloaded before he rose cautiously and called out, "Anybody home?"

Nothing. He walked over to the bar and peered over. The barkeep wasn't dead on the duckboards; he'd apparently just vacated the premises, likely for his health.

Longarm was sure he'd left Boss O'Brian just outside. But O'Brian sure didn't seem interested in what had been going on in here. That figured too. Longarm moved to the shattered window for a look-see before he outlined himself in any doorway where folks might expect to see him. Then he grimaced and said, "I'll be damned. There might be some justice in this cruel world after all."

Boss O'Brian lay on his back in the dust, his spur rowels hooked over the edge of the boardwalk. He wasn't taking a sunbath. Garcia's shotgun blast through the window had put what looked like a cherry pie smack in the middle of O'Brian's chest. He had his gun in his dead hand. He'd moved to the window when the fun and games began, likely to pick the winner off, whoever it might be.

Longarm saw folks coming down the street, slow and cautious. He holstered his Colt and stepped outside as the town marshal came in to comment on the noise. The man stared morosely down at Boss O'Brian and said, "I sure hope you didn't do that, son."

"Nope, I never," Longarm said. "You'll find a dead Mex inside. He opened up with a shotgun as me and O'Brian come over to wet our whistles."

The town marshal stomped past Longarm into the saloon, and Longarm saw Thayer pushing through the growing crowd. Thayer gagged when he saw what a mess the shotgun had made of his yard boss. He asked Longarm the same question and got the same answer. It seemed that everybody just naturally expected him to gun Boss O'Brian, for some reason.

The town marshal came out and stuck out a fist, thumb pointing downward. "Dead as a turd in a milk bucket. Who got him, Crawford, you or old O'Brian there?"

Longarm said, "I disremember hearing O'Brian getting off a round, so I reckon I must have put most of the lead in the ornery rascal. Who the hell was he?"

"Didn't you know him? His name was Garcia and he was supposed to be a bad hombre."

Longarm looked down at the body in the dust. "That sounds like a fair estimate. He was laying for us in there with the shotgun, and I'd hardly call that friendly."

"Are you saying he had no call to go for you, Crawford?" Thayer asked.

"Hell," Longarm said, "how do we know he wasn't after O'Brian? I'm new in Laredo. O'Brian and the Mex might have been after the same gal or some such. I don't mean to tell anybody how to play detective, but you might have noticed the bushwhacker was shooting at O'Brian, not me."

"You sure did a good job of stopping Garcia's clock," the town marshal said, "but I can put her together simple enough. Boss O'Brian and the Mex must have had a few words some other time and place. The sneaky Mex knew O'Brian drank here regular. So, not having the balls for a fair showdown, he was laying for him, not expecting him to show up with anyone to back his play. I can see from the holes he left in the premises that he must have fired at both of you. If he'd had a lick of sense, he'd have lit out the back way when he saw there was two of you coming. No Mex birthed of mortal woman could hope to take on two growed white men and live. He must have been likkered up."

"Maybe," Longarm said. "I didn't smell his breath before I fired. You'll likely want me to make another statement to the coroner, huh?"

The town law nodded wearily. "Yeah, just drop by when you get off work. You know the way to the doc's. I'd sure take it kindly if you tried to cut down on these visits, though. I ain't saying this was your fault, but things was sure a lot more peaceable 'fore you come to town."

A couple of deputies came legging it up the road. The town marshal pointed at O'Brian with his chin and said, "I'm sure glad you boys saw fit to set the cards aside for a spell and earn your keep. One of you go fetch the undertaker. Tell him we got two customers this time. I've a hunch we may have a handle on that earlier shooting over to the Mex quarter, too. If Garcia was feeling ornery enough to fire a shotgun at two growed white men, it seems only logical he'd be up to blowing away that barkeep at Mama Felicidad's."

One of the deputies said, "Hey, old Chino got hit by a ten-gauge too, Jim!" The town marshal stared at the deputy. "I just told you that, damn it," he said softly.

Longarm saw they didn't need him at the moment. He stepped closer to Thayer and said, "Well, O'Brian can't tell me what I'm supposed to do next. So I reckon it's up to you, boss."

"I suppose you figured on stepping into his boots?" Thayer said.

"Somebody has to, don't they?"

Thayer shook his head and said, "You're fired, Crawford." Then he reached in his pocket and took out a gold piece, adding, "Here's your couple of days in lieu of notice. You're too much trouble to have around, no offense. I don't know who you are or where you came from, but folks sure die a lot in your vicinity, and you're making me nervous."

Longarm took the money, put it away, and sighed, "I've been trying to break the habit, but trouble just seems to follow me around. I thought you said you needed a good gunhand on your payroll."

Thayer snorted. "You're not a gunhand, you're the Black Plague. I deal in cattle on the side, not private wars. I don't know who you are. If your name was really Crawford, you'd have a rep I could check out better. I doubt if John Wesley Hardin ever put as many men on the ground as you in such a short time. Poor O'Brian said you were trouble looking for a place to happen, and I should have listened to him. It's been nice knowing you, Crawford, but I just can't afford to have you anywhere near me."

"Oh? Are you suggesting this town's a snug fit for the two of us?"

Thayer glanced down at his dead yard boss and asked, "Do I look stupid? Nobody's trying to run you out of town, Crawford. But if you don't mind some friendly parting advice, I'd fork a bronc and ride if I was you. No grown man with brains is about to try and take a gent like you, but a rep like yours draws would-be gunslicks like honey draws ants!"

Before Longarm could answer, Thayer turned on his heel and went inside the saloon, likely to find his barkeep and find out what had gone wrong.

Longarm headed the other way, trying not to grin. The chess they were playing was getting interesting, and Thayer's last move had worked to both their advantages. He'd already figured out that going to work for the rascal wasn't going to help, for they'd been suspicious of him from the start. He'd been wondering how to quit or get fired without their knowing he was onto them. He fingered the gold coin in his pocket and decided to use it to do some celebrating before he had to get back to work that evening.

Longarm's parting wages paid for some drinks, another hot bath, and a good steak-and-potatoes dinner at the Drover's Hotel. By then it was getting dark enough to head over to Mama Felicidad's *posada*. It wasn't just because he was ashamed to be seen with her in broad daylight; he didn't want anyone in town connecting him up with his Mex friends.

Felicidad's cantina had been shut down by the law, as the town marshal had said, so he found her and Palomina alone in the kitchen when he came up to the back door. Felicidad said she had to hang about and talk to her own Mex lawyer about getting the ban on her bar lifted, so she told her little niece to run Longarm out to her stock spread in their buckboard.

Longarm offered to drive. A tactical error, as it turned out. He followed Palomina's directions until they were out of town a ways, and then, as they drove through a tunnel of live oak, Palomina started trying to unbutton his fly. "I wish you wouldn't do that, honey," he said.

Palomina said, "Stop the horse."

He shook his head. "Not hardly. We are on a public highway in the first place, and I want to scout your aunt's place for sign in the second. Maybe we can work something out later."

"Pooh, we can't do it out at Tía Felicidad's. My childish brother is out there, watching the property for her. It is almost dark and nobody else is on the road. Let's do it now."

"Damn it, girl, get your fool hand out of my britches!" he said. "I can't think of two things at once, and right now I'm thinking about stolen cows. Just simmer down and later I'll give you some undivided attention."

They drove another quarter-mile and turned into the gate of a small spread surrounded by a cactus hedge and guarded by yapping yellow dogs. A kid in baggy white cotton duds came out of the 'dobe with a shotgun, saw who they were, and cussed the dogs quiet as Longarm reined in. Palomina's kid brother offered to coffee and bean them, but Longarm said he wanted to look out back for sign. So as he got down and helped Palomina to the ground, the boy went in and got a bullseye lantern.

Longarm and the young Mex boy went out back, where the missing cows had been pastured. The boy showed him a gap in the cactus hedge, and when Longarm shone the light on it he nodded and said, "Yep, those cactus pads were cut, not trampled. Too much grass in here for much sign, but I see where a cow with a lame hind leg was herded through the gap. He was moved too sudden for it to have been a volunteer move."

The boy said, "That would have been the black *chongo*. I noticed he had a bad leg, *Señor*."

Things were looking up. Longarm said, "A black steer with crooked horns ain't hard to spot at a distance, even when he ain't limping. What's your Aunt Felicidad's brand, *muchacho*?"

"Brand? We don't got no brand, *Señor*. Tía Felicidad buys calves and yearlings for to fatten up. We don't breed them. We are only feeders."

"Shit, you mean none of the stolen cows have registered brands, for God's sake?"

The boy brightened and said, "Oh, they got the brands they came with. Is that any help?"

"It is if you remember any."

"Ah, I see. The black *chongo* wore a letter K, only lying down with it's short lines up."

"Lazy K. That's one," grunted Longarm. He stepped through the gap in the cactus, shining his light on the ground. He held it on one hoofprint and said, "Another one of your aunt's cows had a split hoof that's healed. He wouldn't limp, but he leaves a good sign. Can you place old Split-Hoof?"

"*Sí*, I remember when we doctored it. The steer is a calico, red and white. It has ordinary horns. It was branded with the letter H, only the letter had a little curving line under it, like so."

"Rocking H." Longarm nodded, shining the beam around some more. The other cows had all just left the usual marks, but two out of thirteen were something to go on. He spotted the hoofmark of a pony. There was nothing remarkable about the print, but it verified that the cows hadn't busted out on their own. The boy said, "I followed the trail by daylight as far as the main north-south road. There, of course, I lost it. They must have turned south to Mexico, no?"

Longarm shook his head. "Doubt it. That road leads into Laredo, and thieves don't hardly ever come that bold. They likely ran 'em north a spell and then headed west. The Rio Grande gets deeper to the east. I doubt that anybody would be dumb enough to try and ford the river anywhere near Laredo. No friends of El Gato would steal his aunt's cows, and unless they've heard, some of 'em are staked out along the river waiting for Garcia to try for Mexico. Did you hear about Garcia getting killed late this afternoon?"

The boy blinked and then smiled. "No, but I am not displeased to learn this, *Señor*. Who got the *cabrone*?"

"Never mind. Your aunt's cows were stolen before it happened, so if the thieves know anything, they'd be expecting Chino's friends to be watching the near crossings. They likely ran the cows into some brushy draw to hold 'em for nightfall, which is now. They couldn't know Garcia is dead since they're farther from town than you, and you didn't know it until just now. I figure they'll run 'em west through the darkness and figure on swinging south to the river just before dawn. Your aunt said you had a pony and saddle I could use. Where's it at?"

The boy looked embarrassed. "We tried for to borrow you a mount from Hernan Lopez, but he would not part with it for free. Hernan is a very selfish pig, I think."

Longarm swore softly. He knew that a mounted man made better time than cows being driven by hands who didn't mean to draw much attention, but he didn't have much of a lead, damn it. If he went back to the hotel and got his rifle, then picked up a mount from the livery in town, he'd still likely make it, but that would mean certain interested parties would know he'd ridden out under a hunter's moon.

He took out his Ingersoll watch and shone the bullseye beam on it. Thayer would have left his office by now. There might be somebody watching his room at the Drover's Hotel, but there might not be. He'd have to chance it. He'd likely need the Winchester in any case.

He went around to the front and told Palomina they had to get cracking. As they headed back to town she asked, "Where do you wish to stop for to make love, my *toro*?"

He just whipped the cart horse with the reins and drove faster. She said, "Not so fast. It is dark and we could turn over." He didn't answer and she said, "Ah, I see why you are in such a hurry. You wish for to do it right, in a bed, no?"

He told her she was right. So that calmed her down and he started to figure out how they were going to put it over on old Felicidad, this early. She said, "My Tía Felicidad has no business, with the cantina shut down, but she never goes to bed before ten." "Tell you what, then," he said. "I'll drop you off and leg it over to my other hotel to see if it looks safe to sneak you up the backstairs."

Palomina laughed and said, "Oh, that sounds like fun. I like to be sneaky. Don't you?"

He didn't answer. He wasn't sure how he felt about sneaking her into the Drover's Hotel, but right now he had some other sneaking to study on. He had to sneak into Mexico, against orders, without either Billy Vail or the *rurales* finding out about it. Old Billy would likely fire him if he found out. *Los rurales* might be even more testy if he allowed his fool self to be spotted crossing the border.

Chapter 8

Longarm took his things to the livery in Laredo and hired a big white stud with a long mane and a big bushy tail. Its name was Showboat. He knew that sooner or later the gang would hear he'd ridden out. He hoped they'd think he'd just tired of Laredo's unhealthy climate. If they suspected he'd jumped the border, he wanted the *rurales* looking for a tall dark *gringo* on a flashy white horse.

It was cutting the time close, but his next move was to ride to the army camp that had gotten him in so much trouble by being named after Dr. Crawford Long too. As a federal agent, he was accustomed to using the services of army remount depots. But remount officers could be a pain in the ass, and he didn't have time for the usual bullshit. So he rode up to camp headquarters and asked to see the CO, who turned out to be a reasonable sort. Longarm identified himself and said, "You can check me out with Army of the West HQ by wire, if you make it quick. They'll tell you how me and Matt Kincaid of Easy Company, Outpost Nine, worked right well together on another government case."

The CO said, "I know your rep, Longarm. What's your pleasure?"

Longarm explained, and the soldier told him, "I can let you have a good chestnut mare who covers ground and takes her time to tire. But what if somebody notices the U.S. brand, down Mexico way?"

"They'll likely think I stole her and be a mite more fond of me. I'll save time by jumping the border where you boys are guarding the river crossing. If there's one place nobody in the bandit business will be expecting me to cross, that should be it."

The CO said he'd run over to the army stables with Longarm to save explanations and leave fewer men on post aware of what was going on. He said he doubted he had many Mexican spies in the outfit, but soldiers talked on leave, and most of 'em screwed Mex gals if they could afford it. As they crossed the parade together, he asked Longarm, "Assuming you don't get picked up by the *rurales* just inside Mexico, and assuming the cow thieves you're after really mean to cross farther west, how will you know which ford to stake out? There's any number of good places to sneak a cow over the water between here and the Big Bend."

"Hell," Longarm said, "I don't mean to be hunkered down and waiting. If I've timed it right, come sunrise I should be poking along the south bank a couple of hours behind 'em. I'll pick up the sign when I see where one lame *chongo* and a split-hoofed calico moseyed up the bank."

The CO nodded. "Of course. I wasn't thinking. Any man riding alone and well mounted should have no trouble catching up with a herd. But what do you do when you catch up? I've heard you're good, but taking on a gang of Mexican outlaws in their own country sounds mighty risky. There's no way you're about to persuade them to come back quietly, cows and all."

"I ain't after the cow thieves, and while I'm fond of the lady who was left with an empty pasture, she has the wherewithal to replace thirteen scrub cows as soon as her old cantina is back in business selling beer and beans."

"You're sure going to a lot of trouble if you don't mean to recover the cows or arrest the thieves, Longarm."

"Yeah, this job does get tedious at times. My badge ain't

very big medicine in Old Mexico, though. So I won't move in on the thieves as I trail them. What we're trying to find out is where the stolen cows *come back* from Mexico, and who's in on it that we can arrest."

"Jesus, if I understand the Laredo Loop, you could wind up trailing those stolen cows all the way west to Arizona!"

"I said the job gets tedious from time to time. That's why I only aim to do this once, if twice can be avoided."

When they got to the stables, the CO told the army hostler to shift the Texas saddle from the white stud Longarm was leading to the mare called Osage. Since the order came from high places, the hostler didn't ask questions. The CO asked if there was anything else he could do for him, and Longarm said there was. They left Osage for the moment and went over to the telegraph shack. It was a relief to be able to transmit messages in the clear for a change, so Longarm sent a mess of wires. He didn't have time to wait for any answers, but the CO said he'd hold any that came in until Longarm got back.

He shook the CO's hand and left the army man to go back to his wife and supper. On the way back to the stables, he stopped at the suttler's and went in to see if he could do something about himself, now that he had a less spectacular mount. The suttler sold local souvenirs, or would have, if the army paid better. Longarm saw a big straw sombrero gathering dust on a top shelf, so he bought it. It smelled like a haunted haymow, even after the suttler dusted it off, but seen from a distance, a man riding through Mexico under a Mexican hat would attract scant attention. He went back to the stable, bunched up his Stetson, and put it in a saddlebag, then put on the foolish-looking sombrero and rode out.

The almanac promised a moon for later that night, but it was still dark as a coal bin when Longarm and Osage rode into the guard detail at the ford. Somebody yelled, "Halt!" Longarm said he had a pass from the CO, so they didn't shoot him. He asked if *rurales* were posted on the far side, and the soldier who handed his pass back said he hadn't seen any at sundown, and added, "They generally watch the places where we ain't."

That seemed logical enough, given a manpower shortage on both sides. *El Presidente* Díaz didn't care if anybody *left* Mexico, empty-handed at least, and he probably figured the U.S. Army would notice anybody who was running off Mexican livestock, kidnapped women, and such.

Longarm heeled Osage down the bank and into the water. The river was low, but still stirrup-deep this far downstream. Shallow-draft sternwheel steamboats had been known to make it as far upstream as Eagle Pass once. The steamboats seldom ran these days. The run was discouraging, with surly folks on the far bank putting bullets through your wheelhouse just to see if they could hit it.

He didn't know what made the Tex-Mex border so unfriendly. It likely had something to do with the way folks in these parts made their hot tamales too peppery. But nobody was waiting to blast him out of the saddle on the far bank, so Longarm figured he'd be all right until the moon rose.

The almanac hadn't lied; the moon came up an hour after Longarm jumped the border. It was a good thing it did, for he found himself riding through a pear flat, and it could smart to hang a knee up on a ten-foot prickly pear. There was something about Mexico that agreed with cactus. They grew as far north as the Wyoming High Plains, albeit stunted down to one or two tiny pads in some sheltered draw. They got bigger to the south, and the border states and territories boasted some fair-sized cactus. South of the border, the thorny stuff started thinking it was tall timber. He lost the moonlit sheen of the river to his right as he threaded his way through the pear flat. He reined in, dismounted, and unlashed his bedroll. He took out the folded gunbarrel chaps he'd thought to pack as soon as Billy Vail mentioned the border country. They were of light elkhide, cut close, without batwings or fancy conchos to hang up on a mesquite branch.

He buckled the waistband under his gunbelt and bent down to fasten the snaps as he folded the hide around his legs. The Texas saddle, of course, had *tapaderos* of stout bullhide covering the stirrups, and the martingale on Osage's breast afforded her some protection, but he sure wished the saddle had come with *armas*. He could only steer her between the heavier-looking stuff and kick the rest clear while hoping for the best.

He lashed the roll back behind the cantle, and as long as he was afoot, he had a friendly drink with Osage, cupping canteen water in his palm for them both. Neither one of them was thirsty yet, he just wanted to assure the old mare he was on her side and that she didn't have to worry about him being one of those fool riders who treated his mount like a machine.

He generally talked or sang some to his mount, alone on the trail, like most riders. He knew Osage couldn't savvy why he didn't want to be overheard singing Yanqui cowboy songs in Mexico, and a silent rider tended to spook a mount on a long ride. Old Osage didn't try to bite his hand, so he figured they were going to get along.

He remounted and rode on, navigating by the stars and moon. The cactus jungle was a bitch. The only advantage he could see to it was that the cow thieves couldn't even think of crossing in these parts.

They finally left the pear flat and made better time crossing an open stretch. He watched for sign in the bright moonlight, but didn't see a thing. He wasn't expecting to. Next to driving cows through cactus, nothing beat overgrazed and dusted-out desert as a pain in the ass. Even when cows weren't hungry, they didn't cotton much to the notion of leaving water and grass behind to head out into bone-dry dust flats. They came to another pear flat that was even bigger, and by the time they made the far side the sky was growing pearly to the east and the land ahead looked more reasonable. It was flat, scattered brush, with summer-killed grass here and there, but like the rest of the border country, it was mostly bare dirt. Longarm swung Osage back into the cactus jungle, dismounted in a clearing he remembered, and said, "We'll just have us some grub while we wait for the light to get less tricky. There's a way to ride at night and a way to ride by daylight, but when the world's all gray and shadows, it don't pay to move about much."

He grubbed the mare first, of course. He'd brought a sack of oats, lashed to the front swells. But he knew Osage would like green pear better, once he peeled the thorns. He took out his pocket knife, cut off a pad of pear, and skinned it out for her. Osage, being an army mount, was sort of hesitant about eating Apache-style, but after she'd sniffed warily and risked a nibble, she went for thornless cactus with some enthusiasm. Most critters did. Mexican folks even used cactus for salad greens or pickled candy. Longarm didn't want her bloating on too much greenery, so he topped the pear off with a couple of handfuls of dried oats and said that if she didn't mind, he'd like to eat his own meal now.

He grubbed on a can of cold baked beans, washed down

with a can of tomatoes. He'd rather have had coffee for breakfast, but he didn't want to make a fire just now.

After a time, the sun peeked over the rim of the world, and, as a cactus wren was cussing them out upon awakening to find them under her nest, he mounted up and rode out across the flats to the west.

They had gone about a mile when Longarm reined in, looked around to see nobody in sight, and told Osage, "They crossed earlier than I would have. See that line of cow tracks across your bows? Well, one of the dozen or so head had a split hoof and another was limping. So it was them."

He sat his mount, thinking, as he fished out a cheroot and lit up. He knew he'd have heard even a small herd in motion from where they'd been hunkered in the cactus a mile back. The windless night had been quiet enough to hear your own heartbeat. As he'd expected, the thieves hadn't spent much time covering their tracks. They'd run the cows across by moonlight and were making a beeline due south, as though they were going someplace they had in mind when they jumped the border.

Longarm reined Osage around and said, "Let's find out what's so all-fired interesting down that way. But maybe we'd best drift over to the side a quarter-mile or so, in case that trail they took ain't a public thoroughfare a stranger would be welcome on."

It was an old Indian trick, but a trick that didn't work never *got* old. Folks who were expecting to be trailed watched the trail behind them. As the sun rose higher it was easy enough for Longarm to keep the arrow-straight streak of trampled dust in view as he rode more or less parallel to it, riding behind a rise or drifting off through the brush from time to time before swinging back close enough to see that it was still there and still headed due south.

He spied a windmill peeking over the horizon ahead, and told Osage, "Well, we know where they headed, so let's come at 'em from another direction altogether."

He heeled his mount at a forty-five-degree angle to circle wide of the windmill as he watched its sunflower blades hanging motionless in the sun's slanting rays. They worked their way around to the south, and when they cut the north-south trail again he didn't see the familiar hoofmarks of the stolen cows. He saw that other cow tracks and some ponies had gone both ways, but the limping *chongo* and the split-hoofed calico were likely enjoying a cool drink from that windmill's tank about now.

Longarm dismounted at the bottom of a rise, tied the mare to a bush, and took off the sombrero as he legged it up the slope to peer over it, between two clumps of mesquite.

The windmill rose above what was either a small village or a mighty big home spread for a hacienda in such dry country. A mess of one-story adobes circled a central plaza, and it looked like they even had a wayside *posada* if the lettering in blue on the adobe wall meant what it said. He saw stock corrals off to one side, near the windmill tower. One corral had about a dozen horses in it and another held at least a hundred head of cows. He couldn't tell from this distance whether any of the cows had banged-up hooves, so he went back down, mounted up, and said, "Well, we're riding in, old girl, and if I get shot I'll never speak to you again."

He rode up the trail from the south, as bold as brass. As he made it to the plaza, a woman called her kids inside and shut the door. Longarm reined in near the *posada* and dismounted to tether his mare to the hitch rail out front. No other horses were tethered there, but a man dressed in riding duds was lounging in the doorway, staring at Longarm thoughtfully. He was dressed Mexican, but his accent was pure Texas as he asked, "Where do you think you're going, stranger?"

Longarm glanced up at the blue letters over the portal and said, "Inside to wet my whistle, of course. I've rid a long ways and the sign says they sell eats and drinks here."

"Maybe they do and maybe they don't. How come that chestnut packs a U.S. Army brand?"

"Does she now? Funny, I never noticed. I disremember where I, uh, bought her."

The Mex-dressed man blocking the doorway said, "If I was you, I'd fork back aboard and ride another long ways, stranger. This is a quiet little settlement, and hoss thieves ain't welcome here."

"You the town marshal, old son?"

"Shoot, we don't need no town marshal. Folks hereabouts can take care of such trouble as drifts in. I ain't asking you to ride on, stranger. I'm telling you."

Longarm smiled thinly and said, "Let's study on that. You ain't the town law. Are you the owner of that *posada* you seem so possessive about?"

"Do I look like a Mex landlord? Who I might be ain't none of your business, stranger. Just ride on, like I told you to, and you'll find life more peaceable, further along."

The door behind the unfriendly cuss opened. Another man dressed Mex and talking English asked, "What's the trouble out here, Trigger?"

Trigger, if that was indeed his name, said, "No trouble. I just told this here stranger to move it on up the road, and that's what he was just aiming to do. Ain't that right, stranger?"

"I said I was studying on it," Longarm replied. "How far north is the Rio, and is there a friendlier place to shade and wet my whistle 'twixt here and there?"

The second man had spotted the government brand on Osage too, and Longarm could see he'd bought the part about his not knowing the country to the north when the man said, "Ain't nothing between here and the border. Where'd you say you was riding from, stranger?"

"I didn't," Longarm answered, adding, "your young friend here passed a rude remark about my pony, so you boys can do your own homework. I can see it's two to one, and nobody needs a drink all that bad, so I'll just be on my way and the two of you can go to hell." He turned, and had started to mount up, when the older of the two men suddenly laughed.

"Hey," he called, "don't get your shit hot. I reckon it won't hurt to buy you a beer. Come on inside, stranger, and let's be more civilized."

Longarm turned back around to face the two men with a less surly expression on his face this time. "A little civilization never hurt nobody," he said, "but this 'stranger' stuff is getting tedious. My name's Crawford in case anybody's interested, and I gather the young fellow here's called Trigger. What do they call you?"

After a pause, the man said quietly, "Boss. Just Boss."

"Fair enough," Longarm said, and Trigger stepped to one side as Boss led Longarm into the cantina part of the rambling *posada*. The cantina was empty, save for a sleepy Mex barkeep talking to a barefoot waitress in a peon skirt, standing next to the bar.

Boss led Longarm to a corner table, where the tall deputy could see that he'd already started working on a bottle. Longarm moved around to sit with his back to the rough adobe wall, facing the semidark room.

"That's my chair you took, pard," Boss said. "I reckon you'd be more comfortable here in this other one."

Longarm shoved the bottle and the glass next to it across toward him and said, "Not hardly. You know the folks here. I don't. I'll just keep my back to the wall for now, if it's all the same to you boys. But I'll buy you both a drink, for I wouldn't want you thinking I was surly."

Trigger frowned and asked Boss, "Are you going to let this saddle bum talk to us like that, Boss?"

Boss said, "Simmer down," and took the chair that put his back to Trigger and the bar, adding, "I generally jaw some with a man before I make up my mind one way or the other about gunning him."

He held up three fingers without turning his gaze from Longarm, who put his hands on the table as a polite stranger should, while he waited for the next play.

Boss said, "This ain't a regular town you're in. It's the headquarters of El Rancho Moreno. It used to be a town. That's why there's still some old signs up. But you might call this cantina a private club for Don Fernando's guests and help."

Longarm nodded up at Trigger and said, "I stand corrected, and I'm sorry I acted a mite muley about what I took for a public saloon. This Don Whomsoever must be mighty rich if he can afford to buy whole villages. How come you call it Rancho Moreno? Is that the family name or is it 'cause the country around here is so brown-looking. Moreno does mean 'brown' in Mex, don't it?"

"Don Fernando's last name is Moreno, and you don't want to know how he takes over towns," Boss said. "How come you only know a little Spanish if you're riding around Old Mexico on a mighty suspicious-looking horse?"

Longarm tried a slightly embarrassed expression as he said, "That just might be the reason I've decided to head back across the border. I can talk a little Mex, but you're dead right about folks down here being curious as hell."

The girl came over with a tray of *cervezas*. Longarm smiled up at her and said, "Grassy-ass, ma'am," as Trigger shot him a look of dismissal and took another chair to lift his beer. Boss poured his shotglass full of tequila, downed it neat, and washed it down with a slug of beer. When he could breathe again he said, "Your Spanish is awful. How the hell did you manage to find about the safe crossing to the north if you can't hardly talk to nobody?"

Longarm gave a snort. "Hell, this gal I met the other night talked American, and if I have to, I can get most notions across by moving my hands some. She said some Mex border raider— I disremember his handle—crossed just north of here from time to time. I figured if the infernal Rangers let a greaser get across, I ought to be able to make her."

The other two men exchanged glances. Boss then turned his gaze back on Longarm. "Was this gal talking about El Gato, do you remember?"

Longarm frowned, took a sip of beer, and said, "Yeah, that was the coot's name, now that you mention it. It means 'the cat' in Mex, ain't that a bitch? I know how to say 'dog' in Mex too. A dog is a *perro*, right?"

Boss grinned. "I can see you've been taking a lot of Spanish lessons. I don't reckon you ought to try and cross due north of here, Crawford. Not for a day or so, at least."

"Do tell? Trigger here was just acting sort of insistent about it."

"Yeah, well, that's why I'm the boss and he ain't. The Texas law might be interested in that particular ford at the moment. We wouldn't want you to get picked up just after having a drink with us."

Longarm took another sip, put down the mug, and said, "I wouldn't like that, neither. How come you suspicion the law is interested in that there crossing? Has old El Gato been raiding north again?"

Boss said, "Close enough. It'll be getting too hot to ride in a spell. So why don't you just siesta here, whilst I consider a better way for you to get home?"

He got to his feet, pointed at his private bottle, and said, "Stay out of that, Trigger. I'm going over to the main house to have a talk with Don Fernando. Needless to say, you boys can have all the *cerveza* you want, but leave Rosalita alone. She's private stock too."

Longarm knew most of that had been meant for his ears.

As Boss jingled out, he smiled at Trigger and said, "He sure seems like a friendly cuss."

"Yeah," Trigger said. "I got to see about putting some spurs and hats on our new cows. You stay here and leave both his tequila and *mujer* alone, hear?"

As Trigger got to his feet, Longarm pasted a puzzled look across his face and said innocently, "I may be a mite green for Mexico, but I have worked stock some. I've never seen a cow wearing either spurs *or* a hat, and customs can't be *that* different down here."

Trigger laughed. He didn't see fit to tell the foolish-looking stranger that the spur and hat were Don Fernando's brand. But Longarm didn't mind; he'd already made the connection. He'd poked a mess of Spur and Hat brands aboard the cars up in Laredo. Don Fernando was the official owner at this end of the Laredo Loop. He'd trailed Mama Felicidad's stolen cows right smack into the lion's den, and now that he knew where it was, how the hell was he about to ride back out?

Chapter 9

Longarm was glad he'd kept his story loose when Boss came back with a Mexican in a fancy maroon-and-gilt-braid *charro* outfit, for he could see that the Mexican recognized him too.

The man who'd been introduced as Don Fernando sat down, smiled, and said, "Ah, you did hide out and ride as far as Monterrey after you shot that hombre on the train. My brother said he thought you got off at Laredo, but I think on my feet too. The porter told us the Texan you killed in the dining car was from Laredo. Who but an *idiota* would get off at the hometown of a man he'd just shot, eh?"

Longarm stalled with another sip of *cerveza* as he pondered how to answer that. Don Fernando might not have friends in Laredo who kept him abreast of the latest news, but that hardly seemed likely. So Longarm shook his head and said, "I reckon I'm one of them *idiota* gents, then. I didn't know the gent who started up with me hailed from Laredo. I sure found out as soon as I tried to get a job there, though. Men with guns was coming at me from every which way. So I lit out on the first horse I found untended and jumped the durned border. Only things ain't been as peaceable as I figured down here, neither. So I'm heading back where folks don't think I talk funny."

Boss looked interested and asked, "How come you shot that gent on Don Fernando's train from Fort Worth, Crawford?"

Longarm was more interested in what Don Fernando and those other Mexican folks had been up to in Fort Worth. But he ran the scenes on the train through his mind anyway, to make sure he didn't mess up. He had Don Fernando placed now. He'd been the quiet one. So the man fussing at the pretty *señorita* was likely the brother he'd mentioned. Longarm hadn't spoken to any of them, and the only one who'd heard enough of the conversation to matter was old Petunia-Molly, and she wasn't here. So he shrugged and said, "I ain't sure why the rascal started up with me. He said I'd gunned a pal of his, up Dodge way, but I can't say for sure he wasn't just a bounty hunter."

"He wasn't," Don Fernando said. "Pecos McGraw was a business associate of mine."

Boss looked startled and gasped, "Great day on the mountain! Is *this* the gunslick who took Pecos McGraw?"

Longarm dropped a hand off the table, not wanting to look *too* foolish, as he sighed and said, "I sure wish you hadn't said that, Don Fernando."

The Mexican opened both palms wide on the table and said quickly, "Hey, hombre, let us not have foolish misunderstandings, eh? Pecos was a big boy who should have known how to take care of himself. Everyone knows he started the fight with you, for whatever reason. I said I had had business dealings with McGraw. I never said he was a friend."

Longarm made a show of looking more relaxed. "It's good to know I'm with more civilized gents here. I'm purely sorry if my shooting McGraw made trouble for you, Don Fernando, but it was me or him. So if you ain't sore, let's say no more about it."

Boss took another slug of tequila and marveled, "Jesus, Trigger started up with the man who took Pecos McGraw and he's still alive to talk about it. Wait till I tell him. He won't know whether to shit or go blind!"

Longarm shrugged and said simply, "I'm a peaceable cuss, if folks will let me be."

The dapperly dressed Mexican made a gesture like a man

brushing flies from his face and said, "Pecos was not important to us. Just an associate of more important people I have certain dealings with. As you proved the other night, a gunhand of his skill is easily replaced. Have you ever had the same sort of discussion with Apache, *Señor* Crawford?"

"I've swapped lead with an Indian or two in my day, but it was my understanding the Apache are at peace this summer."

Don Fernando smiled thinly and said, "On your side of the border, perhaps. *El Presidente* Díaz has not seen fit to issue the same rations to our pagan *indios*. A rather rude young Apache chief called Alejandro has been begging guns and ammunition from your BIA, and using them on *rancheros* over in Sonora. *Los rurales* have complained to your government about the repeating rifles Alejandro says he needs for to hunt rabbits. Alas, certain past misunderstandings seem to have caused Washington to turn a deaf ear to our enlightened despot."

Longarm figured that even a drifter usually knew where he was, so he said, "I don't see what your problem is, here in Tamaulipas. Sonora is a couple of states over, ain't it?"

The Mexican nodded, but said, "I have to make a delivery to some cattle dealers in Arizona Territory. It has occurred to me that both you and my cows would be safer crossing that far west, eh?"

"Through Apache country?"

"A minor problem, given enough riders, with guns they know how to use. I will pay you the wages of a top hand, and you won't have to herd at all if you're willing to scout for us. What do you say, Crawford?"

Longarm stalled by sipping some more *cerveza*. Boss frowned and asked in Spanish, "Are you sure you know what you are doing, *Patrón*?" and Don Fernando replied, also in Spanish, "What do you think he is, a range detective? I was there when he killed one man. The lawyer tells me he's killed others since. His story makes sense. He's a gunman on the run, trying to live down his reputation and not having much luck."

"You may be right, *Patrón*, but it makes me nervous to think of riding with a homicidal maniac, too!"

Don Fernando chuckled. "Relax. He is less likely to shoot you than Alejandro and his braves, no? I was there when Pecos started teasing him in the dining car. He is not as unreasonable as his reputation would lead one to believe. Just make sure you keep Trigger from bothering him. Trigger has a big mouth, and this new boy seems to be part sidewinder. You know how it is with sidewinders, eh? When they rattle, the wise man moves back a pace or two. I knew what was about to happen long before poor Pecos did. Pecos was a lot like Trigger in some ways, now that I think of it."

Longarm had drained his beer mug and put it down. Don Fernando said, "Forgive us if we seem rude, Crawford. I was discussing some branding with Boss here, and I find I express myself easier in my native language."

Longarm nodded as if satisfied. The son of a bitch spoke fancier English than he and Boss put together, but since he wasn't supposed to know what they'd said just now, he saw no need to comment.

Boss said, "Well, if Don Fernando vouches for you, I'd say you ought to study on his offer, Crawford. We'll be crossing the border near Tombstone. It's a nice little town. Ever been there?"

"No," Longarm lied, "but I heard it's a tough mining camp. So I dunno, gents. That sounds like a long dusty drive from one peck of trouble into another, with Apache in between."

He was going to let them talk him into it, of course. But this game was getting risky as hell, even if nothing went wrong, and Longarm could already think of a mess of things that could. He only brought a couple of them up. He could hardly point out that the Justice Department figured to fire him five minutes after it learned he was in Mexico against Marshal Vail's direct orders. If he thought too hard about what would happen if somebody recognized him while he was surrounded by a wolfpack of hired guns, he'd likely scare himself out of going. So he asked a few dumb questions about Arizona law.

Boss had gotten so interested in talking him into signing on that he'd forgotten his original reluctance. He said, "Hell, we got the law around Tombstone fixed, and I'll introduce you to a gal at the Birdcage who admires tall cowboys."

Longarm drummed the table as if trying to make up his mind, and when Don Fernando signaled the waitress for another round of *cerveza*, Longarm asked, "How many head are we herding all them miles through Apache country, and more important, how many guns will be riding with us?"

Don Fernando said, "You will start with only a few cows and two dozen riders. You will be picking up more cows along the way at other *ranchos* south of the border. But the numbers need not concern you, since you will be acting as a scout, not a trail hand, eh?"

"I'm not as concerned about cows as I am about Apache. How many braves does this infernal Alejandro ride with?"

Don Fernando looked uncomfortable and said, "*Quién sabe?* Perhaps thirty. It is difficult to count raiders on the run at night."

The pretty waitress put another beer in front of Longarm. He could see now why they were so anxious to sign on hired help. Two dozen guns against a larger band of unreconstructed Apache armed with repeating rifles was cutting things a mite thin, even if those hired guns were better than average. He knew they had him down as a lethal drifter without much sense, and since he'd hesitated enough to show that he wasn't a total idiot, he shrugged and said, "What the hell, I may as well give it a shot."

Don Fernando smiled and said, "*Bueno*, it is settled then. We shall not be leaving for a few days. We are waiting for some more cows from, ah, another *rancho*. Meanwhile, of course, you are on the payroll. Boss will show you the ropes and see that you are comfortable. Forgive me, but I must return to the main house for the moment. I have paperwork and it will soon be siesta time in any case."

He rose and left. Boss was staring sort of owlishly at nothing in particular. Tequila with beer chasers could have that effect on a gent.

Longarm said, "I'd best run my mount over to the corral and let her take her own siesta before we worry about where I'm to grub and bed down, eh?"

Boss nodded but didn't answer as he helped himself to another snort. So Longarm got up, went outside, and untethered the mare. He led her across the dusty plaza and between two outbuildings to the corral he'd noticed when he came in. There were other horses standing listlessly in the corral, swatting at flies with their tails and nibbling the dusty straw someone had thought to fork over the rails to them. There was no visible wrangler on duty. It was a mite early for a siesta, but some old boys liked to get a head start on everybody else. Longarm opened the gate and led the mare in. He spied a water trough across the way and led her to it to drink while he unsaddled her and rubbed her down with a fistful of straw. He forked the saddle and gear over a corral rail and started to unbridle her.

As he did so, he spied a bunch of riders coming in. There was one man wearing a civilian *charro* outfit. The four men with him were dressed *charro* too, in identical outfits with ammunition belts crisscrossed over their short jackets and two-gun *buscadero* rigs around their hips. They wore identical high-crowned sombreros, set straight on their heads, and they rode too proud to be anything but *rurales*, the dreaded federal police that kept Mexico so "stable" for the Díaz dictatorship.

Longarm told the hairs on the back of his neck to lie down as he finished tending to his mount. They weren't after him; they were headed for the fenced-in cow pasture north of the horse corral. They reined in and one got down from his horse to take a piss right out in the open.

The civilian had a pad of yellow paper tacked to a plank in his free hand. He dismounted, tethered his horse, and climbed up on the rails for a look-see at the fenced-in cows. Longarm knew better, but he climbed over the rails of the horse corral and walked over to them anyway. That was the trouble with being a lawman. The job didn't allow a man to use his common sense when trouble bared its fangs at him.

As he approached, one of the *rurales* eyed him appraisingly and called out, "Hey, *gringo*. Where is everybody?"

He asked in Spanish, so Longarm answered, "*No comprendo Español, Señor.*"

The *rurale* who'd questioned him said something about Longarm's mother that would have gotten him killed in more civilized parts. Another *rurale* shushed him and spoke English as he said, "My comrade asked you where everyone is. We have brought the brand inspector for to look at Don Fernando's cows."

"I just work here," Longarm said. "I reckon you'd find Don Fernando up to his house if you'd find him anywhere. I'll fetch him for you, if you like."

"*No es importante*. We are in the hurry."

"Well, I'll just trot over to the cantina and fetch you boys a pitcher of *cerveza*. If you're allowed to drink on duty, that is."

The English-speaking *rurale* translated. There was a round of laughter and he said, "We may be persuaded to bend the rules on such a hot day."

So Longarm jogged over to the cantina and went in. He told Boss about the inspection team and added that it might be a good move to stay on the good side of them. Boss didn't answer. He was still upright in his chair, but the tequila had gotten to him. Longarm went over to the bar and told the barkeep to fill a pitcher. He didn't get an argument when he added that it was for *los rurales*. The waitress made the sign of the cross and mentioned that she was taking the rest of the morning off behind a locked door upstairs.

Longarm lugged the suds back to the inspection team, not too puzzled about the fact that not another living soul seemed to be showing his or her head outdoors right now.

He saw that all four *rurales* had dismounted and were hunkered against the shady wall of a 'dobe while the brand inspector ticked off the brands he read on the far side of the pasture fence. Longarm handed the pitcher to the one *rurale* who spoke English.

The Mexican thanked him and said, "You are most *simpático*, for a *gringo*. How come you are not afraid of us, eh? Most people run and hide when they see *los rurales* coming."

Longarm smiled down at him and said, "I never got to vote for your *Presidente* Díaz, but I admire the way he keeps things tidy down here. I used to be afraid of policemen when I was a small boy. But I reckon a man with a clear conscience has nothing to fear from men who're only trying to do their duty."

The English speaker translated as he took a slug of beer and passed the pitcher. Another who hadn't gotten any yet growled in Spanish, "I'll bet I could make him show some fear. Hey, you boys want to see a *gringo* dance?"

Longarm didn't betray his understanding, and the friendly one said, "Hey, Pablito, for why do you wish to be so unfriendly on such a hot day? The *gringo* is trying to be nice. Leave him alone."

"Bah, when people try to be nice to us, they are usually hiding something. Maybe if I shot at his feet he will tell us why Don Fernando needs so many *gringo* bastards on his payroll, eh?"

"Leave him alone, Pablito. He may be what you say, but

Don Pedro makes no trouble and pays his taxes, so who cares why he likes *gringo* help?"

The pitcher went around and came back to the English speaker. He handed it to Longarm and said, in the tone of a friendly bully used to getting his own way, "See if the inspector would like a sip."

Longarm took the pitcher over to the brand inspector and held it out to him. The inspector spoke good English. He sighed and inhaled a deep draft before handing it back, saying, "Thank you. It is most fatiguing to ride about on fool's errands on such a day as this."

Longarm glanced casually over into the pasture as he replied, "I reckon you're looking for stolen cows, huh?"

He could see the red calico and the black *chongo* that had been stolen from Mama Felicidad, mixed in with the other cows, and he doubted that many of them had been dropped and weaned in these parts, since most had Texas horns. The brand inspector tapped his pad with his pencil and said, "It's just a stupid formality, but who am I to question orders, eh?"

"Yeah, orders do get tedious. But I don't see why you bother, with Don Fernando's herd, I mean."

"What do you take me for, a lax or corrupt official?"

That was indeed what Longarm had taken him for, but he saw he might be wrong as the brand inspector tapped his pad again and said, "I have a complete list here of Mexican cows missing in this state. It is true I have yet to find Don Fernando in possession of another citizen's livestock, but, forgive me, one must do his duty, even among friends."

The English-speaking *rurale* called out, "Hey, *gringo*, bring that *cerveza* back, eh?" So Longarm had to leave the brand inspector to his brand inspecting. He took the pitcher back, said something about having to do other chores, and left before they could send him after more beer. He went back to where he'd left his saddle and gear, picked them up, and legged it to the *posada*. *Fair is fair*, he thought. *The Mex law ain't any dumber than our own, but it sure beats hell how easy it is to steal cows in these parts!*

Maybe someday they'd have a central file for all cow brands so a suspicious lawman could just send a wire and check things out the same day. But, while he could see how a central file in, say, Washington might work in theory, he knew it wasn't practical. Even with a lot of help playing typewriters and maybe jawing back and forth on that newfangled telephone, his notions on central files sounded too complicated to work. And even if it could work, he could think of a mess of things more important than cow brands to keep track of. Hell, it could take days to find out if a man was wanted anywhere for murder or bank robbery, if you could find out at all. Lots of old cases sort of fell behind a drawer, and some offices were as lazy as hell about answering a lawman they didn't owe, even when they had something on file. He'd seen that the Mexican inspector had at least a hundred Mexican brands he had to track down. Had he known for a fact that some of those cows back there were listed as strayed or stolen in Texas, he likely wouldn't have done much about it. But Longarm was relieved to have at least one solid answer to check off. The Mexican government had a lot to answer for, but cow theft wasn't one of them. *El Presidente* Díaz wasn't working with the Laredo Loop; he just didn't give a shit about it one way or the other.

Longarm wondered how he was going to work that into his final report in a way that wouldn't get him fired.

The barkeep showed Longarm to a cool, shady room with a rope-springed bedstead. The room had a single slit-window opening on to the plaza. The barkeep said to drop his saddle and gear anywhere he felt like, and not to bother him anymore until after *la siesta*. As he was leaving, Longarm asked him where Boss was, and the Mexican shrugged and said, "*Quién sabe?* Perhaps he went up to *la casa*. Perhaps he is with his *mujer*. Does *el señor* take me for the Grand Inquisitor?"

He closed the oak door after him on the way out. Longarm put his things in a corner and checked the action of his Winchester before leaning it against the wall closer to his bed. He heard hoofbeats and went to the slit to look out. The *rurales* and the brand inspector were riding out.

Longarm wasn't unhappy to see them go. Few people were. He supposed it took tough lawmen to police a tough country, but the *rurales* bullied in too personal a manner for real professionals. He knew the dictatorship had trouble recruiting decent Mexicans to push their kith and kin around, so Díaz had to hire the sort of gents who'd usually be found robbing banks on the far side of the border. Most Mexicans who believed in justice tended to be *banditos* if they were tough, or just stayed as far away from the law as they were able, if they didn't like noise.

Longarm tossed his straw sombrero on the bed, but didn't follow it. He knew a few hours' sleep wouldn't kill him after being up for so long, but he was too keyed up and too aware of his surroundings to lie down like a lamb in the lion's den. *La siesta* was boring as hell if you didn't aim to sleep or get drunk. Getting drunk wasn't much fun, alone, so he moseyed out to the cantina to see if he could maybe find a newspaper or something to occupy his next few hours. Nobody would be stirring between now and three in the afternoon.

The door leading outside was barred inside the cantina, and the barkeep was off sleeping, getting laid, or both. Longarm resisted temptation as he ignored the bottles behind the bar and poked about for something less likely to fuzz his head more. He'd already put away more beer than he should have on top of a meager breakfast. He was a big man and it took a lot of beer to get him drunk, but his gut was filled with suds and he was sort of glad he was alone, between the belching and the farting.

He didn't find a newspaper. Don Fernando didn't seem to hire many intellectual hands. But he found a deck of cards on a corner table, so maybe he could play some solitaire and see who won.

He headed back to his room, and met the pretty little waitress in the gloomy hallway. She whispered, "Have *los rurales* left, *Señor*?" "Yep," he replied. "But you don't have to be so formal. I'm called Custis by my friends."

"I am called Rosalita. I am glad those *rurales* left. They can be most wicked to young women."

He said something he figured would be reassuring and headed around her to his room. She followed him. He supposed, since she worked there, she could go anywhere she had a mind to. But when she followed him inside and shot the bolt on the door after closing it behind her, he said, "The barkeep said I was to bed down in here. But if it's your room, I reckon I could look about for another."

Rosalita's breathing sounded kind of ragged as she stared down at the floor. She said, "Custis, you must help me. I do not like this place. I wish for to go home to my people."

Longarm sat down on the bed and began to deal himself a hand, spreading the cards on the blanket. Rosalita knelt on the floor at his feet, putting her hands on his thighs as she asked, "Did you not hear me?"

"Yep. Last time I heard this tale, it cost me one hell of a fight in an alley. But go ahead and hand me your pitch, honey."

"I am a simple farm girl," Rosalita said. "My village is not far. But I am afraid to run away from these terrible men."

"You're talking about some folks I just went to work with. How do you know I won't tell 'em you've been mean-mouthing them behind their backs?"

She put her head in his lap and sighed, "I knew as soon as I first saw you that you were not like these others. They are outlaws, Custis!"

"No fooling? I thought I was joining a monastery. Speaking of celibate orders, Rosalita, ain't you the *mujer* of Boss?"

"Bah, he tells everyone that, but I am not his woman. He drinks like the fish, and even if I *was* his woman, he would not be able to treat me like one. About my plan to get away—"

"Honey," he cut in, "I don't want to hear your plan. I signed on to herd cows, not to escort wayward girls back home. If your village ain't all that far, what's stopping you from just leaving on any of the loose horses I see all about us?"

"I am afraid. I am only a woman. Don Fernando holds me here against my will and they watch me every minute."

"Sure they do. That's why you're in here with your head on my lap. I'd be a fool to say I don't find you tolerable attractive, but for God's sake sake, how dumb do I look?"

She rubbed her head in his lap like a cat as she purred, "I do not think you are dumb, Custis. I think you are the *caballero* I have been waiting for. You are not like these others. Like me, you are trapped here, and together we can get away, no?"

"No. In the first place, since you speak English and were listening to our conversation all the while, you know I'm wanted in Texas for some misunderstandings with the law. In the second place, even if I wasn't an outlaw, I told you I'd played this game before. So why don't you just go back and tell Boss I passed his test, huh? It was sort of crude, but so was Boss, now that I study on it some."

Rosalita suddenly laughed. "I told him it would not work. But I do what I am told. I am so glad I can tell them that you resisted a chance to cross them double."

He dealt the ace of spades and growled, "Swell. What's keeping you? What you're doing with your head against me like that is getting past a simple test."

Rosalita ran her hand up Longarm's thigh to his fly as she purred, "So I noticed, and you are *muy toro*, too!"

He turned from his cards, staring down at the part in her dark Indian hair, and said, "Look here, sis. There's tests and then there's tests. I don't owe *anybody* that much loyalty!"

She started to unbutton him as she said, "The test was to see if you would cross them double. It is over. I will tell them you are an honest outlaw."

"Then what the hell are you after now?"

She reached into his pants, hauled out his member, and began to play a love song on it as he muttered, "Ask a dumb question and you get a dumb answer."

So he started working on his other buttons as Rosalita gained his undivided attention. . . .

During a break, she warned him that Boss was sort of jealous and that they'd have to get it all this afternoon, in case Boss woke up for some of the same tonight.

"We were dumb to do it at all, and I wouldn't have taken you up on it, had not I seen Boss drunk as a skunk with my own eyes," he told her.

"You will not be riding out with the others for a few more days, no?"

"I follow your drift, but this will have to be it, pretty lady. Boss sent you to test me this afternoon. So it won't matter if somebody tells him you were in here with me behind a locked door. Not during *this* siesta, anyway. But it might make him testy if we were to make a habit of it, and I mean to ride damn near to California with the cuss. I ain't about to stay awake and watching my back *that* long!"

She fondled him and sighed, "Ay, I have started to miss you already, Custis. But perhaps you are right. Can we do it again before I must go back to *la casa*?"

He had already mounted her before he frowned and asked, "What do you mean, '*la casa*'? I thought you worked *here*. What are you doing up to the big house?"

"I serve as the *chica*, for to clean the rooms in *la casa*. How often did you think we have customers here in this *posada*, since it's been taken over by Don Fernando?"

He was losing interest in conversation by this time, but he said, "If you don't run a regular cantina here, the next few days figure to be mighty slow for me."

She arched her back sensuously and purred, "I can see you need it every night, you naughty boy."

"Takes one to know one. Where the hell does a man go for some excitement around here at night? When you ain't available, that is? You wouldn't have a sick friend for me to look after, would you?"

Rosalita laughed and replied, "The *mujers* in this little ghost town are all spoken for. But there is a crossroads village a few miles south where the girls like Anglos, even if the men do not. You must have passed it riding in from the south, no?"

"Oh, sure, I remember the place. Didn't know they had much action at night. Maybe I'll just go and... never mind, right now I seem to be fixing to do some *coming*!"

Rosalita said she was of a mind to do the same, so they did, and parted friends. Longarm felt like he wouldn't want a woman for a week, but what the hell, if they had a telegraph office at that little town down the road, he might be able to get out of one hell of a ride through fire, salt, and Apache.

Chapter 10

They didn't have a telegraph office in the crossroads village, the gals were downright ugly, and Rosalita had been right about the natives not liking Anglos all that much. So he paid for his one beer and got back aboard Osage to head back to the Spur and Hat. He felt sort of annoyed with himself for taking the chance. Nobody had said much when he announced after siesta that he craved some expensive booze and cheap women. But Boss and Trigger had both looked sort of thoughtful.

It wouldn't matter as long as he got back sooner than he could have if he'd done anything sneaky. He noticed that the sky was still red to the west, despite the stars winking down at him. The trail led over a brushy rise he remembered, and he knew he was over halfway back to Don Fernando's. But as he topped the rise, a rifle hammer clicked back, and before Longarm could do much about it, he found himself surrounded by white-clad Mexicans, afoot, with rifles trained on him from every which way. If he was lucky, they were only highway robbers.

He reined in and said, "Howdy. Nice night, ain't it?"

A burly Mexican said something about Longarm's sister that wasn't true, and as he tensed to go down fighting, since he figured to go down in any case, a familiar voice called out, "*Momento! Es mi amigo!*"

Longarm saw El Gato riding closer aboard his own black brute and said, "I'd be a liar if I said I was sorry to meet up with you right now, old son."

El Gato asked, "For why are you in Mexico, *Señor* Crawford?" and Longarm said, "I was trailing your Aunt Felicidad's cows. Her whole herd got stolen."

El Gato glowered darkly. "*Sí*, I know. They are at Don Fernando's *rancho*. We have been considering ways to recover them and perhaps make a profit on the others. Alas, as you see, I do not have enough men. Don Fernando has hired a big gang of well-armed professionals. We might be able to pick them off one by one, if the thrice-accursed *rurales* were not in the neighborhood, checking brands."

Longarm said, "Let's study on this, old son. I've been trying to figure out what an Americano could do about a crooked rancher down here, and I ain't come up with much. But meeting up with you has dealt some new cards into this game. Hang onto your guns and don't get overwrought until you hear me out, for at the moment I have signed on with Don Fernando as a hired gun."

El Gato gasped and asked, "For why would you wish to do such a thing, *Señor*? Was not my Tía Felicidad kind to you?"

"Kinder than she had to be. Simmer down. They got your aunt's little black *chongo* and I spotted her split-hoof calico in the pasture too. But they won't be driving them off, this trip. They have to rebrand 'em and give 'em time to heal before they head 'em off to the west. Don Fernando is sending others he stole in a day or so. Your aunt's cows will still be here. And more important, most of the hired guns you're worried about *won't* be!"

He didn't have to explain further. El Gato sighed like a cat who'd just spied a mouse he'd waited a long time for. He said, "Bueno. There will never be a better chance to burn the *ladrone* out. We will kill everyone but the *pobrecitos* and leave the place a pile of embers as we take back Tía Felicidad's cows, and perhaps some other things of value, eh?"

"That's up to you, El Gato. I ain't interested in the *bandito* business down here in Mexico, and I can see you know your chosen trade. I've got to ride back before they start looking for me. Will you sort of lay low and let me ride out with the others before you hit the *rancho*?"

El Gato said, "Of course. We never shoot our friends. I shall take my men back to my hideout in—"

"Don't tell me where," Longarm cut in flatly, and again he didn't have to explain to the smart young bandit leader. El Gato said, "Go with God, *mi amigo*," and then he yelled softly, "*Vamonos, muchachos!*" and the whole gang sort of melted away in thin air. Longarm sat Osage quietly until the chittering of crickets in the brush told him he was alone. He muttered, "I can see why they call him 'the cat.' Let's get it on home, Osage."

He reined in before the *posada*-cantina to find Trigger in the doorway again, as though the owl hoot didn't have anyplace else to hang out. As Longarm dismounted, Trigger said, "They want you up to the big house, boy. Don Fernando's made some changes in his plans, so you'd best get cracking."

Longarm left his mount where she was tethered and legged it across the plaza and up the slight slope to the ranch house he'd yet to visit. Some old boys never walked when they could ride, but Longarm liked to be on his own two feet when and if he had to draw. And until he found out what was going on, he'd keep drawing in mind.

It would have been more polite to just sashay up to the front door under the veranda light, but Longarm had been shot at, doing that a couple of times, so as he approached the house he skirted to one side and decided to have a listen and a look-see first.

He got on the dark side of the place and eased into the inky shadow it cast. Scouting adobe houses with foot-thick walls wasn't as easy a task as reconnoitering a frame dwelling. Mexican folks didn't like windows much, so there was only a slit here and there along the clay walls. But he heard voices arguing and moved closer to listen in.

It sounded like a man and woman. The woman was saying the man was full of shit and the man was calling her a whore and worse. He knew who the contending parties were. He remembered how Don Fernando's brother had been mean-mouthing his *mujer* on the train that night. Apparently they were still at it.

He doubted that anybody would be having a family quarrel if they meant to ambush anybody else, so he went around to the front door and knocked. A servant let him in and led the way to a big room where Don Fernando and some other Mexican gents sat at a table with Boss. Don Fernando introduced Longarm all around and told him to sit, so he did. The crooked Mexican cow dealer said, "We are leaving earlier than we expected, and taking some of these other dealers' cows."

Longarm started to ask what the hurry was, and one of the other Mexicans said, "Those stupid Yanquis with their stupid fears about the health of our *vacas*! I ask you all, have any of you seen one cow with hoof-and-mouth in this district? Of course not. It is all a Yanqui trick to keep our beef off the Americano market!"

Don Fernando said, "The Americans have declared a quarantine against hoof-and-mouth disease, as Don José says. It is most distressing. The last time this happened, our own government was most tiresome about a health inspection, and there is no telling when we may expect them. All in all, I feel it wise to leave a little early with perhaps fewer cows, eh?"

Longarm nodded but didn't answer. He wasn't too surprised to hear the runor about hoof-and-mouth, for he'd started it himself by telegraph from the army camp to see if it would put a crimp in the Laredo Loop. He wasn't sure how things were likely to work out for El Gato, with Mexico City sending in more hired help, but that was El Gato's problem. If a man aimed to live as a bandit, he couldn't count on not dying as a bandit.

They'd all eaten, but some were smoking and a bottle was being passed, so Longarm lit up and leaned back, keeping his ears open and his mouth shut.

The man Longarm remembered from the train as Don Fernando's surly brother came in with his wife. She was wearing an expensive mantilla and a Paris gown to go with her fancy powder and paint. As Don Fernando introduced them to Longarm, she took the seat offered to her and smiled up at him as innocently as hell, considering.

He'd thought Rosalita, the cantina gal, had looked sort of familiar, but he hadn't even thought to connect her to the

Mexican woman he'd seen on the train that night!

Rosalita hadn't been sent to test him by Boss. Her brother-in-law, Don Fernando, had been the one playing slick. Longarm saw why they told every new man that the pretty spy pretending to be a waitress was spoken for. He wondered if she tested all the new men as thoroughly as she'd tested him. If she did, he owed her husband an apology for thinking his suspicions were probably unfounded. Hell, he'd only called her *puta*, *vaca*, and other ordinary things a man might call his wife. Rosalita wasn't just a flirty bawd, she was a totally dedicated female Casanova who got a kick out of doing her husband dirty. None of the others at the table were looking at her as Rosalita smiled and batted her eyelashes at them. Longarm wondered if it was possible that every man in the room had had Rosalita. Knowing Rosalita, it seemed likely.

But what the hell, he knew he'd passed her test and that she'd said as much to Don Fernando, for the Mexican said, "I'll be leading the *vaqueros* on the trail, Crawford. Boss will be in command of the guard detail, with you as his segundo."

"What about old Trigger?" Longarm asked.

Don Fernando grimaced and said, "I want a man with brains backing Boss. Trigger has earned his nickname more than once, but Trigger looks after only Trigger in a fight. I have heard about some of your activities north of the border from my American lawyer and associate. Frankly, he warned me you were a maniac, but Alejandro is a maniac too. I was not displeased to learn that you survived two ambushes in as many days. Any man with good reflexes can live through a showdown in a saloon, but it takes more intuition than Trigger has, to know when one has been set up. So the discussion is ended. We leave at dawn. I advise everyone who is coming to turn in early, eh?"

Longarm rose, and as he made for the door, Rosalita got up to show him out, her husband shooting daggers with his eyes as he tagged along behind them. In the doorway, Rosalita said, "I am glad you will be coming, *Señor*."

Her husband was within earshot, so Longarm just said good night and lit out. Boss called after him, and he stopped to let him catch up. As Boss fell in beside him, he said, "I'd best be the one to explain all the new plans to old Trigger. He was sort of proud of being my segundo."

"I noticed," Longarm replied. "It's no never-mind to me if he stays the same. It'd save some hard feelings, and what the hell, I'd still be about if you needed me."

Boss shook his head. "You heard what Don Fernando said. We'd best get it settled. By the way, that low-slung *buscadero* that Trigger wears has a swivel holster."

"I noticed, but I thank you for mentioning it. Do you really expect him to be so testy about my getting his job?"

"I told Don Fernando he would be, but he never listens."

They got back to the cantina. Trigger wasn't in the doorway, so they went in. Trigger was leaning against the bar, drinking seriously. He looked at Boss and said, "Well?"

Boss said, "I tried to speak up for you, old son, but Don Fernando wants a man with more experience."

Trigger swung his gaze to Longarm, licked his lips, and said, "Does he now? Well, the only way a man gets a rep for experience is to have himself some of the same. You reckon you could take me, Crawford?"

Longarm sighed wearily. "Don't know. Since I don't mean to try, we'll likely *never* know, will we?"

"I could take you, you son of a bitch."

"I sure wish you wouldn't, Trigger."

Trigger picked up his glass of tequila with a disgusted look, made as if to drink it, and hurled the contents in Longarm's face as he slapped leather!

Longarm had been braced for something, but tequila in the eyes sure smarted. He couldn't see a damned thing as he crabbed to one side, cross-drawing, and fired blind where he hoped Trigger still was. He fired again for effect and then, since he was still alive, he wiped his tearing eyes and blinked to clear them.

Trigger was sitting on the floor in a puddle of piss, with his back against the bar and a puzzled smile on his face. Boss's voice spoke next to Longarm.

"You hulled him bad, Crawford. There ain't a doc for ten miles, neither."

Longarm blinked tequila tears as he reloaded his gun and muttered, "Just leave him be, Boss. He don't need a doc. He needs an undertaker, but it ain't come to him yet."

Trigger started to say something, gave a defeated little sigh, and keeled over on his side. Longarm said, "See what I mean?"

Boss said, "Well, I told him you was too big a boo for him, but nobody never listens to me in these parts. You don't want *my* job, do you? For if you do, just say so and you'll find me more agreeable about stepping aside."

Longarm holstered his six gun and said, "Don't worry, Boss, I wouldn't take your job even as a gift."

Don Fernando had said they'd pull out at sunrise, but the small herd was on the trail before the last stars winked out.

Longarm suspected that the untimely demise of Trigger might have had something to do with it. Trigger had been disposed of informally under a compost pile, and it was agreed they'd say no more about it. But for a man who was said to own the district, Don Fernando acted as nervous around the *rurales* as anyone else did. That was a good thing to know. Mexico had a fair army, and while Uncle Sam had whipped Mexico once, it was sort of a relief to be able to report—if Longarm ever lived to—that while the government down here wasn't worried much about stolen *gringo* beef, it also wasn't in business with the cow thieves of the Laredo Loop.

Don Fernando and his ilk doubtless had one or two crooked Mexican officials on their payroll, but that was manageable and only to be expected in a world that Longarm had long since learned wasn't run on the level.

Don Fernando was riding point with the chuckwagon and other vehicles, of course. Longarm, as a security man, was well out on the north flank, for if there was one place they didn't want a stampede to head, it was the U.S. border.

Unfortunately, they were too far south for Longarm to consider that as a move. They'd likely turn the herd well inside Mexico, and he'd have given himself away. It would get worse as they kept heading west, for the Rio Grande (down here they called it the Rio Bravo), trended ever more to the north as they moved the infernal cows.

The herd was small, so they had far too many riders for any honest outfit. That meant anybody who wasn't watching a cow might be watching him. None of the others had said much when Boss announced that the new man was segundo. Nothing beat shooting the *old* segundo to make folks keep such thoughts they might have to themselves.

Longarm had hardly gotten to meet any of the others, but

he knew that by the time this damned drive was over, he would have heard each and every man's life story, over and over. Herding cows was a lot like being in jail with other gents. And in fact, if things worked out according to Longarm's plan, some of these old boys would get to spend some time in the same. As he'd expected, the mixed gang had mostly Mexican *vaqueros* actually tending the cows and doing camp chores. The hired guns were mostly Mex-dressed Anglos, like himself. Longarm had allowed himself to "remember" a mite more Spanish by now; it meant he could give such orders as he had to on the trail, and he'd gotten all the juice out of his dumb act that he was likely to. Trigger was no longer in business, and Boss was the only one left with whom Longarm had pretended stupidity. Boss might remember and he might not. Boss wasn't too bright, sober, and he wasn't sober often. Longarm was a mite puzzled by Boss. He couldn't figure out why Don Fernando had him running the guard detail.

As they topped a rise and saw that the sky was getting light enough to throw shadows, Longarm heard a distant crackle of what sounded like gunfire. It was coming from behind them. Far behind them. So he paid it no mind.

One of the other hands rode up beside him and called out, "Hey, segundo, did you hear that?"

Longarm reached in his shirt pocket for a cheroot as he nodded and said, "Yep. Sounds like heat lightning, over to the east."

"Come on, the damned sky is clear all the way to God's asshole. Who ever heard of lightning from a clear sky?"

"Ain't you ever heard of a bolt from the blue? What do you reckon it was, if not lightning?"

"Sounded a lot like gunplay to me. Sounded like it come from back near the ranch we just left."

Longarm lit his smoke and said, "You could be right. Why don't you ride forward and tell Don Fernando?"

"Well, if I heard it, he must have heard it too, right?"

Longarm didn't answer. He didn't think many of these gunslicks were honest cowhands. Who in hell was going to hear far-off gunshots, with a herd of bawling critters and rumbling wagon wheels between him and the distant sounds?

But Longarm knew that later on someone might compare notes. So he heeled Osage forward and rode around the herd to fall in beside the Mexican *ranchero*, mounted on his fancy black Spanish barb. Longarm called out, "One of the boys says he heard what might have been some gunshots, way back. Want me to ride back and check it out, *Patrón*?"

Don Fernando looked at the sky and said, "No. It was probably my brother shooting at tin cans again. Every morning about this time he gets up and kills a row of tomato cans for some reason. It is a most annoying but harmless habit."

So Longarm dropped back. As he took up his position on the herd's right flank, he heard more gunshots and muttered, "Jesus, El Gato, couldn't you have waited a respectful spell?" But when Boss rode over to him with a worried comment, Longarm was able to say, "It's all right. I just told Don Fernando, and he says it's his kid brother, showing off for Rosalita with his gun."

Boss laughed. "That figures. She told me his *other* weapon was small and foolish."

Longarm didn't answer. If Boss wanted to brag about having Rosalita, that was his business. Longarm didn't believe in comparing notes about a gal behind her back, and Boss hadn't told him a thing he hadn't already surmised.

He hoped El Gato and his crew wouldn't shoot Rosalita, but he figured her for a survivor. El Gato had said they wouldn't kill any *pobrecitos*, and if the girl had any sense at all, she'd dress poor and hand El Gato the same tale she'd fed him about her family background.

They were passing a rise that was a little higher than most. Longarm rode over to it, more to keep any other scout off it than to see anything he'd be surprised about.

He reined Osage in and peered into the sunrise. It was hard to see with the sun in his eyes, and most folks would have taken the drifting haze over to the east for clouds with the sun shining redly through them. But there wasn't a cloud anywhere else in the cobalt-blue bowl of the Mexican sky. He said to his mount, "They told us true when they said they aimed to burn the rascals out, didn't they?"

The mare didn't answer, so Longarm dropped off the rise and fell in on the herd's flank again. Boss was off scouting some coyote turds or something, so nobody asked if he'd seen anything, and he didn't have to tell any more fibs.

The east end of the Laredo Loop was sort of messed up.

He had six or eight notions on how to put Thayer out of business, now that he knew for a fact that the rascal was Don Fernando's Anglo confederate.

All he had to find out now was who ran the other end. He knew there was no way in hell he'd completely end cow thievery in the foreseeable future, but if he ever managed to clean up all the crime in the world, he'd be out of a job. A man had to eat the apple a bite at a time. If he could manage to stay alive long enough to get some more names and addresses down for Billy Vail, this particular case would be wrapped up and some other lawman could worry about the next case. He reached for a smoke, but decided he'd best save it for later; if nobody killed him between here and there, he knew he faced one long, tedious time on the owlhoot trail. It didn't seem likely that they'd pass through many towns with tobacco shops and such.

Longarm had been on other trail drives, and each time he'd made himself a promise never to do such a fool thing again. But trail driving was something like childbirth or a toothache. Between times, folks tended to forget how much they'd really hurt until they found themselves in the same fix again.

The first few days weren't so bad. The country kept changing as they headed the illegally acquired beef up the Babia Sabinas Valley, with the low and rolling Burro Range keeping Texas off their flank to the north. Longarm got to know the others better, and since nobody could be expected to ride one mount all the time, he had some fun teaching other ponies from the remuda that just because a man didn't sit his saddle Mexican-style, there was no call to think you could buck him into a cactus patch.

He made mental notes as they picked up an odd head here and a dozen there at scattered little spreads along the way. It was easy to see how they'd come over the Burros after a midnight swim in the Rio Grande, for he recognized a few well-known Texan brands, blotted with a slash and replaced by Mexican picture-writing.

They picked up a trio of hardcases in the dusty pueblo of San Juan. One was Mexican and the others were Anglos wearing *charro* duds. Fortunately, while Longarm recognized one from a wanted poster, none of them knew him. But that was another thing to worry about, if Don Fernando recruited help along the way. At one time or another, Longarm had either chased or arrested most of the well-established owlhoots west of the Big Muddy, and lots of folks on the other side couldn't have fond memories of him. The law didn't post pictures of its own minions, but hardly anybody stayed in prison forever, and he was used to bumping into folks who'd sworn they'd get him when they got out. Generally, when he met up with an old boy he'd met professionally in his six or eight years wearing a badge, they grinned sort of sheepishly and had a drink with him. But more than one had nursed a grudge past common sense, so he'd wound up swapping shots in the damnedest places at the oddest times. He doubted that any owlhoot riding the Laredo Loop had gone straight, so it paid to look new recruits over with care, and should one ride in who knew him, he was in trouble for fair. Longarm figured he could handle most owlhoots on a man-to-man basis, but his back would be to others whenever and wherever he had to slap leather.

But as dull and weary days in the saddle followed more of the same, the distraction of worry started wearing off; there was nothing more boring than herding cows that weren't in a hurry to get anywhere. The goddamned *vaqueros* were too good to spill strays or let the critters stampede once in a while. They just poked them along at a dreary pace from morning to siesta, let 'em graze and rest through the heat of the afternoon, and poked 'em another million years to the next night camp, with everybody moving about as fast as a prissy gal strolled her garden, day after day after goddamned day. The chuck wasn't bad, and Don Fernando served real Arbuckle coffee, knowing his Anglo hands didn't cotton to what Mexicans called coffee. There was enough water in the tank carts for important things like drinking, but nobody washed on a trail drive, and as dust and cow-smell settled into a man's hide, he got to feeling like a lizard with the mange. Longarm noticed that all the others were letting their beards grow, so he didn't try to dry-shave. Perhaps if he met someone from the past, all grubby and bearded under a Mexican hat, they'd forget where they'd seen him before. He knew he wasn't fit company for a woman anymore, but what the hell. Don Fernando didn't drive near any towns or even big villages. So it was getting hard to remember what a female even looked like. The other riders must have noticed this too, for at night around a cow-chip fire, the talk kept getting dirtier as they recounted all the gals they'd ever had or wanted. Longarm noticed that the Anglos talked about sex a lot, while the *vaqueros* bragged more about fights they'd had, or were going to have if they ever caught up with the son of a bitch who spoke to their sister on the street without a proper introduction. He supposed the *vaqueros* were more used to the long, lonesome nights out under the stars. They'd been in the business longer. The hired Anglo guns included a few real cowhands who'd gone wrong after deciding there had to be a better way to make a living, but a lot of them were just plain crooks who had no other trade. Since the War, a lot of folks out West were just slumgullions from back East, looking for more opportunity than the better-policed Eastern cities afforded a boy who didn't want to carry bricks or work in a factory. A couple in the outfit were such piss-poor riders that Longarm knew they had to be good gunslicks. Others had been out here long enough to know which end of the horse the shit fell out of. A husky, red-faced kid called Bowery had the makings of a tolerable drag rider, if he ever changed his mind about the difficulties of raising cows instead of just stealing them. Bowery talked funny. He reminded Longarm of that other cuss from the New York East Side, Billy the Kid. He sure hoped Bowery wasn't as quick on the draw, if push came to shove sometime.

One that talked even funnier was called Boston. The others teased him about his Boston accent, but Longarm had talked to folks from Boston, and while they sounded a mite odd, they didn't talk like that. Old Boston sounded like a prissy schoolmarm, shaved even though no gals were looking, and kept washing himself with canteen water and a cake of lavender soap he packed in his possibles. Boston wore a silver-mounted S&W double-action .45 in a tooled-leather holster. It had pearl grips too. It would be sort of interesting to see if Boston shot as pretty as he looked, but Longarm figured it made more sense to steer clear of him in camp. Boston had a bitchy way of answering back when the others teased him, and Longarm knew that his kind—if he was that kind—fought better than most old boys gave them credit for.

The one who teased Boston the most was a big Arkansas gent called Shorty, since he only stood six foot six on the ground. Shorty was from a spread in the western end of the state, he said, and while he knew more than some of the slum-bred boys about horses, he didn't savvy that if a man didn't want to kiss a gent like Boston, it was best to leave him alone.

Longarm had learned to tolerate a certain amount of sodomy in a cow camp, jailhouse, hobo jungle, or such. But some men had less patience. Or maybe the life alone among men attracted a certain number who preferred things that way. Longarm was willing to live and let live, as long as they didn't ask him to join in. He'd suspected for some time that he was a man who admired women, so he'd never felt the need to prove this by rawhiding gents who walked funny. But Shorty couldn't seem to leave Boston alone. Longarm wondered what Shorty's problem was, but it wasn't his place to horn in. Had he been ramrodding the outfit, he'd have taken Shorty aside and explained a few facts of life to him. But he was only the segundo. Boss was supposed to keep order in camp. Longarm thought about mentioning the growing feud to Boss, but decided that if Boss couldn't see it, he likely wouldn't savvy the danger. So Longarm just made sure he spread his roll at night as far from Boston's as he could get without leaving camp entirely.

That notion grew more attractive by the minute as he read his mental map and noticed how tempting the Big Bend of the Rio looked on it. Then they stopped at a little *finca* nestled in a brushy draw, and picked up a dozen cows that had just crossed through the Big Bend country. He saw that he had to keep track of these outfits, strung like beads along the Laredo Loop. The owlhoots still didn't know he'd messed up the east end of the operation. He still had to do it at the other end, some damned way. If he could nail the main American operators, and if the State Department could send a list of Mex brands to the occasionally cooperative *rurales*, it might be a spell before the border started leaking so many cows again.

As they headed out across the Chihuahua Desert, Longarm learned why Boss was so important to Don Fernando. He'd figured there had to be some damned reason.

They'd driven across the greasewood and pear all day, so the sun was low to the west and in their eyes when Longarm noticed that the cows at his side were bunching up. He figured the lead riders had stopped for some reason. He heeled the pinto he was riding forward, and saw that the *vaqueros* out front had indeed halted the herd leaders. The advance wagons were circled a quarter-mile on. Longarm clucked his mount into a lope and rode out across the flats.

As he swung around the wagons and reined in by Don Fernando, Boss, and some others, he started to ask what was up. Then he stared into the sunset and saw the line of silent mounted figures lined up across their trail. They were black against the orange skyline, but he could see they all wore the same high-crowned sombreros. He said, "They look like *rurales*. What's the play?"

Boss said, "Don Fernando thinks they may be *rurales* too."

Boss turned in his saddle to see who was handy. Longarm hadn't paid much mind to the other hands near the wagons, since he figured they were more or less on his side for the moment. Boss said, "Boston, you and Silent ride on my left. You there, Bowery, fall in with Crawford and cover my left flank. We'll just walk our mounts forward easy, and have us a better look at whoever they might be."

Don Fernando said, "I am sure they are *rurales* and I have papers to show them, Boss."

Boss said flatly, "You and your *vaqueros* stay here and hold the herd if it gets noisy, hear? Let's go, boys. Smile pretty and follow my lead."

So the line of five rode out to meet the riders ahead. There were nine of them, a corporal and his squad, if Mexico had issued those *rurale* hats. Four extra guns to consider if they were something else. Longarm found the way Boss had talked to El Patrón sort of interesting too. He'd met arrogant servants before. On the other hand, if Anglos gave the orders when push came to shove, even down here, it meant the real leaders of the big operation were based on the U.S. side of the border. That was sort of comforting. But how the hell was he supposed to tell Billy Vail about it, if he got killed in a country he wasn't supposed to be in?

As they got closer, the *rurale* squad got more convincing. They had on *rurale* uniforms, *bandoleros* and all. They were sitting identical bay ponies at attention. As Boss held up a hand and reined in, the leader called out, "Hey, hombre, who are you and where are you going with all those cows, eh?"

Boss drew his sixgun and blew the speaker out of the saddle.

Longarm's mount spooked, which seemed more reasonable than anything else that was going on. But as Boston drew his pretty .45 and opened up, Longarm decided they must know something he didn't, and since the *rurales* were shooting at him in any case, he rolled off the bucking pinto, filling his fist on the way down, and came up spitting dust and lead.

He nailed one as Boss spilled another off his mount and Bowery and Boston emptied two more saddles. The *rurales*—or whatever they were—wanted no more part of them and wheeled to light out. Longarm put a round in one man's spine as the rider called Silent fired for the first time, having taken time to draw his saddle rifle from its boot, and that was the end of the two at the far end of pistol range.

Longarm's pinto had run back to the wagons and been caught by a mounted *vaquero*. So Longarm reloaded as he walked over on foot to have a look at the men they'd put on the ground. Boss rode to join him. Longarm stared down at a dead man in *rurale* duds, grinning up at him from the dust. Then he holstered his weapon and asked Boss, "How come we just shot these lawmen, Boss? Don Fernando said he had papers to show 'em."

Boss spat and said, "They wasn't *rurales*. Watch the skyline. I doubt their sidekicks will come in closer now, but you never know with these Chihuahua bandits."

Longarm shaded his eyes as he squinted into the sunset. Sure enough, while he couldn't see anybody, he spotted the dust they were stirring up as they lit out like scalded cats to the southwest. He nodded and said, "I follow your drift. But how did you know these fake *rurales* were fake? They still look like *rurales* to me, but a mite the worse for wear."

Boss said, "They likely gunned a *rurale* here and a *rurale* there until they had the wherewithal to get cute with us. *Rurales* ain't that popular and they do fall down a lot. But I could see right off they were just *banditos*. You see, I gets *feelings*."

Longarm bent, opened the dead man's *charro* jacket, and felt inside for ID. He didn't find any, so he said so.

Boss nodded and said, "I told you I get feelings. I'm like an old Injun fighter when it comes to lawmen. I can smell me a lawman a mile off in the dark, and these boys didn't smell like lawmen, so they had to be something else."

A big gray cat started purring in Longarm's gut. But he managed not to show it as he said, "Well, I'd best walk back if I ever aim to ride again. I've heard of men who have powers like yours, Boss. I'd sure hate to be a lawman trying to sneak up on you."

Boss laughed dryly and said, "It can't be done. You remember how suspicious Trigger was when you rode in that day?"

"Yeah, he was sure a surly cuss, now that I think back."

"I only needed one drink with you to size you up. I could see right off you was a good old boy, like me. Had you been any kind of lawman, I'd have gunned you down a long time ago."

Longarm managed a light laugh as he asked, "What in thunder would I be doing down here if I was packing a badge, Boss?"

"Getting kilt, if anybody guessed it. But like I said, I've always been able to separate the sheep from the goats. You want me to ride you double?"

"No thanks, it ain't all that far, and my legs are stiff from riding all day."

He started legging it for the wagons, maybe five city blocks off. Boston fell in on his other side and asked if Longarm wanted to ride with him. So Longarm repeated what he'd said about his legs. Boston licked his lips and said, "One does get kinky in the saddle, doesn't one?"

Longarm kept walking as he turned back to Boss and said, "It's good to know we trust each other, Boss. But tell me something. How come Rosalita come to test me if you didn't suspicion me in the first place?"

Boss chuckled lewdly. "Hell, that was likely Rosalita's notion. I was there when she told her husband and brother-in-law that she'd been playing cantina gal to see if you'd doublecross us. I never mentioned to either one what the barkeep told me about how much fun the two of you had that afternoon."

Boston sniffed and said, "Oh, hell, Mr. Crawford, you weren't another of that nasty girl's victims, were you?"

"I'm afraid I was," Longarm replied, "but it didn't hurt much. How was it when she tested you, Boston?"

"Good heavens, you don't think *I'd* touch that little slut, do you?"

"Every man to his own taste, I reckon. You sure shoot good, Boston."

Boston shrugged and said, "You're not bad, either. But we don't seem to have much *else* in common, more's the pity."

Chapter 11

It only took about a million years to cross the Chihuahua Desert. They picked up more stolen cows at a spread between the María and the Cosas Grandes, a couple of seasonal rivers that came down out of the Sierra Madre to die as salt lakes under the desert sun. They drove the growing herd west into the Sierra Madre country. There should have been an easier way to move cows, but there wasn't. Aside from the fact that it was mostly slabs of bedrock set on edge like tombstones, the Sierra Madre was infested by ticks, scorpions, poisonous snakes and lizards, and Indians it could make a man broody to think about. A Mexican *ranchero* on one of the little spreads where they'd picked up cows had told them he didn't know for sure whether Alejandro and his Apache were doing the burning and killing to the west, or whether it was just their homegrown Yaqui. Longarm hoped it was Apache; Yaqui could get downright ugly. The Yaqui weren't as famous as the Apache because the U.S. Army didn't have to fight 'em and the Mexican Army knew enough to stay the hell away from them. No white man really wanted to fall into the hands of either tribe, but while Apache generally let a captive die after a few days or torture, the Yaqui had made a study of the art and tended to do things to folks that the Apache found a mite shocking.

Both tribes were night raiders who preferred not to tangle with a party as big and well armed as Don Fernando's in broad daylight, although there was no call to get overconfident about that. So Longarm got less sleep in the hills as they kept going west. He was up, walking picket with his rifle, the night Boston had it out with Shorty.

They'd bedded the herd down for the night in a shallow *rincón* with a water hole in its palm and rimrock all around. Longarm posted Bowery and another hand up on the rimrocks, with orders to stay awake if they felt like seeing the sun come up again. He didn't care much for the place Don Fernando had picked. The *rincón* was a good place to hold a herd, but a hell of a place to meet up with Indians. He didn't think any braves could slip over the rimrocks, once the moon rose. But aside from the grama grass Don Fernando favored for his night bedding, the little mountain nook had a lot of cactus on its slopes. Longarm had gotten to know Indians pretty well in his time. He knew how infernally patient they could be. White raiders tended to sneak up after they waited for you to bed down. Indians had started out with bows and arrows, so they tended to be still-hunters. It was a deadly technique, if you had the patience of a spider and nothing better to do with your time.

When a white man wanted a deer, he moved into the brush that deer favored and crashed about until he flushed one close enough to shoot. Most Indians knew deer didn't move in daylight if they didn't have to. So an Indian out for venison made his way to some likely game trail, hunkered down, and turned into a stump until eventually the sun started going down and the deer left their hiding places to feed. The Indian just stayed put, like Tar Baby, and soon or later a deer would come by, not worried about stumps, and wind up in the Indian's pot.

Both Apache and Yaqui hunted men the way more friendly Indians hunted deer. It seemed tedious, but Longarm could think like an Indian if he had to. So he knew that if he'd been an Apache that afternoon, and knew a cow trail led through here, he'd just hunker down in a clump of pear and stay put until everybody settled for the night.

Hence, with the area secured around the edges, Longarm

thought it might be a good notion to scout all the pear clumps closer in. A man with his head on straight doesn't announce his intentions while sneaking up on a pear flat that could be filled with Indians, so Longarm walked softly, neither smoking nor breathing harder than he had to. None of the pear clumps near the campfires had anybody hiding in them, so he moved up the slope to see what there was to see.

He heard before he saw. A girlish voice coming from a clump of pear said, "Oh, you're too big. Let me lick it some more for you before you fuck me."

Longarm frowned. He was sure he'd have noticed if any gals had joined up with the outfit recently. He'd been suffering awesome erections for some time now.

A deeper male voice said, "Oh, that's nice, but watch them teeth, damn it!"

Longarm circled upslope, knowing that was the last place the secluded lovers would expect anybody. He felt sort of like a Peeping Tom, and he had a good idea who was in there, but the sounds were enough to make any man a mite curious. So he eased in, parted the cactus pads cautiously in the moonlight, and peered into the sandy clearing circled by the pear.

It was Boston and the hand called Silent. They were both naked as jays, and lay on a saddle blanket amid the cactus. Silent was on top, his pale rump bobbing in the moonlight, and it sure looked like a man going hot and heavy with a gal. But that was old Boston on the bottom, smiling up at the sky with his arms and legs wrapped around Silent. Longarm hadn't known they could do it that way. When he'd thought about it at all, he'd assumed the one playing the gal got on his hands and knees to take it in the ass.

He grimaced and eased back, his curiosity satisfied. As long as they weren't Indians, he supposed they had a right to act silly. They weren't hurting anybody else, and if it hurt Boston to be cornholed, he could just ask Silent to stop. It was nobody else's business.

As Longarm scouted another clump and drifted down toward the campfires, he wondered if he should have warned those naked boys about getting caught like that by skulking Indians, but he couldn't see how he could have, without being impolite. They'd had their gun rigs handy on the piles of duds nearby, so what the hell.

As he got a tin cup from the chuckwagon and hunkered

down by the nearest fire, Shorty from Arkansas asked, "Hey, what's happened to Boston? I ain't seen him for a while."

Longarm said, "I did, a while back. He went off to take a piss, I reckon."

Shorty grinned and said, "He's likely jerking off, you mean. He's been gone a spell now. How long does it take a man to drain his durned old pecker?"

Longarm sipped his Arbuckle and observed, "That'd be his business, I reckon. I ain't interested in what other men do with their peckers, Shorty. How come you are?"

"Shoot, I ain't no queer," Shorty snorted. Then he leaned closer and confided, "Boston is. He thinks he's a gal. Ain't that a bitch?"

"Man could get hurt talking about another fellow that way, Shorty."

"Shoot, everybody knows Boston's queer. He advertises."

"He shoots good too. Can't you think of something better to talk about? Who do you reckon is going to win the election this November, Shorty?"

Shorty got to his feet, tossed the dregs of his tin cup into the cow-chip fire, and said, "I reckon I'll see what's taking old Boston so long."

"I wouldn't, if I was you," Longarm said. But Shorty moved off and the tall deputy didn't see how he was going to stop Shorty without being a tattletale. So he didn't. Maybe Silent and Boston would invite him to join the party. It would depend on how he approached them, most likely.

Boss came over and hunkered down, asking, "What's going on?"

Longarm said, "Don't know. Shorty's pestering Boston again. I told him it was dumb, but he don't listen good."

Boss nodded. "I suspicion Shorty's hot for Boston's ass. They say Boston can be accommodating that way. You ever try that, Crawford?"

"Not with a man. Why? You inviting?"

"Not hardly," Boss laughed. "I've yet to meet up with a man as pretty as my fist. I told Shorty to stay away from Boston too. But he can't seem to listen. How would you handle it if you was me, Crawford?"

Longarm replied, "Ain't no way, short of firing both."

"That's what I figured. But I don't like to have queers along.

It can lead to trouble on the trail."

A pistol shot rang out in the night, and as Boss stiffened, Longarm put his own cup down and said, "I'd say it just did. Shall we see who the survivors might be?"

The whole camp was on its feet and milling about now, so Boss yelled, "Simmer down, boys. Me and the segundo here will see what happened."

As he started up the darker slope, Longarm fell in at his side and suggested, "Walk a mite slower, Boss. Give the gals time to get dressed."

Boss stopped among the cactus clumps and called out, "Hey, Shorty?"

Boston stepped out of the pear, buttoning his shirt. He said, "I just shot him. He attacked me."

"He *what*?"

"Attacked me. Tried to rape me. He called me a queer and said if I didn't let him cornhole me, he'd beat me up, so I shot him."

Boss looked at Longarm, who shrugged and said, "That sounds reasonable. I know *I'd* have shot him if he'd asked me to bend over, and we both told Shorty to quit picking on old Boston here."

"Where is he now?" asked Boss, as the hand called Silent came out of the pear, fully dressed and grinning like a dog caught eating shit.

Boston said, "I left him over there in that pear clump he dragged me into. Silent came as soon as he heard the shots."

Longarm suspected that Silent had come long before that, but he said, "There you go, Boss. I'd say it was defense of a maiden's honor. No offense, Boston." So Boss shrugged and said, "Well, what's done is done. But let's not make a habit of this, Boston."

Boston looked down and said, "I'll try to be good. Nobody else in the outfit has been making advances... damn it."

The Laredo Loop worked both ways, so Longarm wasn't surprised when they met up with another herd a week later, going the other way. His big mistake was riding forward on Osage when he saw Boss and Don Fernando jawing with the other gang by the side of the trail. They were not too far south of Tombstone, and he hoped the riders just over the border from

Arizona Territory could tell him if the States were still there. He knew Billy Vail must think he was dead by now, so he wondered if they had any newspapers with them. It might be interesting to read his obituary.

As he reined in, they were jawing about Apache. The leader of the other outfit said they'd tangled with Alejandro or some other Apache the day before, but that they'd driven the rascals off. It wasn't hard to see why. It was a big, mean-looking outfit with only a few cows to worry about.

The other owlhoots had been on the trail less time, so they didn't need shaves much. Longarm spied a familiar face in the crowd and tried to hide his own by lighting up a cheroot, covering his bearded jaws with cupped hands and hoping his big straw hat cast plenty of shade. It was sort of discouraging to see Johnny Cross out of jail again after all the work he'd gone to, arresting him a few years back. He didn't know whether Cross had escaped or been let out, but he sure hadn't reformed. He'd been stealing cows the *last* time Longarm had tangled with him. He'd been one of those broody sons of bitches at his trial too. He'd spent a lot of time glaring across the courtroom at Longarm, saying dumb things about looking him up later.

Longarm couldn't hold the match all day, so he said something about tending to his chores and swung Osage around to ride off. He thought he'd made it, but then Johnny Cross yelled, "Longarm!"

Longarm whirled in his saddle and drew and fired as Cross yelled, "He's a copper!" and went for his own guns. Longarm's bullet took the side off his face and spilled him from his saddle, but by then the damage had been done, so Longarm shot Don Fernando, seeing that he was between him and the nearest cover. Then he heeled Osage into the mesquite as Boss swore and fired toward the spot he'd just vacated. Osage took the hint and started busting brush like she'd been raised in Texas. A rifle squibbed and something humming like a big bee plucked Longarm's straw hat off. He knew that would have been Silent. He saw no need to stop and pick up his hat, since he had a more sensible one in his saddlebag and he'd never liked the damn silly sombrero anyway. They broke into a clear space and Longarm fired five blind shots to his rear as he headed Osage into more mesquite, figuring it was the least he could hand them as a going-away present. He ran his mount through the thickest brush he could find, then he reined in to listen as he reloaded his pistol, holstered it, and drew his Winchester from its saddle boot.

He heard no sounds of pursuit. That wasn't hard to figure. He'd have been cautious about riding blind through tanglewood after a grown man with guns, too. He glanced at the sky and muttered, "All right, that way must be north," and heeled Osage forward some more. He doubted that they'd try to cut him off between here and the border; he wasn't all that far from the Arizona line, and their real business was herding stolen cows through Mexico. He reined in on a rise a mile or so farther on, and had a look back anyway. He saw the rising clouds of cows on the move. Damn it, the outfits had combined and were both headed east. That meant he couldn't set up an ambush on the border, even if he made it to more civilized parts.

He fished out his watch and swore. There was no way he'd make Arizona this side of sundown. Even if he did, no posse he could recruit on short notice was about to invade Mexico with him. The sons of bitches were going to get away, and after he'd wasted damn near the whole summer on the infernal case!

He studied every potential move he could make. Then he patted his mare's sweated neck and said, "We sure messed up, Osage. They'll be on the prod for us to try and ghost 'em, and even if we could, there'd be no sense in us following them. We know where they came from. They ain't going anyplace where my badge means shit."

Osage didn't answer, so he sighed and said, "Well, let's see if Boss was telling us true about that redhead at the Birdcage in Tombstone. I'm sure not going to have much *other* fun! Billy Vail is going to nail my hide to the barn door for this. It ain't enough that I took off all this time without sending wire one. It ain't enough that I rode into Mexico against direct orders. What's really going to vex him is that I'm coming back empty-handed, like a kid playing hookey and then catching no fish!"

He'd lost the cheroot he'd lit before all hell busted loose, so he lit another. He took his regular hat out of the saddlebag to shade his head from the cruel sun before it fried his brains.

Not that they were worth much, he reflected disgustedly. Then he clucked his mount north, cussing soft and low.

Things happened that way, he tried to tell himself. No lawman made all his cases. It was like chasing women. It was more than the Good Lord likely intended for a man to make every gal and catch every crook. Hell, it might take some of the fun out of the chase if you never lost. But damn it, he hadn't taken all this time and risked his ass so many times to ride home empty-handed! Most cases only took a day or so before you knew, one way or the other. This was worse than getting married and finding out your bride hated screwing!

He topped another rise and looked back. Yeah, the sons of bitches were all headed east together to hole up and wait for the law to lose interest. He saw some blue smoke rising, closerby. The cheroot he'd dropped in his mad dash had started a brushfire. He licked a finger, held it up to the wind, and said, "Hell, it ain't even burning the right direction, old girl. Have you ever had one of those days when everything just went wrong?"

The spreading brushfire was no menace to him either, since it was moving slowly south with the prevailing wind in these parts. He hoped nobody important lived down that way. It hardly seemed likely, since the map said it was busted-up canyon and scablands all the way to the Yaqui River.

They dropped off the rise to head north across a flat sandy draw. As they approached the next high ground to the north, the sun flashed on a silver concho. Longarm looked up at the ridgeline. That's when he saw the Indians, about a hundred goddamned Indians, and of course they'd already seen him!

Longarm reined in to consider his options. If that line of mounted redskins lined up on the ridge were Apache, he really ought to be thinking about turning around and heading south, fast. But there were a mess of outlaws down that way who didn't like him worth mention, either.

The Indians started moving slowly down the slope toward him. He knew that if this Alejandro was off an American reservation, there was maybe one chance in ten of getting him to show some respect for an employee of the federal government from which he'd gotten all his nice new guns. Even at that, the odds were better than those offered by Boss and the rest of the gang.

Then, as he got a closer look at the approaching tribesmen, he grimaced and said, "Old girl, we are in a pickle. Them ain't Apache, damn it. They're Yaqui! So let's get the hell *out* of here!"

A mile to the south, with the cows strung out along the trail, Boss and the leader of the other gang were still discussing Longarm's sudden departure. Boss was hurt that he'd been such a poor judge of character and was talking about sending at least a few old boys after Longarm. But the leader of the other gang, a smiling killer called Kibbie, said, "Forget the son of a bitch. If he makes it through the Apache bewixt here and the border, there's nothing he can do about us now. We'll get rid of these critters at the holding ranch I told you about and just fade into the scenery until our pals in the States send word that the law's lost interest."

Boss shrugged and said, "Makes sense. Who the hell was that Crawford?"

"Don't know. He gunned Cross too sudden for Cross to say. But Cross did yell 'Longarm,' and if that's who I think it might be, Cross was dumb to be yelling when he should have been shooting. There's a federal deputy they call Longarm. He's supposed to be good."

Boss said, "He *is* good, whoever in hell he is. But what's the use of wondering? We'll never see the likes of him again."

Then Longarm rode over the crest of the rise to their left, firing as he came. He guided his mount with his knees as he held the reins in his bared teeth, the Winchester in his right hand and the sixgun in his left. Boss gasped, "Thayer was right! He *is* a homicidal maniac!" And then Boss died as a .44 round took him over the eyebrow while he was still trying to get his gun out.

Kibbie rolled out of his saddle as his pony danced to the roar of the guns. He drew his pistol on the way down and was just getting to his feet when Longarm tore through the herd and out the far side, scattering cows from hell to breakfast in a bawling explosion of beef.

Kibbie yelled, "Dawson! Mill 'em, damn it, mill 'em!" Then he saw Dawson lying facedown a few yards away, and could only stand there cussing until the long, ragged line of mounted Yaqui chasing Longarm busted out of the chaparral and charged in, whooping like the Hounds of hell.

"Aw, shit," Kibbie muttered, as he stared morosely down at the arrow in his chest and somebody emptied all the bones out of his legs. Kibbie never knew how lucky he was to die so clean, facing Yaqui.

Longarm never looked back as the Indians descended on the cow thieves. The party was getting rough and noisy, and it was time to leave. But at least one Yaqui must have kept him in mind, for he felt a thud and Osage staggered and kept going, an arrow protruding from her big brown rump. Longarm waited until they tore through the far wall of mesquite before he holstered his sixgun, reached back, and yanked the arrow out on the fly. The head was barbed, so his rough surgery left a godawful hole spouting blood with every stride, but the good old army mount could run better without the arrowhead in her ass, and she did.

A bullet hummed through the chaparral at their side, ticking off twigs like a stick running along a picket fence, so Longarm knew the Yaqui hadn't forgotten what they'd originally set out to do. He knew his wounded mount couldn't keep this up much longer, for Osage was winded as well as bleeding. He took the reins in his now-free left fist and swung her to the west as another whizzing bullet ticked his hatbrim. Riding broadside to the only two Yaqui who were chasing him enough to matter, Longarm aimed the rifle in his right hand at their horses, spilling the one with the gun ass over teakettle. But it took two hands to reload the chamber of a Winchester, so he tried to put some distance between himself and the one with the bow and arrows. The lightly armed Yaqui kept chasing him, lobbing his arrows high and leaning down to retrieve them as he rode on at a flat lope.

Longarm muttered, "Aw, shit," and slowed enough to fumble the arming lever open and shut with his rein hand. Then, since the Yaqui couldn't seem to take a hint, Longarm reined in, steadied Osage, and blew the dumb Indian's skull apart.

He heeled Osage around, saying, "Let's head for that brushfire smoke we started, yonder to the west." But Osage had trouble getting started again and he saw that he'd made a tactical error in letting her stop. He said, "Damn it, girl, this is no damned time to founder on a man! Just get me through that smoke and we'll say no more about it!"

He started whipping her on the unwounded cheek of her as

to gain her undivided attention, and the bleeding mare staggered on. None too soon, either, for the next time Longarm looked back, he saw that the Yaqui had gotten tired of shooting the same outlaws over and over, and some of them were coming after *him* again!

He didn't know where Fort Sill had gotten Osage, but she sure was a good mount, considering she was bleeding to death. She might have felt a mite lightheaded from loss of blood, for she started moving fast again and never balked as he guided her into the brushfire he'd started a while back. Riding into a brushfire aboard a dying mount wasn't the smartest thing he'd ever done, but what man with any brains at all was about to be taken alive by Yaqui when he could burn to death?

He knew there was a fifty-fifty chance they'd only get smoked and singed a mite if the mare didn't quit on him just yet. Mesquite and other dry chaparral burned hot and fierce, but it burned quickly and there wasn't all that much in any one place, as dry as the country was. So it was mostly a matter of avoiding the brightest-burning scrub while just bulling through sissy stuff like burning grass. Few horses would have been as willing, but Osage was in such poor shape that she didn't know how brave she was acting.

They tore out the far side of the fire, a couple of miles from the shot-up thieves lying around the scattered herd's recent position. He didn't know if the Yaqui horses were as foolish. He didn't wait to find out. He saw the high green wall of a big pear jungle over to his right, so he headed for it as fast Osage could still trot, which wasn't all that fast.

The badly wounded mare staggered smack into the cactus and kept going, unaware of the thorns that were bloodying her more and trying to tear her rider's chaps off. Longarm reined in under a good-sized canyon oak growing in an open clearing among the cactus walls. He reached up to grab a low limb and said, "Just hold steady, Osage. I'm going for a look-see back the way we came."

He climbed high enough to see over the top pads of the cactus jungle he was just inside. To the northwest, the tangle of high pear ran over a mile and topped a rise to keep going. To his east, the blue smoke of the wildfire rose in a buzzard-high wall, but he saw that it was thinning as the brush burned itself to ash. He didn't see any Indians yet, but he knew they'd be trailing his sign, and he'd left a mess of it.

He saw some of the scattered cows running about, bawling and wild, but even if a dozen of them crossed his trail, it wouldn't stop a good Indian tracker, and Yaqui were supposed to be good.

"Hell," he muttered, "I may as well have left them my calling card."

He started to lower himself back down to his saddle, but then he noticed it wasn't there. He called, "Damn it, Osage, come back here!"

But the wounded mare paid no mind as she stumbled off, favoring her hurt side as she carried his saddle, possibles, and rifle in the general direction of Mexico City. He doubted that she'd get that far south, but since the Yaqui were down that way somewhere, he didn't see fit to chase her.

A smoke-spooked longhorn snorted and pawed dirt as the dying mare came his way, so Osage spooked too, and headed west, which didn't help him much. He knew the Yaqui would come busting into view any minute, and he had no desire to be caught out in the open, on foot, with one pistol and a derringer in his vest, when such an event occurred.

The best place for him to be heading, next to the Black Cat Saloon in Denver, seemed to be north, afoot or otherwise, through the cactus. Old Osage had passed out of sight into some thin chaparral now, and he could hope the Yaqui would follow her trail without searching the pears, since anyone could see the mare had staggered in and out of the cactus. But Osage wouldn't get far, and when they caught up with her to find the saddle empty, they'd just circle, looking for the place where he got off.

He heard the dull clink of a cow bell and hoisted himself higher to see where it was coming from. An old salt-and-pepper she-cow was poking about, red-eyed, for something to eat or drink after inhaling nothing but dust and smoke for a spell. She wore the bell tied around her neck on a horsehair collar. He knew she was a bellwether cow, or what the Mexicans called a *madrina*. She hadn't come from Don Fernando's herd, so the other owlhoots must have had her leading their own stolen cows. He hadn't had time to inspect them much before the shooting started. But wherever she'd come from, there she was.

The bellwether smelled the cactus juice that had been left when his wounded mare busted through below. She sniffed and came closer, sticking her nose on thorns and bawling in frustration. Though it smelled good, it felt awful.

Longarm reached out and cut a cactus pad with his knife. He skinned it fast and tossed it down by the hungry, thirsty cow. The bellwether sniffed it suspiciously, gave it a nibble, and swallowed it with a contented burble. One bite hardly mattered, of course, so she looked up, saw Longarm in the tree, and stuck her tail up, pawing the dust. He spoke softly and tossed her another peeled pad. She ate it and, having gotten the message that the funny critter in the tree was responsible, looked up at him and asked for more.

A Yaqui on a spotted pony came through the smoke a quarter-mile off and reined in. Longarm moved down the oak trunk and clucked softly to the bellwether as he dropped more cactus for her. Bellwethers were half-tame to begin with, since they were used to lead and steady the cows meant for beef, and since a good bellwether was seldom slaughtered, they could get sort of like pets, considering they were still range critters given to moods of ill will toward anything dumb enough to walk about on two legs.

He dropped her another tidbit, talking nicely to her. She was used to being fed by human hands, all right. She moved under his perch, chomping cactus. He cut a whole stack of big green flapjacks and decided that if it was going to work at all, it would have to be soon, for the Indian out there had spotted the mare's trail and was staring thoughtfully at the wall of cactus by now. Longarm couldn't see this, of course, but he knew what *he'd* be doing if he were a Yaqui, about now.

Longarm lowered himself gingerly onto the bellwether's broad salt-and-pepper back as she was bending down to tongue up some more fodder. She didn't like it very much. He grabbed the rope around her neck and braced himself as he tossed another cactus pad over her horns to hit the dust a few paces out. The bellwether was more hungry and thirsty than interested in bucking him off. She likely figured she could do that, and gore him too, whenever he stopped serving her those delicious cactus pads, so she moved deeper into the cactus jungle, following the line of fodder he tossed just ahead of them. When he ran out of the ones he had, he reached up and gathered more. If there was one thing they had plenty of right now, it was cactus.

Longarm resisted the temptation to try and hurry her. She

was moving him away from the Yaqui slower than a cat shitting through a funnel, but the important thing was, she was moving him *away*, and he wasn't leaving bootmarks, either!

Indians ate beef, the same as anyone else, but since the Yaqui had no iceboxes, they only ate a few cows at a time. He'd left them a widely scattered herd to round up and barbecue as they saw fit. He doubted that any barelegged Indian would want to track through cactus very far, if all he noticed was the hoofprints of another cow.

They got a hundred yards or so into the pear before he thought he might be wrong. He stiffened as he heard two Indians talking, just out of sight behind him and the bellwether. Then one of them said something important-sounding and the voices started fading away as they likely followed the tracks and blood spatters of the steel-shod mare they'd spotted under his now-empty tree.

The bellwether stopped and sniffed at the last pad he'd tossed ahead. She ate it, belched, and waited. He tossed another, and this time she headed right over. As she lowered her muzzle and he tossed another, she kept going without breaking stride. He grinned and said, "You're learning, cow. Let's put some distance between us and those Yaqui, and by the time we run out of cactus, I might well have figured out how to climb down off you without getting killed."

It got even sillier. The bellwether seemed to be a longhorn-Hereford cross who ran to size and indifference. His weight didn't bother her, once she'd gotten used to the notion that the hitchhiker on her broad back was a well-meaning little critter who brushed flies from between her horns and kept feeding her juicy tidbits. As they wound through the cactus he kept cutting off more pads and tossing them ahead, spacing them farther apart now, for there was a limit to how much greenery even a hungry cow would eat at a time. If she decided to sit down for a spell and chew her cud, he didn't know how in hell he'd talk her out of it.

Something else came busting through the cactus to Longarm's side, and he started to reach for his sixgun. Then he saw that it was a walleyed grullo yearling looking for its *mamacita*. He'd forgotten the bell clanking softly down there as the old Judas cow plodded along. The lost yearling, of course, had heard it and decided to rejoin its herd for company. Cows were like that. Folks would have had a hard time eating beef, had cows been more independent-minded.

He reached for the horsehair rope to get rid of the bell, for if other cows could hear it, the Yaqui couldn't all be deaf. But he hesitated, for this took studying. If any Indians in the neighborhood had noticed the distant clanks of the cow bell and hadn't dismissed them as just a damned old cow bell, they'd have gotten here by now. He and the old *madrina* hadn't gone far enough to matter. Next to the way the human ear pricks up at a far-off sound, nothing attracts more attention than the sudden *stopping* of a familiar noise.

He left the bell cord uncut, muttering, "Damned if I do and damned if I don't." It could be mistake either way. But like his daddy used to say, "When in doubt, don't." So he didn't.

The infernal bell seemed louder than he'd first noticed. The grullo yearling walked behind them, asking the bellwether where they were headed. That was a good question. If they left this cactus patch in daylight, he might learn more about Yaqui notions on hospitality than he wanted to know. But there was plenty of lush feed in here, and he didn't see why he couldn't just keep them moving in a circle until it was safe to dismount and run like hell for the border. Nobody would notice his footprints until sunrise, and by then he should have made it, unless Arizona was farther north than he figured. He tossed a pad down a lane to their right and the bellwether stopped, thought about it, and grudgingly ambled over to ingest it. Then she raised her horns and headed due north again. Longarm realized that, now that she'd settled down a mite, the old bellwether had her bearings and was doing what most cows tended to do when nobody was herding them with a lot of waving and yelling. She was heading for her home range!

Longarm said, "Now look, cow, I'm homesick too, and I've been down here longer than you have, but this is a hell of a time to break cover, so let's just have us another delicious yum-yum, right?"

He tossed a pad to the right again. The bellwether ignored it. He swore softly. The trouble with cactus pads was that a little of the rich, juicy fodder went a long way for a critter used to living on dry grass. The old bellwether probably felt kind of like a kid that had had its fill of penny candy. The grullo

173

behind them bawled wistfully and Longarm tossed him a pad, saying, "Aw, shut up."

He stiffened as he heard another movement off to the left. Then a red dehorned she-scrub joined them, lowing happily to find herself in such fine company. Having two children to lead reminded the bellwether of her station in life and she started walking faster. Straight for the North Pole, like she knew where she was going.

Fortunately, the cactus tangle ran north and south too, but not as far as Longarm would have liked. He figured they were only a couple of miles from the last Yaqui he'd spotted when he saw that they were running out of cactus cover. He got his bearings on the thin smoke over his right shoulder and checked the time with his Ingersoll. Then he said, "Come on, cow. I want to go home too, but not full of arrows!"

A lop-eared dun yearling with an Arizona brand joined them as the bellwether neared the north end of the cactus tangle. It had horns too long to be reasonable and rolled its eye thoughtfully at Longarm as it spotted him aboard its *madrina*. He couldn't dismount without gunning at least two or three of the brutes, and the minute he did, he'd start leaving human footprints in any case. So he patted the bellwether's neck and sighed, "I sure hope you know what you're doing, old gal."

He hunkered down, trying to look like cow fat, as the bellwether broke cover and plodded north with her charges in tow. Nobody put an arrow up Longarm's ass, and as they topped a rise he risked a look back. There was nobody following them but cows. But Jesus, where were all those cows coming from?

Half-wild range cows had good ears and didn't like unfamiliar country. The shooting and whooping had spooked them every which way through the chaparral, and now that it was over they wanted no more to do with Mexico.

So those cows that the Yaqui hadn't shot or driven home for their own supper started homing in on the familiar clanking of the *madrina*'s bell. And as the herd re-formed around him, Longarm saw that the Yaqui had modest appetites and had likely ridden off somewhere to show off their new ponies and guns. He started to tally his stock. Damn, he and the bellwether seemed to rounding up some of Don Fernando's Texas beef too. The cows stolen to the east had never met the bellwether and her friends before, but any cow likes company, and once she had a dozen head trailing her bell, things sort of snowballed.

They had cows to the right of them, cows to the left of them, and bawling cows running to catch up behind them. The only direction Longarm didn't see cows was out in front of them, for the bellwether set a mile-eating, brush-busting pace, now that she'd figured out the way home. Longarm relaxed a bit as he saw how much dust they were raising. Anyone out front could see him sitting up here like a fool, but nobody from the rear could pick out a man-sized target in all that billowing dust, and since nobody seemed to be trying, he knew the Yaqui weren't interested in becoming cowboys.

The bellwether settled down to a pace midway between a fast walk and a trot. Longarm felt uncomfortable as hell, but what was a man to do? He'd get gored for certain if he got off, and it beat walking all the way to the border. Wherever that was.

The trouble with the border between Arizona and Sonora was that you had to guess. Back in '48, when Uncle Sam took most of the continent away from Mexico, they'd agreed on the Gila River as the border. Then the railroad surveyors had decided the north bank of the Gila made a poor roadbed for the rails, so Uncle Sam told Mexico he was buying the south bank and moving the border south a hundred and fifty miles or so. Since the land Uncle Sam claimed was mostly desert, infested with reptiles and wild Indians, and Uncle Sam offered to pay cash, Mexico said it was jake with them. They'd been a mite pissed off later, of course, when Yanqui prospectors found copper, silver, and gold all over the otherwise worthless landscape, but by then it was too late to argue, given the size and condition of the Mexican Army.

All this was ancient history to Longarm, but the imaginary line on the map made it hard as hell to figure out where one was, since the country looked the same no matter which side of the border you were on. Mean as hell.

Like the history books said, it was mostly downright nasty desert and chaparral, with a dry wash here and a lava flat there. The few settlers in the area lived around such water as there was, a day's ride or more apart. There were enough copper miners in Bisbee and silver miners in Tombstone to support a few small truck farms and cow spreads, using irrigation and such grass as a tough longhorn could rustle up by strolling some. He didn't think they were far enough west to be headed for Bisbee. Tombstone was farther north, almost in line with the new copper camp smack on the border.

So while Don Fernando had said he meant to deliver the stolen Texas beef near Tombstone, the bellwether and her friends had been stolen somewhere else. That made sense, when you thought about it. The crooked dealers in Tombstone wouldn't want to draw attention to their end of the Laredo Loop by selling their neighbors' cows in Texas. So the Arizona critters keeping company with him right now had been taken a valley or so to the east of Tombstone, likely off spreads feeding the Apache at the Chiricahua agency. . . . Son of a bitch! So *that* was why Alejandro and his braves had jumped the reservation!

The Apache hadn't broke the peace; the cow thieves had. Alejandro hadn't ridden down into Mexico to raid and burn. It was the Yaqui who'd been doing that. Knowing Alejandro was on the prod, the Mexicans had figured it was him. The Apache had just been looking for their government beef!

He stared about in the dust, and sure enough, over there on that blue calico yearling he could see the new ID brand of the Interior Department over the older marks of a civilian spread the Indian agency had purchased it from. Most of the cows hadn't been rebranded. That made sense two ways. The Apache weren't too professional as cowhands, and the thieves had culled out agency cows that hadn't been restamped yet. Just like they'd done with that other federal beef over by El Paso.

He patted the cow he was riding some more and said, "Well, I sure hope you're headed for the spread you were raised on instead of that Apache reservation, for I'd sure hate to meet a pissed-off Apache while I was riding his bought-and-paid-for beef.

He might have known the bellwether belonged to the Indian agency, since she was a trained Judas cow. He was stuck aboard her most of the day. Even when the herd found some grass in a draw and stopped to eat it down to stubble, he couldn't get off without getting gored, stomped, or worse. Now that he had no tidbits to throw in front of her, he had no control at all over the big bellwether. He tried steering with his knees, but she pawed dirt and cussed him so he decided to quit while he was ahead. If she started bucking, he was in trouble. Longarm could stay aboard most broncs, but he had no saddle to cheat with and no rider could count on staying aboard every time. So if she was willing to live and let live, he saw no reason to discuss the matter further.

He felt like the time he'd floated down the Big Muddy on a raft, except the raft had been more comfortable and he'd had a gal aboard to talk to when they went through white water, out of control. He just had to ride with the current, or the herd, until they got under a tree or something.

He managed to take a leak without falling off. But if he ever had to drop his britches, he'd be out of luck. Pissing had wet his boot, and a damfool steer sidled up to lick his foot until he kicked it away, telling it not to act so disgusting. All the critters were drooling-thirsty, for they hadn't been watered for a spell. So when they topped a rise that afternoon and spied a waterhole nestled in the bottom of the draw ahead, the cows started bawling and tear-assing down the slope toward the water.

The bellwether, having gorged on cactus, remembered her dignity and walked down the slope more sedately. All this would have been fine with Longarm, had not there been some others using the water hole. On the far side, a ragged line of Indians sat their ponies soberly, letting them drink. Longarm said, "Hold on, cow. Let's just slow down and ponder this a mite!"

The big salt-and-pepper *madrina* paid him no more mind than the flies on her nose, and as she ambled down to join the other cows slurping water across from the Indians, Longarm saw that they'd spotted him. So he waved. Not an Indian moved; they just stared thoughtfully. Apache were like that.

There were a dozen of them. They had new calico shirts and a few were wearing sombreros from the BIA trading post. That part seemed reasonable. But as he got nearer, he saw that every brave had painted a white streak across his face from cheekbone to cheekbone. That signified that they were mad as hell at somebody.

The bellwether walked him right to the waterhole and lowered her muzzle to drink, leaving Longarm face to face with a cat-eyed Apache wearing a black sombrero and holding a Remington repeater casually across his lap as he stared back, sitting his painted pony, silent as a graveyard at midnight and ten times as spooky.

Longarm said, "Howdy. I've been trying to find Arizona Territory, Chief."

The Indian said, "You are in Arizona, White Eyes. Why

are you riding that cow? You look stupid."

Longarm grinned and replied, "I feel even stupider. But somebody shot my horse. These here cows are mostly stolen from the Indian agency, and I've been trying to get them back to their rightful owners."

"You have. Those are Apache cows. We have been trailing them. We lost the trail when we brushed with some unpleasant Yaqui a few days ago. This morning we saw the dust of many cows. We did not understand why they were headed north. We circled to cut them off. We have. I hope you have a good story to tell us, White Eyes."

Longarm said, "I do. They call me Longarm and I work for the Great White Father."

The Indian looked annoyed and said, "Hey, let's cut that Great White Father bullshit. You don't have to use baby-talk with me. I am Alejandro. I am a *cristiano*. I went to school, too."

Longarm laughed and said, "I noticed you speak good English, Alejandro. As to my tale, it's a long one and a pisser. Would you mind helping me off this infernal cow so's we can talk it out comfortable?"

Alejandro said something in his own lingo. It was surprising how musical and pleasant the Apache language was, considering. A younger brave leading one of their spare ponies waded across the water, whipping a cow that was in the way back with his quirt, and got the barebacked spare pony alongside the *madrina* for the white man to ease aboard. It sure felt good to have his legs so close together again. The Indian handed him the single rein of the hackamore bridle, and Longarm said adios to the bellwether and joined Alejandro on the far bank. The Indian said to get to the point, so Longarm offered him a smoke, lit one for himself when Alejandro refused it, and started from the beginning. Alejandro looked a mite bored about trifles like rules of evidence, but by the time Longarm finished, the Apache was grinning. When he got to the last parts, Alejandro laughed right out and said, "You are crazy, even for a White Eyes, but riding with you must be fun."

Longarm said, "I don't know why I make some sidekicks nervous, but I generally work alone, so what the hell. Speaking of riding with me, old son, I don't suppose you and your boys would like to be deputized by the Justice Department, would you?"

Alejandro frowned and asked, "What are you talking about? As soon as those cows are well watered and manageable, we intend to drive them back to our reservation, where they belong."

"Don't get your bowels in an uproar. About a third of that herd belongs to other folks, as you can see if you read brands."

Alejandro shrugged. "Spoils of war. You are a good person, so we won't kill you. You can keep that pony too. But I don't want to discuss who owns these cows anymore. If you ride into the sunset, you will be in Bisbee soon. If you ride northwest, you will reach Tombstone by morning."

Longarm nodded and said, "Tombstone is where I'm headed. I mean to take those cows along too. That's why I'm going to need your help, Alejandro."

The Indian looked incredulous and said, "I was right. You *are* crazy. These cows belong to us. You are one against many. You have a pistol. We have rifles. Do you really think you want to argue about it further?"

"I have to. It comes with my job. I ain't worried about this one bitty herd, Alejandro. They sent me to put an end to the border-jumping thievery, and without too much bragging, I can say I ended some of it. But it ain't over yet. Sure, you can overpower me and take those cows back to your reservation. Then, as soon as they think it's safe some more, the cow thieves will likely run them off again."

"If they try, we will kill them. This time we will be ready."

"That sounds fair. But it seems to me you'd save yourself a heap of trouble and travel if we did her my way. Don't you want to put those cow thieves out of business, old son?"

"I am not your son, but I am listening."

"Right. Here's what we're going to do. We'll drive this purloined herd to Tombstone and run 'em into the yards to wait for buyers. There can't be many honest buyers from the big meatpackers in an out-of-the-way mining camp like Tombstone. That's likely why they chose it as the west end of the Laredo Loop. Some of these cows are Texican, with brands not recorded in Arizona. The confederates of the gang will be expecting them. How do you like it so far?"

Despite his warpaint, Alejandro was smart. He said, "Crooked cattle dealers might bid on beef they know was stolen in Texas, but what about our Apache cows? They are wearing Arizona brands."

"Sure they are, and the records will show they were sold legal, so no brand inspector will be moody about 'em if he spots 'em, which I doubt, since they'd hardly have many brand inspectors in a mining town a day's ride from the border. It sounds more complicated than it is. I'll do the talking, if you boys will help me run the cows to the crooks."

"You do talk a lot," Alejandro said. "What if the crooks are too smart for you? What if they see this is not the herd they were expecting from Mexico?"

"Well, we'll likely have a hell of a fight on our hands."

Alejandro's eyes went sleepy and gentle. He said, "That is the first thing you've said that I really like. Is it true we will be acting as your deputies? None of this bullshit about wild Indians?"

"I'll put it in writing for you. Should I catch a bullet, you'll still be in the clear. So how's about it, old son?"

Alejandro laughed like a mean little kid. "I wish you wouldn't keep calling me your son. My mother was married when I was born. I think you're fun, Longarm, but I will have to see what my brothers want to do."

Alejandro turned away and began to make a speech in Nadene. Longarm could see that Alejandro was speaking up for him when an older and likely wiser Apache raised a mild objection and was shouted down. As the leader spoke, the others started grinning like weasels who'd just noticed an open henhouse door. They seemed to be taking a vote. They raised their weapons instead of their hands, but they all raised something. Alejandro turned back to Longarm and said, "My brothers think you are fun too. We will ride with you and the cows to Tombstone. We will have a good fight. We will ride in singing our death songs and kill the men who steal our beef. I have finished."

Longarm said, "I ain't. Leaving aside women and children, there's a heap of innocent bystanders in Tombstone, and if I was to charge in ahead of painted Apache, we could have some grisly accidents. So before I deputize you boys, you're going to have to agree to do it *my* way."

He saw Alejandro looking sort of pouty, so he quickly added, "You were reared on tales of Coyote the Trickster. Do you want to just brawl like ornery drunks, or do you want to have some good tales to tell your women and children about pulling the wool over some white eyes?"

Alejandro said, "I have always admired Brother Coyote's funny tricks. Tell us what we must do to fool the thieves and make them look silly as well as dead."

Longarm winked. "We'll talk about it on the way to Tombstone."

Chapter 12

Tombstone was a little mining camp, not a cow town, so the herd drew as much attention as a circus parade when Longarm and his deputized Apache drove it in just after sunrise. It would have attracted even more notice, if Alejandro's boys hadn't removed their paint and tried to look more Mexican.

During the night drive, as they'd rested the cows in a watered draw, Longarm had ridden along into a little desert outpost and bought a bunch of pairs of white cotton britches and a lot of straw hats at the general store. Asking the Indians to wear cowboy boots would have been a mite much, but few of the greenhorn mining folks could tell a high Apache moccasin from a boot, with pants hanging over the top fringes. A little girl sitting on a buckboard in front of a shop waved at them, and Alejandro waved back as he cut off a longhorn that drifted closer than was safe to the child's wagon. There were no other incidents as they ran the dusty critters into the yards by the rail spur. As Longarm slid the gate shut, mounted on his borrowed Indian pony, a puzzled-looking man wearing an eyeshade came out of the nearby frame shacks, yelling,

"What's going on here? Who are you and how come you penned up all them cows in our yard? This here's the property of the Southern Pacific, cowboy!"

Longarm said, "I know. That's where they told us to deliver 'em. We work for Don Fernando, down Mexico way."

The railroad man glanced at the impassive Apache riders all around and said, "I didn't think you come from anywhere else. I don't know who this Don Fernando is, but if he told you to bring the cows here, you must be delivering them to Vince Orwell, right?"

Longarm made a mental note that the Southern Pacific didn't seem to know much, and wrote the new name in his brain too, told the man, "That's who I think they said. Where is old Vince this morning?"

"How should I know? I ain't his mother. I didn't know you boys would be loading cows today." The worried-looking man took a sheaf of dispatches from his hip pocket, thumbed through them, and said, "Oh, here it is. String of cattle cars for later this afternoon. I've never savvied why Orwell ships his cows from here. Make more sense to drive 'em over to the main line at Fairbank, on the Pedro. Save some shunting charges and it ain't that far."

Longarm said, "I just work for the outfit. I don't pay shipping charges."

The railroader shrugged and said, "Well, if Orwell's expecting you, he'll likely be along in his own good time. I got to get out of this sun."

He left them, and Alejandro asked what they should do.

Longarm said, "We wait. I just found out the name of the man who's picking up the cows at this end. I explained to you boys how important it could be to take at least one of the bastards alive, didn't I?"

"Yes. I understand Coyote tricks. You will put a blade against his ass and he will tell you the names of others in his business, right?"

"Close enough. We call it plea bargaining. I'm sorry as hell this part is so dull, boys. But all we can do is wait and watch, for now."

So they did, and it was as boring as Longarm expected. The Indians got down and watered their mounts over by the water tank before they looked for shade, hunkered down all about, and seemed to fall asleep on their haunches.

Longarm knew better. He could see they had the area covered from every angle with the guns across their legs. The sun was still low, but getting hotter by the minute. So Longarm rode his pony over by the railyard sheds, dismounted, and sat on the steps to have a smoke.

A big husky-looking gent wearing batwing chaps came out of the saloon across the way and moseyed over to the yards. He paused, looked casually at the cows in there, and walked over to Longarm. He packed a gun on each hip and walked carefully, so Longarm stood up. The big man said, "I'd like to talk to you about them cows, mister."

"Don't get your bowels in an uproar, Curly Bill," Longarm said. "I know they're stole. Don't you remember me?"

Curly Bill Brocus stared hard, blinked, and said unbelievingly, "Longarm, is that you under that beard and trail dust?"

"Yep. Keep your hands away from your guns. I know you're a good old boy, but my Apache pards are covering us and looking moody."

Longarm waved Alejandro over. When the Apache joined them he said, "Curly, this here's Alejandro of the Chiricahua Nation. I'm trying to figure out which of you is meaner, but it seems to be an even-money bet."

Alejandro said, "I have heard of Curly Bill. They say he is a murderer and a thief."

"Hey, watch that 'thief' shit, Chief," Curly Bill said.

Longarm said, "I understand you have a sense of humor, Curly Bill. Do you mind that time they deputized you to help collect back taxes for Cochise County?"

Curly Bill laughed raucously. "Yeah, that was about the first time we met, as I remember. You was on a federal case and I was packing a badge for the hell of it, so we couldn't fight. You understand, of course, I just took that temporary job 'cause some of the ranchers as owed back taxes had said mean things about me selling beef without bothering with all that fool paperwork?"

"I never questioned your motives, Curly Bill. I know you ain't a sissy. What we got here is a similar situation. I know you don't steal cows anymore, since they started the stage line. We may have to have a serious discussion about some U.S. Mail one of these days, but I'm on another case right now, so what the hell. Before I deputize you, though, I'd like to hear how come you were so interested in those cows just now?"

Curly Bill said, "Recognized a brand. There's this hardscrabble little spread just out of town, and they've been good to me. Settler has a gimp leg and his wife is ugly, but they're decent folks and one night when I cut myself shaving or something, they doctored me for a few days. Folks like that can't afford to lose stock, Longarm."

"Nobody can afford to lose as much stock as they've been stealing of late. Tombstone seems to be one end of the Laredo Loop. You heard of it?"

"Sure, everybody has. I'll bet Orwell is the skunk you're after."

"You know him too?"

"Sure. Been meaning to gun the son of a bitch, soon as we elect a more tolerant marshal. Orwell's a prissified dude who come out here about a year ago, acting like his shit don't stink. Can I kill him if I let you deputize me?"

"There's others in line ahead of you, Curly Bill. But I'd sure feel obliged if you'd help me get the goods on him."

"What are we waiting on, then? I know where the rascal lives, up by the Birdcage. If you know he's behind all the cow stealing in these parts, I'll help you run him in and—"

"Simmer down, goddammit. I ain't as free to act as you and Alejandro here. The courts are sort of fussy, and I have to prove my suspicions."

"Sounds tedious, but I'm in. How do we prove this bastard's a crook?"

"By getting him to act crooked, of course. By now he knows the cows have arrived. From here on in, it's a waiting game. If he takes delivery, he's our man. If he don't, I can't arrest him."

Curly Bill scuffed at the dust with his boot and said, "That's why I didn't want to be a county deputy no more. Like I said, tedious."

Alejandro said, "I find this very dull too. My people do not understand the way the White Eyes' law works."

"That's why you're on reservations and we ain't," Longarm observed. "Why don't you boys go have a drink or something? It ain't illegal to serve a Mex, and Curly Bill won't tell on you if you don't tell on him. What the hell *are* you, Curly Bill?

You don't look like most of the white men I know."

Curly Bill said, "I'm a Greek, if it's any business of your'n. I don't reckon we'd best leave you here alone, Longarm. No offense, I know your rep, but Orwell runs in packs."

"Has bodyguards along, huh? That's interesting, and it might even be evidence. How many hardcased gents does he stroll the streets with, as a rule?"

Curly Bill thought for a moment, then said, "He generally has a couple covering his back from up close. If push comes to shove, he can count on more to come running. A gent found that out the hard way one evening, up the street. Orwell has a law degree and talks funny, but he's got a dozen guns here in town that he can call on, and when that rancher stopped him that night to say something unfriendly, Orwell did just that. They made a sieve out of him."

"Town law didn't inquire about it?"

"Oh, that's the slick part. Orwell don't draw, his ownself. He signals his hired bully boys and walks away all prissy while they make hash out of anyone he sics them on."

Alejandro had been staring past them up the street. Now he said, "If we are talking about a silly-looking man in a derby hat, walking between two cowboys, he is coming our way."

Longarm turned, and saw that the Apache's description was accurate. "The show is about to begin. Stand clear and let me tell all the fibs," he said.

The smartly dressed dude in the derby came over, smiling uncertainly past Longarm at the herd in the yards. He nodded to Longarm and said, "I heard you were looking for me, Mr. . . ."

"Jones," said Longarm, knowing Laredo might have wired all sorts of things by now. He added, "Boss and Don Fernando got tied up down in Sonora. Sent me on ahead with the herd."

One of the hard-eyed hands with Orwell asked, "What happened?"

The lawyer said, "I'm afraid you have me mixed up with somebody else, Jones. I don't know anyone named Don Fernando."

"Don't you buy beef?"

"Of course. It's a profitable sideline to my other interests. But if you want to talk to me about that mangy-looking herd, I hope you have some proper bills of sale to show me."

Longarm sighed and said irritably, "Dammit, I told you we had trouble. Ran into Yaqui and got shot up pretty good. Don Fernando had such papers as there was. But the last I saw of him, he was on the ground with a Yaqui arrow in him. Boss and me busted free with most of the cows, as you see. He told me to get them to you as best I could, since he was feeling poorly."

"Oh? What happened to this, uh, Boss chap?"

"He took a round in the side, but don't worry, he'll likely live. He rode for the doc in Bisbee. Boston and Silent rode along to make sure he made it. Boston and Silent are buddies, as we all know."

One of the other gunslingers laughed lewdly, and Longarm knew he'd scored a point by mentioning the sodomists. But Orwell still acted dumb, so Longarm added, "You can wire Boss in Bisbee, dammit."

"Bisbee hasn't strung wire yet. I think we'll just sit this game out, gents. I don't know anybody called Boss, but if he knows me, he'll doubtless get in touch, don't you suppose?"

As Orwell started to turn away, Longarm blurted out, "Dammit, what am I to do with all this beef?"

Orwell smiled thinly and replied, "Sell it, if you can find a buyer. I don't think I'm interested."

He turned away. Longarm spoke loudly enough for Orwell to hear as he turned to Curly Bill and said, "You were right about him being like old Boston. Notice how he walks?"

Orwell stopped dead in his tracks and slowly turned around, still smiling, but his eyes were buzzing like a sidewinder as he asked softly, "What was that supposed to mean, friend?"

Longarm grinned at him and said, "What does it matter, if you don't know who and what Boston is?"

Orwell stared silently, nodded, and said, "My, aren't we tricky?" Then he turned again and walked away, fast. But he must have given his boys the high sign, for neither of them moved and one of them asked Curly Bill, "Are you in or out?"

Curly Bill shrugged and replied, "What can I tell you? I had a drink with him one time."

The two gunslicks studied the odds for another long moment. Then one of them said, "Later," and turned away.

Longarm knew he was licked. They were too smart. There wasn't a legal move he could make to get them to show their true colors.

188

But Curly Bill didn't have such limitations, and he'd caught the drift. He laughed jeeringly and called after them, "Where do you reckon they find all them boys, pard? Boston?"

For gents who'd never known the late Boston, they sure acted excited about being compared to him. The one on the left spun with a snarl, his gun already on the way out, so Curly Bill went for both of his, and the fun and games began!

The saloon across the way exploded armed men on the prod as Curly Bill started blowing holes in the one he'd goaded into a fight. Longarm wasn't sure he was acting as the law allowed, but he dropped the other with a round in the chest as he crabbed for cover, yelling, "Dammit, Curly Bill, you're supposed to get *behind* something!"

Curly Bill didn't listen as he stood with his legs apart, firing both his big .45s, daring the whole world to come closer. An Apache whooped with delight and opened up with his Remington to drop a man across the way facedown in a water trough. That crawfished some of the more sensible ones back into the saloon.

Curly Bill called out to Longarm, "I'll clean out the taproom, old son. Go arrest that prissy Orwell if you want him alive."

Longarm hesitated, but when he saw that Curly Bill was marching on the saloon with some Indians who also seemed to feel bulletproof, he headed up the street toward the Birdcage Theatre. He was about to ask directions, if only he could find someone dumb enough to be on the streets of Tombstone right now. Then he saw a swinging sign that read, "HENRY ORWELL, ATT.," so he cut between two buildings to enter by way of the backstairs.

Longarm had meant to pussyfoot his way into the lawyer's office, but he heard a man whimpering in pain like a little kid. He sounded like he was hurt, so Longarm took a deep breath and burst in, swinging his gunbarrel in a wide arc to cover the room.

Longarm's deputy Apache, Alejandro, had Orwell facedown on his rolltop desk, one arm twisted up behind him while the Apache carved decorations on the white man's rump with his knife. The Indian grinned at Longarm and said, "This is fun."

"Get this monster off of me, Crawford," Orwell pleaded. "I'll do anything you say."

"Take that knife out of his ass a minute, Chief," Longarm said. "He's starting to make sense. I might have known Thayer would have figured out a few things and wired. But you got the name wrong from your confederate, Orwell. My name is Custis Long. They call me Longarm. I'm a deputy U.S. marshal and you're under arrest. But before I run you down to the jail, you mean to give me a full confession, don't you?"

Orwell remembered he was a lawyer, once the Apache stopped carving on his ass. "This is unconstitutional!" he gasped. "You have no right to torture a confession out of me!"

"I ain't touched you," Longarm said innocently. "The man whittling your behind is a recognized chief of the Chiricahua Nation, and I ain't sure just what the Apache constitution says about self-incrimination. Tell you what, though. If you don't want to cooperate with white man's laws, I'll just let old Alejandro take you back to his village to stand trial as a cow thief under *his* laws. How does that suit you?"

"You son of a bitch, this in inhuman!"

"There's a lot of that going around, I hear. You'll be free to repudiate your confession in court, as long as you give me some names and details about your operation. I don't care what happens to you, once you're out of business."

The lawyer passed an uncalled-for remark about Longarm's heritage, so Longarm said, "Stick him some more, Alejandro. I told him I didn't care one way or another about him, but I don't think he heard me."

So Alejandro jabbed Orwell, and the lawyer allowed that he'd be pleased as punch to cooperate, or words to that effect. The Apache looked a bit disappointed, but Longarm was willing to settle for a mess of names and addresses on a pad of yellow paper. Rubbing his rump, Orwell offered to sign it, but Longarm shook his head as he folded it and put it away, saying, "We both know this wouldn't hold up before a judge. But this list ought to do the job, once everyone from the Texas Rangers to *los rurales* gets their copies. You can let him go now, Alejandro."

"Aren't you going to arrest him?" the Indian asked.

Longarm said, "Like to, but I'm too busy to mess with small fry that'll just get off with a slap on the wrist. You'd best find a good place to hide, Orwell. Any of these owlhoots we don't round up with our first sweep will likely be gunning for you. I'm going to spread the word that your pal Thayer cooperated, too. It's sort of a fib, but what the hell, Thayer lies a lot anyway."

The sounds of gunplay had died down outside, so Longarm and the chief went back down the street to see what had happened. They found Curly Bill and some Indians talking to some men with tin stars pinned on their shirts.

Longarm had his own federal badge on, now that he was in the open once more. He joined the group and told the lawmen, "Curly Bill is a legal deputy, gents. What seems to be the trouble?"

The morose-looking town marshal of Tombstone said, "I'd say it was the last act of *Hamlet*. There's blood and brains and dead folks spattered all over the walls inside yonder saloon."

"Do tell? Well, it's all right, they were a worthless bunch of bastards."

"What do you mean it's all right? I know this man. He's Curly Bill, a hardcased desperado known for sticking up stages, cussing in church, and other crimes too numerous to mention."

Longarm nodded and said, "He sure shoots good, too. I told you I'm a federal agent, and old Curly ain't wanted on any federal warrants, so we'll say no more about it."

The marshal shook his head and said, "That'll be the day. I'm holding him and these greasers till the circuit judge hears what they have to say for themselves. You can't just blow folks apart like that in this town. It scares the horses and spooks the womenfolks."

Longarm said wearily, "Well, I'll have to fight you, then, for I told Curly and these boys they were working for me, and mean to back my men up. They ain't greasers, by the way. They're Apache. This gent here is Alejandro, the big cheese of the Chiricahua Nation. Are you sure you boys wouldn't like to reconsider your options? If you ain't heard enough noise today, we'll be pleased to oblige you with more."

The townies figured he meant it. They saw the death in the gunmetal eyes of the big deputy, and the town marshal said, "Well, since you put it that way, we'll just consider this a federal matter. But you sure act surly, if you want my opinion."

Longarm didn't want his opinion; he just wanted to tidy up and get home. "I've got to send some wires," he said. "Billy Vail must think I'm dead by now. You think you can get those cows back to your people, Alejandro? I can't seem to find anybody here who wants to buy them anymore."

Alejandro grinned and said, "We know the way. But what about the other cows, from Mexico?"

"Hell, finders-keepers. Take forever to trace every owner, and since they won't be losing any more, they'll be ahead of the game in the end."

He turned to Curly Bill and said, "You'd best stick with me so they can't lynch you. I wouldn't hang around town tonight, if I were you."

Curly Bill laughed and said, "I was on my way over to Tucson anyway. Heard there was a man over there who's been boasting he could take me. You go on and send your wires, old son. I'll just fade out of sight till I can catch the stage."

"Adios, then, but see that all you ask the stage driver for is a ride. Leastways, until after I've left Arizona Territory. I mean that, Curly Bill."

Curly Bill laughed again. "I know. One of these days we'll find out which one of us is best, but I've pushed my luck enough for one day."

So they parted amicably and Longarm headed for the Western Union office to tell Billy Vail he was still working for Uncle Sam.

He made the message to his office short and sweet, saying he'd make a full report when he got back where it didn't cost a nickel a word.

But he had to explain things more thoroughly to the other lawmen he wired, so the taxpayers would just have to bite the bullet. He informed the Texas Rangers how he'd blocked the east end of the Laredo Loop, and told them who to arrest. He wasn't too fond of the *rurales*, but fair was fair, and since he'd learned that no important Mexican officials were involved, he sent a wire to Mexico City, hoping they'd understand his Spanish spelling, and leaving out a few things he saw no need to worry Mexico about, like having visited their country without an invitation.

By the time he'd notified other lawmen between Tombstone and Texas as to where to plug the leaks in their southern borders, he was getting writer's cramp and feeling bushed. He'd been up all night, and his recent hours hadn't been all that restful either. But until the gang was either picked up completely or scattered far and wide, bedding down in Tombstone seemed a mite risky. If he could stay awake until he got some answers to these wires, he could catch a few winks on the train when he left.

He figured he could kill some time by repairing his battle damages. So, telling the telegraph operator he'd be back in a few hours to pick up any replies to his messages, Longarm started putting himself back together by going shopping. Aside from needing a shave and a haircut as well as a long, hot bath, he'd lost a mess of creature comforts when that fool mare ran off wounded with them.

He hadn't brought his personal saddle, so the only important gear he'd lost was his Winchester, and he could get another rifle when he returned to Denver. He found his way to a drygoods store and bought fresh underwear, a shirt, and socks. He found a new frock coat that matched his pants so well it must have come from the same place as the old coat. Naturally, he'd kept important stuff, like his badge and money, on his person during the side trip around Robin Hood's barn.

He didn't put any of the new duds on immediately, though. He knew he must smell like a goat in a hog wallow. But that could be fixed too, for there was a Turkish bath up near the photographer's shop across from the O.K. Corral. He passed the Birdcage on the way, and glanced in at the ticket window, remembering the redhead who liked cowboys. But all he saw was a sign saying the place was closed for repairs.

He decided it didn't matter, since he'd be leaving in a little while in any case. He went into the baths, hired a private cubicle, and concluded that the little town was more civilized than it looked when the water ran clear as well as hot. He stripped and got in the galvanized tub to have himself a long hot soak. The first scrub turned the water to the color of thin India Ink, so he ran another, and the next time he got out, the water only looked like dishwater. So he quit. It was hard to stay awake in a hot tub when a man felt like he had been dragged through a keyhole backwards.

He lathered his face and shaved. Then he ran another tub, jumped in, and rinsed himself squeaky clean before deciding that would suffice. He dried himself and put on clean socks and such before hauling on his outer duds. The brown tweed pants were still a mite gamy, but everybody who wore boots smelled sort of like horseshit, so what the hell. He hung the gunbarrel chaps on a nail, figuring somebody in town could find some use for them, even though they were too worn and torn to bother taking back to Denver. He adjusted all his hardware and left. His Ingersoll told him he'd killed nearly two hours since sending his wires. If nobody had answered by now, they likely weren't too interested.

But he gave them more time by drifting down to the railroad depot and booking himself passage to Denver, with a Pullman booth waiting for him when he reached the main line. He figured he was entitled to sleep comfortably as the train chuffed through the night. The government was paying for it anyway, even if Billy Vail fired him when he got home.

He went back to the Western Union, and as he passed the saloon from which Orwell's men had been covering him, he noticed that it had opened for business once more. He didn't go in. After a fight, the place would be full of townies reliving it and offering all sorts of second guesses. He and his sidekicks, the outlaw and the Indian, had given Tombstone something to talk about for years. He doubted there'd ever be such action again in such a dinky, out-of-the-way little town. The silver mines would play out, everyone would move on, and Tombstone would be just another forgotten little boomtown sitting empty in the desert.

The telegraph clerk cheerfully handed Longarm a stack of replies, saying he'd never had so much business in one day before. So Longarm gave him one of his new cheroots and lit one for himself as he leaned against the counter to read the wires.

Longarm read Spanish no better than he spelled it, but as near as he could make out, Mexico City was thanking him for clearing up some things they'd been getting around to investigating. *Los rurales* were missing some men near the border, and they were mad as hell about it. They said they intended to check out all the *rancheros* he'd mentioned and ask some pointed questions about that corporal's squad of bushwhacked *rurales*. He could see they still didn't give a damn one way or the other about Yanqui livestock, but it didn't matter. Nobody the tough *rurales* "questioned" was ever going to steal anything again, from anybody.

Texas was delighted to inform him that they'd sent the Rangers to arrest just about everybody in Laredo who'd ever been seen having a drink with lawyer Thayer. But they couldn't arrest Thayer, as he was no longer with us. His business partner had been released early on good behavior from the Texas State Prison. But now he'd been arrested again. He'd come back to Laredo to have a discussion with Thayer about his first trip to prison, and since Thayer had been gutshot and died without making a statement, the Rangers couldn't decide whether the partner was telling the truth about being railroaded or not. Longarm sent them a wire offering the opinion that the ex-convict might just have a point, as Thayer had wound up owning all his property when he was sent to jail.

Other lawmen along the border wired that they'd been having right interesting talks about the business enterprise of small spreads near their borders. Some of the owners would likely get off, and more than one had run for Mexico, now that they'd been exposed and didn't know the *rurales* were after them too.

The *rurales* worked a mite casually for Longarm to admire them as professional peace officers, but he had to admit they got permanent results.

The last wire, from Billy Vail, sounded like his boss was a mite peeved for some reason. It read: "WHERE HAVE YOU BEEN YOU SON OF A BITCH STOP GET YOUR ASS BACK HERE WITH FULL REPORT BEFORE I SEND ARMY NAVY AND MARINES AFTER YOU STOP VAIL U S MARSHAL COLORADO FEDERAL DISTRICT OFFICE"

The clerk had been keeping track of the messages and said, "I took that last one down the way it was sent, no offense. It don't seem decent or legal to cuss like that on the telegraph wire, though."

Longarm chuckled and said, "He must be missing his prodigal son. I was afraid he'd be really sore at me."

He folded the wires and stuffed them in the side pocket of his new frock coat. He only had about an hour to kill before his train left, and decided his best bet would be a quieter saloon. It was hotter than an oven outside now. Arizona was like that, this time of the year.

As he stepped outside, a voice yelled, "Longarm, duck!" So Longarm did as instructed, dropping to one knee as he drew his sixgun and two guns went off before he could figure out why or where!

A bullet tore through the loose side of his coat, tearing open the side pocket and scattering a yellow confetti cloud of telegraph paper as Longarm spotted Vince Orwell, clinging to a post of the covered walk with one hand, his smoking pistol in the other, pointed at the boardwalk.

Longarm held his fire as he saw the lawyer's knees buckle. Orwell shook his head like he was trying to clear it, then fell facedown, half on the walk and half in the sunlit dust of the street. The wet red blosson on the back of his coat seemed the likely reason for his fainting spell.

Longarm saw the town marshal coming closer along the walk, with his own gun still drooling gunsmoke. He lowered the muzzle politely and told Longarm, "He was laying for you. I was wondering why he was out here in the heat, playing cigar-store Indian. So I was keeping an eye on him."

Longarm rose to his feet, holstering his own gun, as he said, "I told them inside I'd be back. And worse, I told them when. That was neighborly as hell of you, Marshal. I admire a lawman who thinks on his feet."

The town marshal shrugged and said, "Hell, it wasn't hard to see the rascal was up to no good. You and your weird sidekicks just made hash of lawyer Orwell's friends, down the street. There wasn't enough evidence for me to consider arresting a taxpaying resident, but I sure wondered why he was still about after a brush with a federal agent, so I thought I'd best keep an eye on him."

Longarm said, "You're all right. I'm sorry I mean-mouthed you before. Let's find some shade and have a drink on it."

The marshal shook his head, pointed his chin at the townies coming up the street for a look-see, and said, "You go ahead. I have to put this rascal on ice and fill out more infernal papers. I did hear you say you were leaving Tombstone, didn't I, Longarm?"

"Catching the next train. If you won't drink with me, we'll just shake on it. What's your handle, pard?"

The marshal shook Longarm's proffered hand, putting his own gun away as he said, "Earp. Virgil Earp."

"Do tell? I know a deputy over in Dodge names Wyatt Earp. You any kin to old Wyatt?"

"He's my baby brother. I've been trying to get him out here to join me. Dodge don't pay all that much, and as you see it gets sort of noisy in Tombstone. Must be the climate tha makes folks so testy around here. But what the hell, if I get Wyatt and my other brother, Morgan, out here as deputies, we'll likely quiet things down a mite."

It was figuring to get hotter before it got colder. As his train pulled out, Longarm was sweating copiously, so he took off his coat and folded it before taking a seat on the shady side of the car. The local rattled off across the desert toward the junction where they'd change to the main line. He opened the window. It did help to have some air moving over his hot hide. It was late afternoon, so if he could just hold out awhile, the infernal sun would go down and things would cool off. He'd likely be freezing his butt, come morning. Desert country was like that. But he'd have blankets in his Pullman bunk, so he could look forward to a comfortable night.

A woman in green calico stopped by his seat and asked, "Do you mind if I join you, sir? I can't seem to open the window by my seat, and it's so terribly hot in here!"

Longarm rose, doffing his Stetson as he said, "Sit by the window, then, ma'am. I can see you're a mite flushed."

He'd have done the same for any lady, but she was a right handsome redhead with a low-cut bodice and a tiny waist above her saucy Dolly Varden skirts, and he was glad her window was stuck. She smiled blushingly at him and sat down by his window with a sigh, fanning herself with the timetable in her hand. He rejoined her and said, "It won't be so bad when we change at the main line. Cars are newer and might have shades."

She said, "I certainly hope so, sir."

"You don't have to call me 'sir,' ma'am," he told her. "My name is Custis Long and I'm on my way to Denver. Where might you be headed?"

She laughed and said, "My, what a coincidence. I'm on my way to Denver too. I just lost my job. The place I worked got busted up by drunken silver miners, and I can't wait around unpaid until they open again. My name is Sally Malone, by the way."

"I'm proud to meet you, Miss Sally. You'd be the cashier from the Birdcage, right?"

"Why, that's right. However did you know?"

"I'm in the detecting business. I'm a lawman based in Denver, and if you don't know anybody on Larimer Street, I'd be proud to introduce you to some folks who own theaters and such. I drink regular with one of the gents who runs the Opera House, in fact."

"Oh, we'll have to talk about that along the way. How long do you think it will take us to get to Denver? I can't make sense out of this silly timetable. It seems we have to change trains a lot."

"Yep," he agreed. "Tombstone's sort of off the beaten track. But don't you worry. I'll see you get to Denver. Stick with me and I'll keep you from getting on the wrong trains and such."

"That's very sweet of you, ah, Custis. But I still don't have any idea when we'll arrive."

He said, "It ought to take us no more than a couple of days."

"Oh, dear. I hope I won't have to sit up in the coach more than one night. Do you suppose they'll have a bath on the mainline train?"

He said, "They will in the Pullman cars. But I fear that if you're riding coach, you'll be expected to ride dusty."

He waited and let that sink in before he continued, "I'm riding the Pullman. I reckon I can get the porter to let you come forward to freshen up if I treat him right."

She said, "Oh? How are you to help me keep from getting lost, if you'll be up in the Pullman with the gentry and poor little me has to ride back in the silly old coach?"

Longarm frowned. "That could be a problem, now that I study on it. I sure wouldn't want you getting lost."

He leaned back, smiling softly. It was too early and too damned hot to put his arm up on the seat behind her. But little Sally must have been thinking ahead too. She didn't look at him as she fanned herself flutteringly and said, "I don't have Pullman ticket, but I suppose they wouldn't mind if I spent some time visiting with you, would they?"

"No," he said, "I told you I knew how to get along with porters. We'll talk about it when I supper with you, later this evening."

"Are you suggesting it would be proper for me to join you up in the Pullman car after dark, Custis?" she asked demurely.

He smiled down at her and said, "Don't know how proper it might be, but like I said, we'll work something out between now and then. It's a long trip, so we've plenty of time."

SPECIAL PREVIEW

Here are the opening scenes
from

LONGARM AND THE BOOT HILLERS

thirty-fourth novel in the bold
LONGARM series from Jove

Prologue

The Pinkerton and the marshal reined in their mounts as soon as they topped the ridge, then stared solemnly down at Antelope Junction. This was the place they were looking for, all right.

It was a tank town in the middle of nowhere, a good half-day's ride from Salt Lake City. Both men were following trails that were now getting as warm as the fireboxes in the steam locomotives that stopped here to get their boilers flushed. At the moment a steam engine—looking like a toy in the shimmering distance—had pulled to a halt beside the water tower. Puffs of steam were drifting skyward as the engine's boilers were topped with soft water. Even from this distance the two men could hear the locomotive panting as it slaked its thirst. In the switching yard beyond it, the tangled web of iron rails gleamed fiercely in the late-afternoon sun.

The Pinkerton's name was Charlie Halwell. He was a bluff, heavily built fellow with a deceptively cherubic face, flushed now from the long ride over the blistering salt flats. As he sat his gelding, he mopped his florid face with a polka-dotted handkerchief. He was dressed in a dusty frock coat and checked pants. A battered bowler hat was perched on his head. Only the gleaming Smith & Wesson riding in the holster on his hip seemed free of dust and ready for action.

His companion was Deputy U.S. Marshal Pete Baker, a tall, gangling, white-haired oldtimer who had thrown in with the Pinkerton after the two had met in the lobby of a Salt Lake City hotel the night before and begun comparing notes. The Pinkerton was after Weed Leeper, a train robber whose chief operating principle was to shoot down in cold blood any witnesses who might later be able to testify against him, a vicious maxim that caused him to leave behind an awesomely bloody trail. The marshal was pursuing Smiley Blunt, a killer who had thrown in with Leeper just before their last job—the notorious Tipton Train massacre, in which six innocent men, women, and children had been cut down mercilessly in the course of a robbery that had netted a paltry five hundred dollars.

A deputy U.S. marshal had spotted Blunt on his way through Salt Lake City on another assignment, and had notified the local U.S. marshal's office, which had in turn notified Washington. When Marshal Baker had arrived a few days ago in the city to follow up this lead, and had begun making inquiries with the local federal marshals, he got precious little help until he found himself talking at last to the Pinkerton, whose own sources had spotted Weed Leeper in a small town outside the city less than a week before. It was the marshal's hope that Weed Leeper and Smiley Blunt were still together, and still in Antelope Junction.

The two men could have taken the train, but they had decided to enter the place with as little fuss as possible, and they wanted their own mounts handy in case they had to scour the outlying country for their quarry. More than once, however, during the hot ride, they had cursed their decision. Now, as both men gazed down at the mean-looking tank town before them, they felt a slight chill despite the hammering heat that leaned heavily on their dusty shoulders. Neither Weed Leeper nor Smiley Blunt were men they would choose to meet willingly, but each had come a long way to collar these two vicious renegades, and it was not their intention to turn back now.

Baker turned his pale blue eyes on the Pinkerton, his lean face somber. "Ain't nothin' we can do but ride on down there, Charlie." He smiled bleakly. "We come this far anyway, and my whistle's as dry as a lizard's belly."

"You reckon we ought to ride in together?"

"I been thinking on that. Maybe we better separate, then wait till sundown and come in from the opposite ends of the town. Raise as little dust as possible."

"Good idea. I'll come in across them tracks. You can ride in from the west, along that trail leading from the pass."

Marshal Baker nodded as he glanced in the direction of the pass, then looked back at the Pinkerton. "We could meet in one of the bars—by accident, of course. Then we could go see what the local law can tell us."

Charlie Halwell smiled ironically. "*If* we can count on the locals telling us much of anything, Pete—which I am beginning to doubt, from what I've heard of this place."

Without further discussion, the two lawmen nodded goodbye to each other and pulled their mounts apart, Halwell leaving the ridge to circle toward the tracks, Baker angling down the far side of the ridge in the direction of the trail snaking out of the dark hills to the west.

Weed Leeper sat on the porch of the Lucky Seven Saloon, his chair resting back against the saloon's wall, his ankles crossed and resting on the porch railing.

Weed's face was covered with a scraggly beard, which had in fact given rise to his nickname. Beneath his shaggy brows, two red-rimmed eyes blazed out hatefully at a world he loathed. He wore a black, floppy-brimmed hat, a faded red woolen shirt, and greasy Levi's. Two gunbelts sagged across his gut. Both weapons gleamed immaculately in sharp contrast to the rest of the man, for these two Colt Peacemakers were the tools of his trade, and like all good craftsmen, Weed kept them in mint condition.

At the moment, Weed was watching a lone horseman riding into town from the direction of the railyard. The rider was a heavyset fellow with a single, well-kept sidearm, and he rode with the brim of his bowler hat slanted down to shade his eyes from the setting sun.

Weed chuckled. The man had the smell of a Pinkerton about him. As Weed pondered idly who the poor fool was after, he felt a delicious glow of anticipation deep in his gut. Hell, it had been so quiet around here lately that he had been reduced to beating up on the whores for excitement. This was more like it. As the rider rode on past the saloon toward the livery, Weed smiled contentedly, uncrossed his ankles, and got to his feet. He watched the rider dismount, tie up, and disappear inside the livery down the street, then he strode heavily into the saloon to find Smiley.

Marshal Baker left the livery stable close to an hour later, having already noted the Pinkerton's gelding in one of the stalls. Now, moving through the dusty gloom of the main street toward the Lucky Seven, he became aware of a sullen, watchful silence that seemed to have fallen over the street. Of course it could have been just his imagination, but it seemed to him that quite a few of the loungers in front of the saloons and other places of business were following his progress down the street with more than casual interest.

The marshal's spare frame moved lazily, but his long legs ate up the distance with deceptive speed. While he walked, his sharp eyes noted the usual shops to be found in a tank town: a beanery-saloon for passengers, a blacksmith shop, a large general store, Western Union, an impressive and fairly substantial switching yard and roundhouse beyond the train station. But the marshal's keen eyes noted something else as well. There appeared to be an unusually large number of saloons along Main Street, all of them operating at a pace that seemed surprisingly brisk for a sleepy little tank town in the middle of this barren country.

He passed by the beanery, despite his hunger, and mounted the boardwalk in front of the Lucky Seven. What he wanted more than food at the moment was something to wet his whistle and flush away the dust of too many miles. The moment his tall frame strode through the saloon's batwings, he felt the place go silent. It was an expectant silence, as if his entrance had been awaited eagerly. The bartender leaned forward onto the bar, a grin on his face. A few of the patrons turned about to stare at the marshal coolly, speculatively, like customers at a sporting club waiting for the entertainment to begin.

For a fleeting instant, Baker considered turning about and leaving the place to return when he had found Charlie Halwell. Then he spotted the Pinkerton sitting at a table in the rear, his head resting back against the wall behind him, his bowler hat pulled down so far over his forehead that Baker could not see the man's eyes. A nearly full stein of beer was clutched in his right fist.

He was probably asleep.

This is what Baker told himself as he started across the sawdust-covered floor toward the table. The trouble was, he didn't believe it. He was a man who had stumbled into a waking nightmare, and as he neared the Pinkerton and cleared his throat to greet him, he felt a cold shudder pass up his spine.

Charlie Halwell was sitting too goddamn still.

"Charlie?" he said softly, as he straddled a chair and sat down. "You all right, Charlie?"

There was no reply.

Baker reached over and pushed the Pinkerton's bowler hat up off his forehead. A neat black hole had been stamped in the center of Charlie's broad forehead, and for the first time Baker noticed the dark stain on the wall behind Charlie's head. Baker gasped—the sound coming out like a despairing cry in the silent saloon.

He turned swiftly and saw every man in the saloon watching him eagerly, the slavering grins of wild animals on their unshaven faces. At once Baker realized that it was they who had propped Charlie's dead body up like this and then waited for him to come in and discover the dead man! And now that he had found Charlie, the fun was about to begin. What the hell kind of a place was this? Who were these animals?

Terror slipped like a cold knife into his gut.

Someone sat down at the table behind him. He turned and found himself looking into Smiley Blunt's amused face. Standing behind Smiley was a man Baker recognized at once from Charlie Halwell's description as Weed Leeper. There was a sixgun in Smiley's right fist, its enormous bore staring up at Baker's face.

"Charlie didn't want to die, Deputy," Smiley told him. "Bleated like a stuck pig, he did. Said you'd be along to kill me if I didn't let him go. Is that right, Deputy? You going to kill me 'cause I blasted this here Pinkerton?"

Pete Baker moistened dry lips. He was a dead man, and he knew it. But somehow he managed to control his voice. "I come a long way to collar you, Smiley. And now I got a better reason than I had before. You give me a fair chance, I'll take you."

"Guess maybe if I gave you a fair chance, you would take

me, at that." Smiley's grin broadened. "But I ain't goin' to give you that chance."

Baker saw the man's finger tighten on the trigger. He jumped to his feet, clawing for his sixgun. The Colt in Smiley's hand roared. Baker felt his face expanding, filling the universe. A red tide, then darkness washed over him. He tried to grab for something as he was flung violently back. He felt himself floating through the air, twisting slowly toward the floor....

Deputy U.S. Marshal Pete Baker was a dead man before he came to a sprawling rest on the floor, his shattered face buried in the crimson sawdust.

Chapter 1

It was a Monday morning and it was raining—which didn't bother Longarm all that much, since the rain cleaned the Mile High City's pungent air and gave him a chance to breathe again. Longarm was weary of his long hiatus in Denver, sick of the swarming crowds, the air filled with the essence of horse manure and coal smoke—and that odd but persistent smell of burning leaves.

Longarm chuckled ruefully as he looked down at the narrow street below his window. He was getting edgy, all right. Any gent who finds himself cheering for rain is about ready to pull up behind the nearest funeral procession.

Longarm left the window, padded stark naked across the threadbare carpet to the dressing table, and peered at his reflection in the mirror. He was a big man, lean and muscular, with the body of an athlete. But there was nothing young about his seamed face, which had been cured to a saddle-leather brown by the raw sun and cutting winds of many a long trail. His eyes were gunmetal blue, his close-cropped hair the color of aged tobacco leaf. He wore a neatly trimmed longhorn mustache proudly on his upper lip, adding much to the ferocity of his appearance. It was a ferocity he counted on at times. He started to turn away from the window when he heard the rustle of bedsheets behind him, followed by the padding of soft feet. He smiled and turned easily, catlike, in time to enclose the tall, red-haired woman in his arms. Dressed only in a filmy gown, she sighed eagerly as she pressed herself hungrily against him.

Longarm sighed also as he bent and kissed her on the lips. Then, reluctantly, he pulled back. "It's too early, Rose," he told her. "Or too late. I have to be at the office on time this morning."

"Why? You said yourself that Vail hasn't had anything for you in a week." She leaned back, pressing her supple loins against his, a wicked gleam in her hazel eyes. "Stay here for the morning. I'm off today. I could have breakfast sent up. We could eat it in bed." She chuckled throatily. "Afterward."

Longarm shrugged. What the hell, he thought, as he felt himself responding to Rose's nearness. Vail could wait. It might make the man angry enough to send him out of this accursed city.

Longarm reached back for the bottle of Maryland rye on the dresser, then ducked under Rose, lifted her gently over his shoulder, and moved across the floor to the rumpled bed. It was still warm from Rose's body, he noted, as he dumped the laughing woman down beside him and pulled the bottle up to his mouth.

Longarm's breakfast in bed took somewhat longer than he had anticipated. Glancing at his pocket watch as he passed the U.S. Mint on the corner of Cherokee and Colfax, he saw that it was almost eleven o'clock. He would catch hell from Vail, he realized, but it did not bother him; he was still remembering the glow of Rose's eager body beside him in the bed.

He was also remembering the tears that followed, that always followed of late, whenever he was goaded into reminding the woman that his job came first and that marriage was at best a long way off for the likes of him. It was getting to be a problem with Rose, and it was one more reason why he was getting desperate for an assignment that would take him far from this city's complications.

He turned the corner and started for the Federal Building, just ahead of him. Once inside, he strode across the lobby, through swarms of officious lawyers who were already sweating themselves into such a fine frenzy that their oil-plastered hair was coming unstuck. At the top of a marble staircase, Longarm came upon a large oak door. The gilt lettering on it read: UNITED STATES MARSHAL, FIRST DISTRICT COURT OF COLORADO.

Longarm pushed the door open and entered the outer office. The clerk glanced up from his typewriting machine, a look of terror mixed with joy on his pink, beardless face.

"Ah, Mr. Long!" the clerk cried. "It's you!"

"That's right, Custis Long. I'm glad you remember. Is the chief in?"

"He certainly is!" the fellow fairly sang. "You are late, Mr. Long! Very late indeed. Marshal Vail has already sent Deputy Wallace to your rooming house. He is most anxious to find you."

"You mean he's as hot as a cat's ass on a stove lid," Longarm said, leaning close to the clerk. "Is that it, sonny?"

The clerk nodded, pulling back anxiously, obviously acutely aware of the Maryland rye on Longarm's breath. "Yessir, Mr. Long. The marshal is very angry. And I must say I don't blame the poor man. You really should get in here on time."

"That so?"

"Yes, Mr. Long, it is. After all, you've never heard of me being late, have you?"

"Sonny, I never hear much of *anything* about you."

The clerk sniffed haughtily and returned to his precious typewriter. "I suggest you go right on in, Mr. Long."

Longarm straightened, swept past the clerk's desk, and, with a short knock on Billy Vail's door, opened it and marched in. Billy Vail was pacing his small, cluttered office. He halted his pacing when he saw Longarm, his normally florid face even redder than usual.

"Where in hell you been, Longarm? You already missed the morning train north."

"Was I supposed to be on it?"

"You sure as hell were!"

Longarm slumped into the red morocco-leather armchair across the desk from his superior and tipped his head slightly as he regarded the marshal. "Maybe you better tell me what this is all about, Billy."

"Goddamn right I'll tell you," the man said emphatically as he sat down in his swivel chair and began poking anxiously about for a file folder among the blizzard of paperwork cluttering his desktop. "And I'll thank you to show me a little more respect. You can start by not calling me Billy and by getting in here on time!"

Longarm leaned back in the chair. He was impressed. Billy Vail was really hot under the collar this time—which meant he had something for Longarm that demanded immediate action. The tall deputy smiled contentedly.

"All right, Marshal Vail, sir," he said, reaching into his coat pocket for a cheroot. "Where am I headed?"

"Salt Lake City, dammit! If I can find that—" With a grunt of satisfaction, he pulled a file closer to him and flipped it open. "Ah, here it is," he said, squinting down at the directive he had received from Washington.

Billy Vail probably needed glasses. He also needed exercise. After half a lifetime of chasing outlaws, gun runners, and assorted hardcases all the way to hell and back, he had been set down behind this desk and promptly gone to seed; it was a fate Longarm vowed he would never let overtake him.

Vail looked up at Longarm. "Salt Lake City is old territory for you, Longarm. You should have no trouble handling the authorities in that polygamous paradise, and of course that's important. We don't want another war with those damn Mormons."

"What's the problem?" Longarm asked, lighting his cheroot. "The Avenging Angels back to their old habits, are they?"

"I'm not sure. Washington's not sure, either. All we know is they are missing a federal officer who was last seen two weeks ago in Salt Lake City. He was on the trail of Smiley Blunt, a hardcase who had joined up with a pretty mean son of a bitch, name of Weed Leeper. Leeper's specialty is robbing trains, then killing any witnesses in cold blood. I recognize the name of the deputy U.S. marshal. Pete Baker. He's an old sidekick of mine. Tough as a railroad spike back when I knew him, but maybe a mite too old now to be chasin' high-line riders. If he's dead, as Washington fears, I'd like to see you take care of the gunslick responsible."

"Be my pleasure, Chief."

Billy Vail looked at Longarm solemnly for a long moment, then nodded curtly, as if that settled it. "Well, I'd sure appreciate it. I'm hogtied to this here desk, so I'm leaving it up to you."

He pushed the folder across the desk to Longarm. "Look this over. Something spooky's goin' on thereabouts. Seems like too damn many no-accounts have been traced to this tank town outside Salt Lake City. This ain't the first peace officer who's disappeared after heading for it."

"And no one can get the Mormon authorities to get off their duffs and investigate."

"You got it. We're lucky they even bothered to inform Washington of Baker's disappearance after he set out for the place. Since it's inhabited by Gentiles, as far as the authorities in Salt Lake City are concerned, they can pave their way to their own hell and be damned. Besides, the town apparently serves as an excellent source of amusement for those members of the Church who can afford the short train ride out there."

Longarm opened the folder and glanced down at it. "Antelope Junction," he said. "Has a nice ring to it, at that."

"Just see what the hell's going on out there, Longarm. And see what you can do to find Pete Baker. I'd like one more drink with that cussed beanpole before I toss in my spurs."

Longarm stood up. "I'll do my best, Chief."

"Oh, hell," said Vail. "You can call me Billy."

Longarm smiled.

"If you don't make a habit of it, that is."

Longarm was still smiling as he passed the pink-faced clerk. The timid little jasper was obviously unhappy that he had not heard more of an explosion when the tardy Longarm entered Billy Vail's office, and he did not look up from his typewriting machine as Longarm passed. If he had, Longarm would have swatted him smartly with the file folder he was carrying.

As Longarm rode the hack from the train station and looked out at the broad, neatly paved, well-laid-out streets of Salt Lake City, he was impressed once again. Most of the construction he had noticed on his earlier assignment had been completed, though work was still going on at the site of the Temple. When he saw the huge blocks of granite waiting to be lifted into place, he wondered if the Mormons would ever get their Temple completed during this century. Still, even if they did not succeed in completing it during Longarm's lifetime, there was no denying the remarkable stamina and devotion to their faith that such a mighty project represented. The Mormons would not be driven from this settlement. Not this time. They had come to stay.

If only, Longarm reflected, the Mormons could invest their city with a little more joy. The stolid faces of the women, the grim countenances of most of the men, together with the drab, no-nonsense garb affected by both sexes, seemed to cast a pall over the city, despite the undeniable impression of prosperity that met Longarm's eyes on every hand. Perhaps these Latter-Day Saints should seriously consider easing some of their restrictions on alcohol, coffee, tea, and other stimulants.

The hack pulled up in front of Quincy Boggs' impressive, three-story residence. Longarm paid the hackman, mounted the front steps, and rapped smartly on the heavy oaken door. A tall butler pulled the door open.

Longarm stepped inside. "I am Custis Long. I believe Mr. Boggs is expecting me."

"Why, yes he is, Mr. Long," the butler replied, closing the door. "He is waiting for you in the library. I trust you had a pleasant journey."

"Nobody shot at me or tried to cheat me at cards, if that's what you mean," Longarm replied as he handed the man his hat and traveling bag.

"Yessir," the butler said. "Very good, sir."

Quincy Boggs, his lean figure still trim, strode quickly toward him, hand outstretched, as Longarm entered the library. The man looked hardly a day older, Longarm commented to himself as he shook the man's firm hand. Waiting in the library with him was the youngest of his three daughters, Audrey. She smiled impishly as Longarm shook her father's hand. Longarm went over to greet her. Taking her slim hand in his, he gallantly brushed it with his lips. If her father had not aged much in the many months gone by, Audrey had certainly grown up considerably. She had been an impish sprite before; she was a boldy provocative young woman now—and what he read in her eyes almost intimidated him.

"Welcome back to Salt Lake City, Longarm," Audrey said.

"We do hope you'll be staying longer this time."

"Yes indeed," said Boggs. "It is just Audrey and myself inhabiting this big house now. Emilie and Marilyn, as you have probably guessed, have only recently married. Audrey and I would be delighted to have you consider this your home during your stay in Salt Lake City."

Longarm thanked him and the two men sat down, Longarm in an armchair, Boggs on the leather sofa against the wall.

"I'll get something to drink," Audrey said, darting for the door.

"Apple cider, I'll bet," laughed Longarm.

"Wait'll you see!" Audrey cried, disappearing from the room.

"Well now, what nefarious business brings you to Salt Lake City, Longarm?" Boggs asked. "Your telegram said only you'd be visiting as soon as you arrived."

"What do you know of Antelope Junction, Quincy?"

"Seems to be a fine place to go if you want to spend money in a sinful fashion. That's all I know about it for sure. It's a deadly place for those who live there, I understand, but it's no skin off my nose—or that of any other devout Mormon— how these children of Satan assassinate each other."

"After all, they're just Gentiles," Longarm commented. "Is that it?"

"Unfortunately, yes." Boggs threw up his hands in mild resignation. "We have heard of the bloodshed and have sent our people out there to check on it every now and then, but all they have ever found is another grave in boot hill, which is certainly nothing out of the ordinary, Longarm. Not for Antelope Junction. It is a rowdy, sinful place. Prostitutes. Gambling. Drinking. Brawling. A devil's brew. But it is out of our jurisdiction."

"And besides, there might be a few devout Mormons anxious to use the place now and then for blowing off steam."

"Alas, Longarm, the sins of the flesh are with us always. It does no good to deny this lamentable fact."

Boggs looked at Longarm with just the trace of a smile on his lean face, his mild blue eyes barely suppressing a twinkle. It was enough for him, obviously, that the Church kept primarily to its mission of looking after its own flock—at least those of its members who would accept its guidance. It could not do much more than that. Man's unregenerate nature was simply too powerful to whip to a standstill, even by the Latter-Day Saints. Antelope Junction was the escape valve, the compromise the Mormons were willing to make in light of this lamentable fact.

With a weary shrug, Longarm settled back in his chair. "I'll want to talk to this local federal marshal of yours, since he's the one sent in the report on Deputy Baker. What kind of man is he? Can I count on him to back my play?"

Boggs shook his head doubtfully. "His name is Walt Deegar. A large, florid man with a belly to match his enthusiasn for food—and multiple wives. The man is up for reelection. He will not be too eager to rock the boat. And as I said, too many devout members of the Church want nothing at all to do with that hellhole out on the flats. 'Let the cursed Gentiles stew in their own damnation' is their motto—a motto that Walt subscribes to wholeheartedly."

Audrey entered, carrying a bottle of Maryland rye, glasses, and a small flask of tomato juice on a silver tray. Audrey joined them with her juice while Longarm asked no more questions about the business at hand and joined Boggs in a noble attempt to punish the bottle of rye, while the three of them recalled Longarm's earlier visit and his successful joust with the deadly Avenging Angels and their terrifying leader—the Elder Wolverton.

"Emilie will be sorry she missed you," said Audrey at last, getting to her feet and stretching her young, lithe body. "But I will tell her that you are in fine health...and just as handsome."

Putting his empty glass down on the silver tray, Longarm smiled up at Audrey. "Thank you, Audrey. And you tell her how sorry I was to have missed her, as well."

"Good night, you two," Audrey said, starting from the room as she stifled a yawn. "I'll leave you both to your fuddled memories."

Then, with a delighted laugh, she disappeared through the door. Longarm heard her light, swift feet on the stairs—and yawned mightily, aware for the first time just how tired he was.

Boggs smiled indulgently and got to his feet. "Forgive me for keeping you up, Longarm. You have had a long day. And

I imagine you'll have another dreary train ride ahead of you tomorrow. I'll have the butler show you to your room."

Longarm nodded and got gratefully to his feet. Even as Boggs spoke, the butler had materialized in the library doorway, and was now waiting patiently to show Longarm to his room. Wishing momentarily that it was Audrey instead who was taking him to his room for the night, Longarm bade Boggs goodnight and trailed the butler up the stairs.

Longarm's long train ride from Denver had left him pretty nearly exhausted. The Maryland rye had warmed him agreeably—as had the visit with Boggs and Audrey—and now he was more than ready for bed. He sighed contentedly as he climbed in between the immaculate sheets, turned down the lamp on the night table, then rolled over to face the window. The city below was quiet, the moonlight just beginning to flood in through the large, multipaned window. He stretched luxuriously and closed his eyes.

The door squeaked as someone entered. Longarm opened his eyes and turned to see a ghostly figure in a long white nightgown turning to close the door firmly. Even in the dim light, Longarm had no difficulty recognizing Audrey's bright, eager face as she swiftly approached his bed, a finger held against her lips.

"Emilie and Marilyn told me I'd have my turn someday," she said, unceremoniously flinging back Longarm's covers and laughing softly. In the moonlight, Longarm's long, naked flanks stood out clearly—as did his thatch of pubic hair. "Mmmm!" she cried. "Look at that!"

Wasting no more time, she stepped out of her nightgown and flung herself into the bed alongside Longarm. Pulling the covers up over them both, she snuggled happily against him.

"Audrey," Longarm said softly, caressing her long curls and holding her tightly against him. "I ain't sure I am in any condition to pleasure you. It has been a long day for me. I'm pretty near dead."

Her hand snaked down between his legs and took hold of him. At once Longarm felt himself responding. Audrey giggled and pushed herself still closer. "You're not dead yet, Longarm. Besides, I hear tell a woman in heat can revive the dead. If he has a mind to, that is."

With a sigh, Longarm clasped her to him and kissed her on the lips. Their tongues entwined. Audrey thrust herself still closer, moaning slightly. Then she pulled her lips from his and kissed his shoulder. He felt the moist heat of her tongue sliding along the slope of his shoulders to the strong cords of his neck. She bit him suddenly. He almost cried out. And then she began nibbling delightfully on his earlobes. All the while, the fingers of her right hand had been working their magic on his back, while her left hand continued to massage his growing erection gently. Abruptly, she pulled her lips from his ears and kissed him again—passionately, her tongue darting, her scented hair spilling over Longarm's shoulders.

A flame of hot desire lanced upward from his groin. His exhaustion vanished magically, and he felt his pulse quickening. Pulling away from her teasing tongue, he laughed softly, than hauled her over onto him, his massive erection disappearing with effortless ease intothe warm moistness of her. It was her turn to laugh now as she flung the covers back and sat up on him, grinding him wildly into her. It seemed as if her body were trying to devour his erection. He grasped her hips and started rotating her fiercely. As they built surely to a climax, she flung herself forward onto him, her corona of straw-colored hair falling over him, her tongue boldly, wantonly past his lips and deep into his mouth to embrace his own tongue—a wild, passionate counterpart to his own thrusting erection.

That did it. He clasped both of his arms around the small of her back, lifted himself mightily under her—and came to a shuddering climax. As he clung to her, he felt her uncontrolled pulsing as she too reached her climax. She came more than once, and each time she tried to pull away, to cry out in her passion—but he kept his mouth firmly on hers until, at last, satiated completely, she collapsed limply onto his long frame. After a moment she sighed and, kissing him slowly, tenderly, pulled her mouth from his and rested her cheek on his chest.

"Mmmm," she said. "That was nice. Now what shall we do?"

Longarm stroked her long blond tresses and said softly, "Sleep."

"But Longarm, the evening is young yet."

"Not for me, it ain't."

He closed his eyes and almost at once felt himself drifting off. Only dimly did he hear Audrey's soft voice in his ear. "All right," she said, her lips drifting with the softness of moonlight over his cheek. "Sleep. But I'll be in early to wake you up."

Thinking of that promise, Longarm fell into a deep, delicious sleep—one that was almost as filled with delight as was the lovely, wickedly imaginative way in which Audrey roused him from sleep in the still, cool hour before dawn.

EASY COMPANY

MORE ROUGH RIDING ACTION FROM JOHN WESLEY HOWARD

____ 05952-8 EASY COMPANY AND THE ENGINEERS #11 $1.95
____ 05953-6 EASY COMPANY AND THE BLOODY FLAG #12 $1.95
____ 06215-4 EASY COMPANY AND THE OKLAHOMA TRAIL #13 $1.95
____ 06031-3 EASY COMPANY AND THE CHEROKEE BEAUTY #14 $1.95
____ 06032-1 EASY COMPANY AND THE BIG BLIZZARD #15 $1.95
____ 06033-X EASY COMPANY AND THE LONG MARCHERS #16 $1.95
____ 05949-8 EASY COMPANY AND THE BOOTLEGGERS #17 $1.95
____ 06350-9 EASY COMPANY AND THE CARDSHARPS #18 $1.95
____ 06351-7 EASY COMPANY AND THE INDIAN DOCTOR #19 $2.25
____ 06352-5 EASY COMPANY AND THE TWILIGHT SNIPER #20 $2.25
____ 06353-3 EASY COMPANY AND THE SHEEP RANCHERS #21 $2.25
____ 06354-1 EASY COMPANY AT HAT CREEK STATION #22 $2.25

Available at your local bookstore or return this form to:

JOVE/BOOK MAILING SERVICE
P.O. Box 690, Rockville Center, N.Y. 11570

Please enclose 75¢ for postage and handling for one book, 25¢ each add'l. book ($1.50 max.). No cash, CODs or stamps. Total amount enclosed: $ _____ in check or money order.

NAME _____

ADDRESS _____

CITY _____ STATE/ZIP _____

Allow six weeks for delivery.

SK-4

LONGARM

Explore the exciting Old West with one of the men who made it wild!

___ 06576-5	LONGARM #1	$2.25
___ 06807-1	LONGARM ON THE BORDER #2	$2.25
___ 06808-X	LONGARM AND THE AVENGING ANGELS #3	$2.25
___ 06809-8	LONGARM AND THE WENDIGO #4	$2.25
___ 06810-1	LONGARM IN THE INDIAN NATION #5	$2.25
___ 05900-5	LONGARM AND THE LOGGERS #6	$1.95
___ 05901-3	LONGARM AND THE HIGHGRADERS #7	$1.95
___ 05985-4	LONGARM AND THE NESTERS #8	$1.95
___ 05973-0	LONGARM AND THE HATCHET MAN #9	$1.95
___ 06064-X	LONGARM AND THE MOLLY MAGUIRES #10	$1.95
___ 06626-5	LONGARM AND THE TEXAS RANGERS #11	$2.25
___ 06950-7	LONGARM IN LINCOLN COUNTY #12	$2.25
___ 06153-0	LONGARM IN THE SAND HILLS #13	$1.95
___ 06070-4	LONGARM IN LEADVILLE #14	$1.95
___ 05904-8	LONGARM ON THE DEVIL'S TRAIL #15	$1.95
___ 06104-2	LONGARM AND THE MOUNTIES #16	$1.95
___ 06154-9	LONGARM AND THE BANDIT QUEEN #17	$1.95
___ 06155-7	LONGARM ON THE YELLOWSTONE #18	$1.95
___ 06951-5	LONGARM IN THE FOUR CORNERS #19	$2.25
___ 06627-3	LONGARM AT ROBBER'S ROOST #20	$2.25
___ 06628-1	LONGARM AND THE SHEEPHERDER'S #21	$2.25
___ 06156-5	LONGARM AND THE GHOST DANCERS #22	$1.95
___ 05999-4	LONGARM AND THE TOWN TAMER #23	$1.95

Available at your local bookstore or return this form to:

JOVE/BOOK MAILING SERVICE
P.O. Box 690, Rockville Center, N.Y. 11570

Please enclose 75¢ for postage and handling for one book, 25¢ each add'l. book ($1.50 max.). No cash, CODs or stamps. Total amount enclosed: $ _____ in check or money order.

NAME _____

ADDRESS _____

CITY _____ STATE/ZIP _____

SK-5

Allow six weeks for delivery.